Mother, Dearest
By
Patrick Scattergood

Copyright © 2019 Patrick Scattergood

The right of Patrick Scattergood to be identified as the Author of the Work has been asserted by him in accordance with the Copyright, Designs and Patents Act 1988.

First published in Great Britain in 2019 by Dark Pond Creations

Apart from any use permitted under UK copyright law, this publication may only be reproduced, stored, or transmitted, in any form, or by any means, with prior permission in writing of the publishers or, in the case of reprographic production, in accordance with the terms of licences issued by the Copyright Licensing Agency.

All characters in this publication are fictitious and any resemblance to real person's, living or dead, is purely coincidental

For Ashley

Who always lets me chase random dreams.

For Cyrus

Who shows me how to dream.

For Golda

Who helped me put random scribblings in to coherent sentences.

For the Elevation Wrestling Academy Team

Who helped me find my confidence again.

Chapter One

As I travel through the chilly night with the rain drizzling on to my windscreen, a bladder full of piss and a belly full of hunger, there is one thought plays around in my head again and again with no signs of stopping. My mother is dead.

The woman who carried me in her womb for nine months is gone forever. She's dead, buried and now little more than food for the worms, maggots and flies that will slowly but surely devour her and yet one thing comes back to me. My mother is dead and I couldn't be happier.

In fact, you could sum up my life priorities in this way. My car is running out of gas, it's held together by luck and rust, I have no idea where I'm going and I need to find somewhere to lay my head before I fall asleep at the wheel of this piece of shit rental. Oh, and my mother is dead. This is as interesting as my life has ever gotten other than the weird genetic mistake that gave me one green eye and one blue. Other than that, I'm a pretty forgettable person living a largely forgettable life. A life of sin and sodomy as my mother once said.

I suppose I should feel sadness. I should feel the overwhelming grief that comes with losing a parent but instead I feel relief, solitude and most of all, I feel happiness. It feels a bit like a warm, comfy blanket being draped over me. Part of me can't help but wonder if I can finally be myself with no resentment for fitting her narrow view of the world.

I catch myself in the mirror as I'm driving, the dial on my dash edging ever closer to 80 miles per hour and I laugh. A leaning my head back, mouth open wide kind of laugh that echoes in the silence of my rental car. A laugh that brings tears to my eyes for the first time that day. Weird isn't it? No tears at the funeral or the wake filled with rapacious vulture like relatives afterwards but tears of laughter in a cheap rental car. So many thoughts run through my head behind the laughter but the one that sticks in my head is that she *really* is dead. She *really* is gone. I *really* am free of her and I am glad. I am happy and I am relieved. For some reason, that makes me laugh even more.

But are you ever truly free?

The voice takes me by surprise and I jerk my hands on the wheel and slam on the brakes. The skid feels like it lasts a lifetime until the rental comes to an awkward, violent stop in the middle of the road.

Please not now. Please I'm begging you, not now. Slowly I allow myself to look in to my mirror, the sound of my breath feeling more like the roar of the sea on a stormy day. Frozen to my seat, I just stare at the empty mirror. There is nobody behind me in the car, nobody behind me on the rain slicked road. I am alone. Maybe it's the lack of sleep playing tricks on my already fragile mind. Admittedly, I haven't slept more than four hours in the last couple of days. That must be it. I'm just tired and my mind is imagining things that simply aren't there. That's the only explanation for it. Surely, it has to be that. What else could it be?

Maybe you're insane? Maybe you've been off your medication for too long?

No, this is not going to happen. Not tonight, not any night. It is simply not going to happen. I'll drive my ass back to the hotel, throw myself down on to the bed and sleep until room service knocks on my door to tell me to get the hell out of there. That's what I'll do. That's exactly what I will do.

No you won't.

Great, I'm even arguing with the voices in my head. Isn't there an old saying about the first sign of madness being talking to yourself?

Yes there is, the second is you arguing with yourself.

No matter what the voice says, it's always my mother's. Her slow voice, soaked in gin and bitterness. The sort of voice that never really goes away, not even after the bitch is dead in the ground.

They say madness runs in the family you know.

My shaking hand turns the volume up on the radio. Some cheesy rock song from the 1980's blares out. I don't truly hear the song or the lyrics or even the rain outside. I just want it to drown my mind out. I want it to silence whatever is speaking in my mother's voice inside my head. I just want it to make it stop. All of it.

Now you're just being downright rude.

It takes me a few seconds to realise that my foot has pressed down on the accelerator and the car is moving through the night again, the headlights shining in front of me as my only guide to where I am going. If truth be known, I don't even know where I am going. I'm just driving as far away from that house as I can get. As far away from the venomous family that raised me and as far away from that gossip filled mess of a small town that I used to call home when I was younger. No doubt my quick and easy escape from the wake will give them yet more reason to gossip about me but I'll never have to step foot in that god forsaken place ever again.

I had been stuck in that house for nearly six god damned hours. Six whole hours of being surrounded by people I didn't know and who didn't know me either. Their hollow words of sympathy feeling like crooked nails being hammered slowly in to my brain again and again.

I honestly had no idea why I was there for long so long or why I put myself through that yet I stayed, did my part, nodding and smiling at the appropriate moments in the mind numbing conversations around me.

Not exactly a people pleaser are you?

Standing there, in amongst those people, I couldn't help but feel the need for an escape that felt more like a necessity, a compulsion to just get away from everything and everyone. Has anyone ever felt like that before? Of course they have. Everybody has. It's not a new sensation, in fact, it is a feeling as old as the world itself. There was one thing however that the people here hadn't realised. I was only there because I *had* to be, not because I *wanted* to be. I had to be there to try to go along with the societal norm of having to grieve for a lost parent. Nothing more, nothing less so take that however you will.

You utter arsehole.

The more these words worked through my brain, the more they felt like a confession. I hadn't been at the house as a mourner or a heartbroken son. I was there as a spectator of sorts. I was glad that she was dead, I was glad that she was never coming back but part me wanted to stand there and make sure of it. To make sure that ding dong, the witch was truly dead. I was her only son in the plethora of near identical, *Stepford Wives* group of daughters. I was surprised they didn't have to wear name badges so people could tell them apart. I was even more surprised that people noticed that I was even worthy of existing in their presence.

You always were ungrateful, even as a child.

A normal person would have shed a hundred tears at the thought of having lost someone so close. A normal person would have spent hours looking at old photographs and remembering fond moments of their lives that they spent together. Me? I spent it stood by the window, on my own and with a scotch in my hand wondering when the earliest I could leave would be. This scotch was not my first of the day and it most definitely would not be my last.

You alcoholic piece of shit.

The glass felt so comforting in my hand. A sign of a true alcoholic I suppose. It sent me back to a time when, as a small child, I would stand and watch the world go by while I'd hold my comforter close to my chest. The only difference being that now, as an adult, the comforter has changed to a glass of chilled scotch.

The funny thing about funerals and wakes is how many people come out of the woodwork and the shadows before a body is even cold in the ground. The worms hadn't even started on their feast and they were already milling around. Hell, for a woman that prided herself on having a near perfect image, she did know some unsavoury people. Uncles that had we had long lost contact with over various scandal filled rumours of wrong doing. One thought to have been the head of a pyramid scheme losing people thousands in life savings. One thought to rather like partaking in the company in barely legal aged rent boys. Somehow, each passing relative that I met, seemed to morally degrade before my very eyes. I felt dirty, sullied, almost ruined with each interaction with these people that I apparently shared a seemingly shallow gene pool with. Was it any wonder that I was such a failure when I shared DNA with these people?

Always ready to blame everyone except yourself aren't you?

Yet she, as a person, liked to be thought of as being cleaner than purely driven snow despite having surrounded herself with people of the same ilk. Heaven forbid you should ever make any kind of mistake. Heaven forbid you should be even remotely different. If you didn't fit her view of perfection, then ostracised you were and that's where I had been for the last five years. There was no family of my own to speak of and that clearly added to my growing list of failures and a job that merely enabled me to exist but not to live. The worst thing of it all was the simple fact that I wasn't even doing that very well.

I would call you an idiot but even that is too successful a term for you.

The radio started to play little more than static with a split second of music so I flicked the off switch so I could drive in silence. Static somehow still crackled through the car so I tried to flick the switch again. I'd only taken my eyes from the road for a split second but that's all it took. The car drifted in to the next lane and the loud angry honk of a car horn shook me from wherever my mind had wandered to while trying to turn the damn thing off. I skidded back in to my lane, managing to keep the car on the road. I cursed the radio under my breath as it tuned in to a station for a couple of seconds to a DJ laughing hysterically before switching back to the incessant crackle of the static that acted as the soundtrack to my second close call of the evening.

I suppose that's just the reward for skimping and renting the cheapest car possible to drive here. Yet here I am, driving with no destination in sight nor in mind.

You get what you paid for you cheap bastard, always do.

And here it comes, that voice ripping me to shreds, pointing out every single little mistake I've made from the day I was born. Even with her dead and buried, the voice still hasn't shut up all day. The rain is making it hard to see through the streaky, dirty windscreen but I know there must be somewhere I can stop and rent a room. These tiny, arse end of the country towns always have somewhere and they're nearly always run by a skinny husband constantly ordered about by his fat, loud wife. It never fails to amaze me just how many stereotypes really are true. I shouldn't be surprised though. This is the sort of town where marrying your cousin is seen as moving up in the world.

I hope you got your listening ears on boy.

The radio jumped back in to life, startling me a little but bringing yet another throaty laugh from deep inside of me as the radio started playing some twee song about buying a pair of roller skates. My laughter and the sickly-sweet song made for strange bedfellows but it kind of summed up the entire day thus far. Happiness in place of sadness and escape in place of support.

The strangest thing had been the simple fact that I felt compelled to turn the car around and drive back to the house I'd not long come from. The house I grew up in. The house that had seen every moment of my growing up and sure as hell had some stories to tell to anyone that would listen but I stayed heading in to what I thought was the middle of nowhere in search of a cheap room for the night.

Cheap. The perfect word for you.

Part of me was glad I did as it didn't take me long to see a grotesquely lit neon sign with half of the letters smashed to pieces. It didn't exactly fill me with hope for a good night's sleep but I suppose it would be a damn sight better than sleeping in this cheap heap of junk so I pulled in to the empty car park with a exhausted sigh.

I started to wonder if the place was open at all as the rest of the lights seemed to have been turned off when a hunched over man exited one of the doors holding a mop and a rusty old bucket.

Getting out of the car as quickly as possible, I called over to him. He seemed to be startled by either my sudden appearance in front of him or by having a random stranger call to him but he regained his composure pretty quickly as he waved me over.

"Yes sir, we are open, not that you would know it thanks to that sign" he said with a wry smile which seemed at odds with his tired and sad eyes. They were the sort of eyes that you just know had seen so many things, both happy and sad but also some things that could haunt a man to his very bones.

"Come with me and we will make sure to get you all signed in and out of the rain." I was intrigued by how his voice seemed to be both welcoming but weary too. A broken shell of a person at odds with the glare of the neon lights, a shadow crossing the world while waiting for its body to turn to dust and be blown away to never be seen again yet looking strangely serene.

The old man sped up and walked over to the solitary lit up room and threw open the door, making a bell clang to announce our arrival. "It's just me up in here tonight so you will have to bear with me one moment while I put ol' Percy and Shirley away" he said as he gestured at the mop and bucket he had in his hands and walked behind the counter.

I wasn't sure if it was the fact that I had been driving for hours, my imagination or something else but the old man seemed to have come to life since we came inside. My eyes darted around the room while I waited for him to come back and the tick of the clock filled the silence.

Faded artwork bought from a yard sale adorning the walls in dusty frames. Check.

A snack machine with out of date snacks inside. Check.

An ice machine with a never-ending buzz and an out of order sign hanging on it. Check.

A grimy looking bell on the counter top. Check.

Peeling stickers hanging from dirty windows. Check.

An armchair in the waiting area that looks like it's held together by patches. Check.

This place was literally one stereotype after another. It was almost as if the owners had searched motels 101 on the internet and copied every single overused thing that they read about to furnish their own place. The whole place seemed to give off a bit of a Norman Bates vibe but it was the only place in town that I had found.

I stretched my arms, legs and back as much as I possibly could and felt a lot older than I actually was.

Everything ached. Everything throbbed including the dull throb in my head that had been there since I left that house.

Who in blue hell names their mop and bucket?

I clamped my hands over my ears and started to hum to myself, hoping that the voice would shut up before the tired but kindly old man returned from putting Percy and Shirley away. I didn't even realise that I was rocking back and forth on my heels until I nearly fell backwards. Cursing to myself quietly, I rested my hands on the counter top and tried to concentrate on the bell in front of me. I couldn't resist a sly smile at the peeling sticker next to it. With some of the letters missing, you could now ring bell for a tent.

These sorts of places always made me wonder if the people that owned them cared about how the places looked or merely went there to die in silence, away from the prying eyes of the world around them.

The sound of a throat clearing snapped me back to reality so I looked up to see that the man had returned from his trek to put Percy and Shirley away. He smiled at me while I tried to focus on his face and found I'd missed half of what he was saying before realising that he was merely asking if I was feeling OK. I nodded and gave some rubbish about being tired and having had a long drive which seemed to satisfy his curiosity on that front.

I signed my name in the visitor log, which hadn't had any entries for the last six months and was given an old looking key. The kindly old man walked slowly with me to the door of my room before being left there with a cheery wave. For some reason I hesitated before going in. I just couldn't shake a feeling from my mind about not being alone despite clearly being the only tenant this place had for a long time. Looking around the night sky, it felt like a hundred pairs of eyes were watching my every move.

Scared of a motel room are you son? That's a new one even for you.

My hand slammed heavily in frustration on the door and I felt it shudder with the impact. Shut up, just shut up and let me get in to this place so I can sleep. I just want to sleep. One full night's sleep, that's all. Is that too much to ask? It had been so long since I had managed to have a full night sleep just to myself. No nightmares, no night terrors, no waking up screaming until my lungs are raw. I just wanted peace, quiet and sleep. That's all.

Oh my dear Naz, do you want mummy to hold your hand? Is that it?

I rested my weary head against the cold wood of the door. Strangely, I felt it give slightly under the pressure. Literally everything about this motel was screaming cheap and nasty at me but at least it was somewhere to put my head down for the evening. Preferably without catching anything but I think that in itself was a 50/50 chance.

The key slid in to the lock and the door clicked as I turned the handle slowly but as the door opened, my body lurched forward. I felt the darkness around me envelope everything in sight and my world disappeared, leaving me spiralling into the shadows that had opened up all around me.

***

The sky was a dark gun metal grey only brightening when a flash of lightning blinded my eyes. It felt strangely calming despite the foreboding that followed every crack of thunder, jabbing at my brain like a championship boxer. The sky itself felt charged with an energy that was both exciting yet dangerous. I knew I shouldn't be here, I knew I shouldn't stay yet I couldn't take my eyes away from my surroundings.

There I was, stood in the middle of the forest with the trees giving me minimal protection from the storm. The rain lashed around me, leaving me feeling like it was soaking through my clothes and through my entire body.

I felt as rooted to the spot as the oak trees around me. It's not that I couldn't move, it's that I just didn't want to. Strangely I felt almost at home here. It felt like maybe I was supposed to be here but that I was here at the wrong time.

The rain gave everything a strange, almost otherworldly shine. All I could think of was just how beautiful and serene the forest was in front of me. I could have happily stayed here for the rest of my life with no regrets but even with the calmness prevailing through my mind, there was one tiny spark of anxiety that just wouldn't go out no matter how hard the storm winds blew. That spark felt like an invincible candle that could withstand anything the world threw at it but still burned brightly at the back of my mind. It may as well have been a neon sign that declared that it was here and was not going to go away any time soon.

A deer stood in the distance front of me. The creature was at least thirty paces ahead of me but I couldn't shake the strange sensation that it was nearer, that it was right in front of me. My mind always liked to play tricks on night's like this but tonight felt different. This felt wrong. Slowly, almost deliberately, its head raised and it pricked its ears forward as if sensing danger nearby.

The creature's eyes stared straight through me, making me feel invisible not only to the deer itself but also to the world at large. I tilted my head to get a better look so that my eyes could adjust to the dark quicker. Still the deer stared and I stared right back. I have no idea why I felt the compulsion to stare back but I did it anyway. That's when I noticed. The deer was staring at me with eyes full of life yet its belly had been split open and its insides trailing through the mud. I felt myself take a shocked step backwards but still it stared. My eyes couldn't leave the vision of its guts hanging from its stomach yet the deer seemed completely unaffected by it.

A crack of thunder shook me from my waking slumber and my eyes darted around my little part of the forest before I turned to look back at the deer. I took a step back and tried in vain to rub the rain from my eyes as it ran down my face. The deer had gone without a sign that it existed at all. There were no tracks in the mud, no sounds, nothing at all. Had it really been there or had I imagined the deer? Was my mind playing yet more tricks on me in this strange place?

I walked forwards slowly as the sense of anxiety in my gut gradually started to take hold. I crouched down and placed my hand against the dirt and felt it squeeze between my fingers as I tried to find something that felt real. My eyes closed as I tried to calm my rapidly panicked breathing. The sense of dread and anxiety grew deep inside me. I could feel it almost like fingers trying to take hold of my heart and squeezing tightly. If I couldn't calm it down then I knew that those very fingers would be tearing me apart from the inside out.

Lightning carved a bright slice across the sky but then froze in mid flash. I sat down and let the mud envelope my legs and hands as I stared at the lightning. Why was it not moving? The trees around me were still, the wind had stopped and the jagged bolt of lightning just hung there in the sky.

I tried to get to my feet yet the mud around me held my body down. My legs felt like a large weight had been dropped on them yet there was no pain, only the panic.

Suddenly the deer appeared silently in front of my eyes with its unblinking eyes once again staring deeply in to mine. My body froze as if I were a toy that had ran out of battery as the deer sniffed at me. A shiver tried to escape my body but it dissipated into little more than a tingle. There was no reason to be so scared of this creature sniffing at me yet I could feel myself wanting to run and not look back but try as I might, my feet stayed exactly where they were. The feeling that I would be here forever started to creep in to my head and my breathing sped up even more.

I wanted to scream out as loud as I could but the only sound that escaped was a deep raspy gasp of air. A tickling sensation started to touch the back of my throat and I gagged violently as if I wanted to vomit yet no bile rose. Still the sensation continued and my breathing became more desperate and evanescent. My body started to feel like I was falling despite being completely prone in front of the creature with the exposed guts that hung, limp and useless in the middle of its four legs.

Finally I managed to pull my hand free from the mud with a sticky echo and I slid my fingers in to my mouth. I felt my tongue and my teeth against the mud-covered fingers. The feeling made me want to vomit as they made their way further in to my mouth before I felt something at the back of my throat. A sharp edge touched the tips of my fingers and I grabbed it as tight as I could and pulled. With a hard tug, I pulled it out and dropped it on to the floor in front of me. Before I could look, the tingling sensation got turned to a burning pain before a sense of nausea took over and I retched violently. A scream slowly escaped as hundreds of bees burst from my throat in an orgy of bile, pain and noise. The buzzing of the bees felt like a drill boring through my brain and I curled in to a foetal position in the dirt as the deer stayed staring at me. Tears mixed with the dirt and the rain on my face as I looked at the creature looming over me in desperation. I reached my mud-covered hand to try to touch it, to try to hold it as if that would help me from the agony that I was feeling.

"Help me", I mouthed with each word like a dagger stabbing the back of my throat.

Still the deer stared at me without a flicker of emotion ever crossing its face despite the hundreds of bees surrounding it, some of which landing on its trailing, muddy guts that were hanging from his sliced open belly making them sway slightly like an out of time pendulum.

"Please."

A smile gracefully looked back at me as the deer snorted and its lips moved from his teeth revealing jagged, pointed fangs as the bees continued flying in circles around us both. The sounds of the thunder, the buzzing and the snorting all mixed in to a symphony of anxiety and panic masking the haggard screams and pleas for mercy coming from my own lips.

The last thing I remembered seeing was a hoof above my face as the sound of laughter started to echo towards me from the open mouth of the deer. It was laughing at me! The damned creature was laughing at me while I was left in the mud like a discarded piece of rubbish.

I managed to make out one word that floated through the storm before my world once again turned in to little more than a silent blackness. A solitary, scratchy word that exploded from the mouth of the deer as it laughed and slammed its hoof in to my head in a shower of mud, bone and blood as my head collapsed under it.

"No, not yet."

Chapter Two

Each laboured breath echoed around the motel room, like a gunshot in the night. The smell of dried vomit assaulted my nose and I felt the nausea heave its way from my stomach and in to the back of my throat with a jolt. My heavy legs swung out of the side of the bed and I sat there for a moment while the feelings of sickness lapped at me in waves, lapping in time with the drumbeat of pain that was throbbing through my entire head. Feeling the bile rising in my throat, I knew that getting to the toilet would be a much better idea than adding more to the already disgustingly patterned carpet that the room had.

Slowly I stood up but the dizziness took me by surprise. I felt almost like I'd been on those stupid tea cup rides you get at hastily erected fairs that invade towns every now and then. As I reached for my glass of water in an effort to calm my head and my stomach, I glanced a look at the clock. It was somehow 8 a.m. and I was still fully dressed in my suit from the funeral, only now it had some rather unsavoury marks and stains on it. Sipping my water didn't help quell the feelings of sickness at all, it just gave my stomach another reason to jerk and lunge violently so I ran in to the bathroom as quickly as my heavy legs would carry me.

The feeling of the cold ceramic toilet bowl against my body felt rather comforting and for a split second, I felt like the nausea had started to subside but it was only a temporary reprieve at best as I looked around the room to see if anything could distract me from the pain in my stomach. The nondescript nature of the bathroom was no help. You could literally be anywhere in the country and you'd have the same sort of bathroom at these sorts of cheap, by the hour places.

A shadowy movement flashed in the corner of my eye and all of a sudden my body shot backwards on to the cold, hard floor. A blinding abdominal pain caused my body to curl up on the floor in a helpless and crude version of the foetal position. The silence of the bathroom being quickly broken by the sobs that came from deep instead my throat. It felt like a release that had been a long time coming but not for the loss of the now buried old woman but for all the years of frustration and judgement that I had long been victim to.

Never could handle your drink could you Naz?

I'd long had a problem with my drinking but I'd never felt like this before, not even after the heaviest of drinking sessions with my work colleagues. It had never felt this bad, not even close. In fact, I could drink and drink and still only have the slightest of headaches to contend with the next day. This wasn't right. This wasn't right at all.

See? You're lying to yourself now. You couldn't even manage to be a normal alcoholic could you? Couldn't even do that right.

The voice was boring through my head quicker and quicker with each word being followed by a vicious stabbing pain in my head. I could feel my cold hands pressed against the sides of my head but it didn't calm me. Maybe I had a brain tumour or something. That would be my luck really wouldn't it? I finally get rid of the old bitch only to find I have a brain tumour. God, if you're really up there and this is what's really happening then you have a really shitty sense of humour.

Slowly, the sickness started to settle and the room felt like it was coming in to focus a lot more as I stayed prone on the floor. The feeling of sickness was steadily being replaced by a feeling of confusion as I looked at the muddy foot prints on the floor and the mud on my suit that disappeared after I slowly and gently rubbed my eyes to ease the pain behind them.

This was a cheap and easy motel room. A room with no thrills and nothing fancy. That much was true and I was as sure of that as I could possibly be while lying on the bathroom floor. It was kind of weird but I wasn't all that sure why I was here exactly. As far as I knew, I was still in my home town but why hadn't I gone further? I'd left the house hours and hours ago, driven for longer than I could remember yet I'd ended up in a seedy motel room *still* in my home town. Had some other force drawn me here? Was it merely an accident I'm here?

Crap alcoholic. No sense of direction. Is there no end to your skills?

I just wished that bitter, twisted voice would shut up but right now, I had a bigger problem. I needed to get to my feet but standing up was almost a military operation. Slowly but surely and with each movement considered and measured, I managed to stand and support my weight by leaning on the back of the toilet. While my head started to spin, I tried to concentrate on the random marks and stains on the wall and top of the toilet cistern.

Every part of me ached and throbbed with pain so with a deep breath and a mumbled count to ten, my feet took me back in to the bedroom. Catching my reflection in the mirror as I past, I couldn't help but chuckle slightly. My walk looked like Boris Karloff's from one of those old Frankenstein horror movies in the 1930's as I shuffled and ambled my way through the room towards the battered old bag that I had brought with me. Like me, it had seen much better days but my clothes sticking out of it in every possible direction gave it a shabby and untidy look. A printed paper booklet stood on top of the bag, making it look like someone wearing a crown. It was the pamphlet from her funeral and in an almost mocking irony, it somehow managed to stand on the pile of clothes sticking out from my bag with a smug feel. The thought that I shouldn't really be surprised hit me hard. Of course it was going to look smug and intruding, it was connected to my dead mother. Why would it look like anything else for a woman such as her?

Thank you.

The confusion in my head started to whirl around in my mind again. I was glad that my mother was dead, of that there was no doubt yet for some reason I couldn't help but wonder if I was missing something about the whole situation. Am I too fucked up to feel anything the way a *normal* person would or is it normal to celebrate that someone who has plagued you for your entire life is dead? The best way that I could think of it would be if I woke up trying to remember the dream from the night before.

I always wondered what I would do when she did go yet here I am in a motel room in my home town. I've driven for hours and ended up in a damned motel less than thirty minutes away from where I'd spent most of my day surrounded by vultures, liars and sycophants. I shouldn't be surprised. I've spent nearly all my life second guessing every single decision and thought that I have ever had and all because of her. The self-doubt that she had left me was crippling at best and soul destroying at worst and for what? To make herself feel better? To hold me up to her daughters as a lesson in what not to do in life? Either way, I could feel the black dog of depression nipping hungrily at my heels and I knew I had to get out of there or it would eat me alive and leave me to put my remains back together again the only way I knew how. With alcohol. A shit ton of alcohol. If I can't forget or drown anything out then I can at least dumb myself to the point of feeling absolutely nothing for a couple of hours at least.

Yeah that's right loser, go find your mind in the bottom of a bottle.

Rummaging through the mess of a bag was a fruitless task, plus I didn't even know what the hell I was looking for. I just knew that I had an insatiable need to look for it as if there was something in there that would change my life. However the stark truth of the matter was that the only other useful thing in there was a dark blue suit, the same damn thing I always wore. The same damn thing I wore every day to work, to the pub afterwards and when I inevitably passed out drunk alone on the sofa. The jacket itself has been missing a button on it for years but for some reason I just couldn't bring myself to throw it away. Stupid really. Having sentimental feelings towards a worn-out thrift store suit jacket yet not to my own mother.

Says it all really about you Naz. Selfish, fucked up, alcoholic. Your own holy trinity.

Sitting on the bed, I found myself rocking back and forth gently to try to help silence the voice, even if for a moment with the funeral pamphlet screwed up in my hand. Deep down in the back of my mind, there was the truth that if *she* were here then there would be a hell of a lot more berating happening. About my appearance, my failed marriages, my job going nowhere. It was almost a never ending list for her. I threw the pamphlet towards the bin but it flopped from the sky with a disappointing scratch on to the carpet.

Can you blame me? You gave me such good material to work with.

Slowly I got dressed in to my clean but well-worn suit, only stopping to stroke the empty button hole where the missing button should be as I looked in the dirty motel room mirror that hanged at an angle on the wall. The reflection in the mirror appeared to be looking back in a mocking tone. At least it wasn't looking at me in pity like most people do so there was a silver lining there.

However the murmur was still in the back of my mind, like two people talking to one another in a crowded and loud bar. It was ever present but until now, it had always been simple to block it out. It had always been relatively easy to disguise it, maybe not fully but enough to get a bit of peace and quiet once in a while. I nudge the rolled up pamphlet with the toe of my well scuffed shoe and quietly sigh. She isn't here any more but still her voice is trying to invade. She is still trying to take charge and to break through the psyche.

Throwing bits of paper around won't change that.

The corridor outside was eerily quiet. No footsteps, no talking, nothing. It felt like a ghost town of sorts. Just like the rooms themselves, the corridors were devoid of anything even remotely warm or showing any personality. Another shadowy movement flashed across the wall next to me. To calm my nerves, I tried desperately to straighten down my shirt and jacket. The voice then forced itself in to my head again.

Damn-it, take pride in your appearance. You look like a bum.

My hands slammed against myself over and over. My head, my body, my face. All targets of the rage I was feeling. If I couldn't drown out that damned infernal voice then at least I could beat it out of myself. Wish as hard as I could, her voice seemed to be getting louder and louder. She died a few days ago and was buried today yet the voice just kept going and getting more and more judgemental. Why can't she just shut up? Why can't she just leave me alone?

Stop complaining and stop making your damned excuses.

Each impact of my fist against my head tried in vain to make the noises stop with furious abandon. Each hit of my knuckles found their mark and still the voice went on. I could feel my body shudder with every single one of my punches.

"Get out of my head you dead bitch. Get out of my head!"

I screamed the words with every bit of anger and resentment that I could possibly muster. Each emotion that I'd kept bottled up inside of me forced itself up to the top and burst forth in each and every word that came out of my mouth. The spit hung from my lips and my breathing became laboured and heavy, my arms limp by my sides and a tiny trickle of blood starting to run from my nose.

The click of one of the room doors unlocking near me silenced every voice that was echoing in my head except for the one telling me to run. The thumping of my shoes copied the pounding of my heart as I pushed at the door to open, oblivious to the fact that the sign on the door was saying to pull. I started to panic even more as my hands struggled in vain with the handle. What would someone say if they found me like this? What would they do? Would they call the police?

Questions flew through my brain like bullets and I looked around me to find a different exit but I could only see this one door as my hands floundered.

"Come on, come on. Open damn you, open."

Finally I dove through the door just as the room door opened and the man who signed me in looked out of the door sleepily and with what little hair he had left sticking up in every direction possible.

"Hello? Is anyone there?"

He looked around confused at the door that was flapping shut as I left as quickly as my legs could carry me. I didn't want to see his face. I didn't want to see the pity that he would no doubt feel when he saw what a useless state I had become all because of a stupid voice that would never be silenced. A voice that would never leave my brain. A voice that will haunt me until my very dying day and who would mourn me then? Would the vultures that are my family members come to my funeral and talk about how good a person I was while eyeing up the family heirlooms and wondering what they could possibly be left with in the will?

I ran to the corner of the street and bent off to try to catch my bearings and to work out where the hell I was going. I may have this urge to run but to where was completely lost to me. People walked past me, trying to avoid even the smallest chance of making eye contact. Impact after impact against me as people barged past and knocked me out of the way as they went about their business. It seemed to be blur after blur after blur as the world around me passed me by. Sparked out of my confusion by a quiet voice, I turned to see a young but stern looking lady holding out an envelope.

"I was told to give this to you as soon as you came out and I've been stood here like a bloody idiot for ages so take it and I can be on my way."

Before I even had it fully in my hand, she'd turned on her heel and was marching off in the opposite direction, her heels making a rhythmic clicking on the path that reminded me of a metronome. Puzzled, I looked at the envelope in my hands. It was blank except for the words OPEN ME written on it in exceedingly neat handwriting. After what felt like a lifetime, an elderly man cleared his throat and muttered that I was to move out the way before he barged past grumpily. Again I stared at the envelope. Was this really meant for me? Why the hell was someone waiting for me? Did they have the right person? So many questions were running through my head that I wasn't sure if I preferred those or the accusing voice of my mother. I suppose it's a bit like a choice between dying of a gunshot to the head or dying because of thousands of bites of angry rats but I suppose it was a choice nonetheless so I decided I'd find the nearest place to sit down and try to formulate some kind of plan to get some answers to all of these fucking questions.

The city around me had most definitely seen better days but it really seemed to be a rather strange mixture. The buildings that I could see seemed to alternate between being boarded up and run-down shells of old shops and fresh new coffee shops and boutiques. My eyes were finally allowing me to adjust to everything around me and yet it still didn't look quite right. In fact, it felt like an unfinished illustration where the artist just gave up partway through to tackle something more important. There seemed to just be such a mixture of styles around me that none of it made even the tiniest bit of sense to my brain.

"Well have you read it yet?"

My head turned to see the girl had returned but managed to look more impatient than before, her arms folded across her chest like a disappointed teacher. I noticed her eyes this time. Behind her square rimmed glasses were eyes that were a deep scarlet red. She was definitely wearing contact lenses of some sort for sure yet the sheer vibrancy of the colour took me by surprise.

I hadn't even had a chance to answer before there was a sudden, blinding pain inside my brain. It felt like someone was taking a chainsaw to the inside of my mind and pulling pieces out through my eyes. A scream rumbled up my throat wanting to escape my mouth but I couldn't even open my mouth. My eyes were clenched shut as tight as they could be to try to stop the piercing light that was trying to push its way through. I could feel the pavement underneath my knees and my hands, I could feel hands on my back, movement all around me yet I felt more trapped now than in any nightmare that I'd ever had.

Well idiot, answer the girl instead of standing there like a damned fool.

"Read it quickly before we lose you Naz. Quickly!"

Her voice sounded frantic, almost scared. I couldn't help but let the feeling of time passing too quickly run through me like a bolt of electricity trying to shock me in to action instead of feeling rooted to the spot.

"Now Naz, now!"

Before I could move, the whole world around me seemed to bend, to crush everything in to one indescribable mess, people changed in to abstract versions of themselves. The shops slowly dissolved in to colourless shapes and finally, my entire world went black and I started to fall.

***

The deer walked slowly along the deserted road, its guts trailing behind him like some sort of grotesque cape. Everywhere was completely and utterly silent except for the echo of its hooves as it walked for a few moments before stopping next to me. Even though I had my eyes shut, I knew it was there but prayed to myself that it would walk on past.

Stop being so melodramatic Naz, you're going to have to see this.

That voice. Even in my dreams it was *still* that infernal voice. Maybe there truly was no escape from her. Not even death. A sharp nudge to my ribs forced me awake and I opened my eyes to see the deer standing over me, clouds of condensation steaming from its nostrils. Its black and lifeless eyes were staring at me as if trying to make me get to my feet via sheer will of force.

"Get up Naz. You need to see this."

The voice came from the deer. I rubbed my eyes. The voice was different and it definitely came from the deer, I was sure of it.

Well you heard the deer, get up.

Great, now I'm hearing two voices in my head and I'm only God knows where.

"Your God has nothing to do with what I am about to show you Naz."

Slowly, I stood up and without thinking, rested my hand on the back of the deer to steady myself. At least I knew the deer was real now or as real as a talking deer with its guts hanging out in a dream could be.

Now you're just being pedantic.

The creature looked at me as if offended that my hand was on its flank so I quickly stuffed both of my hands in to my pockets without really knowing why I chose to put them there. As I looked the deer up and down and seeing the guts hanging out of it and patches of fur missing, I could feel the eyes still staring back at me.

"No need to stare Naz, I'm fully aware that I'm not looking my best right now."

Out of all the weird shit I had seen in my dreams recently, it felt rather strange to be most perplexed by the fact that an animal could talk. Hearing my dead mother's voice in my head. Fine, I'll deal with that despite it slowly driving me to what I'll assume is an end that involves insanity of some kind. A deer with their guts dragging along the floor, disgusting but yes, I'll deal with that too. My dreams coming during the night *and* during the day? Even that I'll deal with as best as I can but an animal talking to me? That just seemed one step too damn far for my shattered mind to comprehend.

I hope you're ready for this Naz.

The deer nudged me with its head and grunted impatiently.

"Are you coming or not Naz?"

With that, it turned and started to walk towards the trees slowly and I walked behind with the hesitation I was feeling growing with each and every step I took. I had no idea where I was being taken to, all I knew was I clearly had no choice whether to go or not.

The further in to the woods we went, the quicker the dread built up around me. Suddenly, I could hear voices and laughter echo around us and we both stopped.

"Are you ready Naz? I have many things to show you and this is merely the first of those."

I shook my head in answer while my eyes darted around to see if I could see where the voices were coming from. A howl of laughter burst forth from a clearing in the distance alongside some muffled talking.

I'm sorry. I'm sorry I couldn't stop this from happening Naz.

Now I know for sure this place isn't real. *She* would never apologise no matter what had happened. A gunshot cracked and I threw myself to the floor in a feeble act of self-preservation.

"Do not fear, nothing can hurt you in this place. You can only see here. Not feel. Now follow for this is the start of it all."

Kneeling and looking at the deer, I tried to make sense of all that I was hearing, all of the things that I had seen here. Nothing was making sense at all. Everything felt real but it couldn't be.

"Come."

The more steps the two of us took, the louder the voices were becoming. I could finally begin to make out the words.

"Get him up there."

"Make sure it's nice and tight, you know what these people are like."

"Boy, all of this is all your fault."

I didn't recognise any of the voices but none of it sounded good. Looking at the deer, I knew it wanted me to walk to the clearing. I knew it wanted me to see what was about to happen but something deep in my gut was screaming at me to turn and run in the opposite direction, ignoring anything that was happening there.

Suddenly I heard a woman scream and the laughter got louder, drowning out the crying and pleading that followed as the deer looked at me.

"You cannot involve yourself. This is already the past. It has already been done and cannot be changed."

Before I knew what was happening, I found myself running as fast as I could to the clearing. I had to get there. Fuck what the damned deer said. I had to try to do something, anything. It sounded like something really horrific was happening there. Someone, anyone had to do something. To just do nothing would make me as guilty as they were.

Bursting through the trees, the men in front of me were laughing and dancing around a tree as a woman lay on the floor sobbing. I couldn't see her face but her clothes looked strange, they looked old as if from the 50's. A man was stood over her, holding her down by pushing his dirty boot on to her side. He had a rifle slung over his shoulder. I looked around to see if there was anything I could use to defend myself with but it was just tree after tree after tree. Without warning, he stamped on the woman and when she doubled over in pain, he kicked her swiftly and violently in the ribs.

"Get away from her!" My own voice carried through the air, shocking even myself but the man didn't budge an inch. One of his friends walked next to him and looked in my direction but did nothing. His eyes were empty and despite looking right at me, he didn't see me.

"He sure is taking a long time to die ain't he?"

He? Who are they talking about? I ran to the two men but I fell, my hand passing through the leg nearest me as the voice of the deer came through the noise.

"I told you Naz, this has already come to pass, you cannot change that which has already been done."

I pushed myself to my feet and looked around and saw a small dirt road which had lead to the clearing near me. On it was an old red Dodge Ram pickup truck with three more men on it. They were whooping and cheering loudly with bottles of beer in their hands and pointing at a tree. That's when I heard it. That's when I heard the sound that nobody should ever have to hear. I heard slow, pained gasps of air. I heard slow sounds of coughing and the creaking of a branch.

Please Naz. Don't look. Please. I couldn't stop it. Please.

I looked at the woman on the floor. The man that pinned her down spat on her. As she turned to wipe her face, that's when I recognised her.

"Mum?"

I dove at the man again and went right through him as if he didn't exist at all, landing in a heap as a shadow danced across the floor. That's when the coughing and the gasps of air stopped. That's when the cheering somehow managed to get even louder.

"Finally. Took his damned time dying that boy."

They all ran to the truck and the wheels skidded in the mud as it sped away taking the cheering with it. The only sounds left were her sobs and the creaking of a tree branch above my head. I didn't want to look but I knew I had to.

The shadow swayed in front of me as I forced myself to look up to see if my worst fears were true. They were. Above me, a body was swaying in the breeze, hanging from a roughly tied noose in the tree. As my eyes moved up the body, I noticed it was covered in blood and two of the fingers on its left hand were obviously broken in an unnatural angle. I couldn't stop watching it sway in the wind despite it being the most horrific thing I had ever seen.

"This is where it all began for you Naz, the beginning of many endings."

I looked up slowly and fell backwards to the floor. The face. That face. I couldn't mistake it no matter how much I wished it wasn't so. It may have been covered in blood from the various wounds and swellings but I couldn't mistake it. I screamed until my throat felt raw. I screamed for what felt like an eternity as the wind took my voice and spread it through the trees.

That face. That bloody, beat up face.

It was mine.

Chapter Three

Sunlight seared into my eyes making it nearly impossible to open them fully, leaving me to squint as tightly as I could. My hands scrabbled to find something to hold on to when I felt another hand take mine. I jerked backwards in shock and tried to focus my eyes so I could see who it was. I could hear a quiet voice talking to me but the words were a jumbled mess in my head. My head rested against a wall behind me and I was pretty sure it was only the brickwork that was keeping me upright.

"Come back to me Naz, I'm here."

The voice was familiar, safe and I somehow knew it was one that I could trust. That hand took mine again and I felt the top of mine being stroked gently. I opened my eyes as wide as the sunlight would allow me and slowly everything came back in to focus. I looked at the floor. The envelope was next to my leg so I picked it up with my spare hand and rushed to put it back in to my pocket before I looked around to see just who was holding my hand.

"Welcome back."

It was the girl who had given me the envelope but this time the stern look had been replaced by a kind one as she looked at me.

"I'm guessing you have a lot of questions now?" she asked nicely.

I nodded, not trusting myself to speak and manage a coherent sentence. The envelope in my pocket felt reassuring but also confused me more. Did that weird vision have something to do with the contents of the black envelope?

The weird thing is, whenever I touched the textured envelope, it awakened a deep need and desperation inside me to open it but it also carried a deep sense of foreboding too. I just couldn't shake the feeling that if I opened it then everything would change. Whether that change would be for the better or the worse I had no idea but right now, I had more pressing matters to take care of. Namely, what the hell was going on?

Don't leave her standing there. At least get her a coffee or something you idiot.

Well, the voice was back to her normal, vindictive self again. Knew it was too good to last.

That was different. You'll see soon enough.

The girl next to me lead me to the nearby coffee shop. A lurid, bright green neon sign outside said 'Welcome' but the view through the window was the exact opposite. A grumpy looking man stood behind the counter holding a ragged looking cloth but he was the only person in there.

I think she felt my hesitation in going inside as she squeezed my hand reassuringly again. "We'll be OK in here, we'll be left alone."

As we walked in, a bell jingled in a high-pitched annoying tone above our heads. On the plus side, at least it was better than *that* voice. Silver lining and all that jazz. The man behind the counter was definitely the only person in here so we grabbed the nearest table. To be fair, it's not like the place was busy so it seemed as good a choice as any.

I looked around and this place had clearly seen much better days. Like the motel I was staying in, it was as if they'd managed to fit every stereotype in to one place but at least it felt safe. Placing the envelope on to the scratched table top, it looked out of place next to a dirty looking vase with a feeble looking flower in and a plastic covered menu with some ominous looking stains on and gave our table a rather strange atmosphere.

"My names Rhea, yes it is after Zeus' mother and yes my parents were hippies so there's three of your questions answered already."

In spite of everything that had happened thus far, I smiled. A real smile. In fact, I didn't remember the last time I'd smiled. Rhea's hand went over mine as I went to pick up the envelope.

"Not here, not yet" said Rhea with a serious look on her face as the man behind the counter walked over to us.

"Aright? What you want?"

I started to read the menu but was distracted by the man chuckling to himself.

"We have tea. We have coffee. If you want anything else then you are shit out-ta luck."

"Well then, two coffees it is then and may I commend you on your rather splendid customer service."

The man turned on his heel and walked off to get our coffees and Rhea smirked slightly when she looked at me.

"Never mind Jim. He's just not a people person."

I let my eyes drift back to the envelope on the table. The calligraphic handwriting truly was a beautiful thing to behold. Each swirl of every letter looked like hours of concentration had gone in to getting it on to the paper looking as perfect as could be. Running a finger over the words definitely gave the realisation that the envelope was definitely not a cheap one and I'm guessing the contents wouldn't be cheap either. The footsteps alerted me to Jim's arrival so I quickly pushed the envelope under the plastic menu.

"Here's your coffees. Want anything else?"

"I thought you said we were shit out-ta luck Jim?"

"I did but I was being nice weren't I Rhea" replied Jim with a deep throaty chuckle as he walked away from our table and out the back door.

The jarring sound of the bell broke my attention away from the envelope as the door swung open abruptly and a red-haired woman gracefully entered the coffee shop. I watched her enter with each movement seemingly casting a spell leaving me incapable of taking my eyes from her as she waited to order.

Eventually, after what felt like an eternity, Jim came out from the back holding a dirty cloth and a semi-annoyed grimace on his unshaven face. Each movement of his face made it look like interaction with anyone was pure and utter torture. Part of me was happy that the shitty customer service was for everyone and not just aimed at me and Rhea.

As the woman ordered a coffee to go, a glint caught my eye. An ornate earring adorned her ear, its modernity juxtaposed by its antique finish. However it was something just above the jewellery that he couldn't take his eyes from. Her ear came to an elf like point. She gasped as she caught his reflection staring at her and hurriedly rearranged her hair to cover her ear. The auburn hair fell across her shoulders and seemed to almost clash with the subtle yet bright colours of her dress and leather jacket. Her hand darted to the counter and grabbed the cardboard cup as she handed over the coins and left as quickly as she entered.

I stared after her and realised that I hadn't breathed the entire time that she had stood at the counter.

"There are many things you are going to learn, going to see and going to hear but it's probably going to be better for your health if you don't stare at people Naz."

"You coulda just asked 'er for a picture ya know?"

Jim's voice shook me out of my dreamlike state and made me realise that I was still staring at where she had once stood.

"Sorry?"

"The picture woulda lasted longer" he said as he gave the counter the briefest of wipes with the dirty cloth as if doing so out of habit and not necessity.

He could definitely sense how uncomfortable I was as a smirk mixed with arrogance crossed his face as he saw me slide the envelope back out from under the plastic menu.

"You gonna open that there envelope or are you gonna make love to it?" he asked with a chuckle.

I slowly took a sip of the tepid and gritty tasting coffee then looked at Rhea hoping that she would be able to realise that I was trying to tell her I was ready to start asking questions now then looked at Jim.

"Thanks for the coffee."

"If that's what it were."

As he once again walked through the back door, I could hear his laughter mixing with the sounds of boxes moving around in the back room. Rhea nodded at me then stood up and gestured for me to follow her as she walked to the back room door before looking back at my no doubt confused face.

"Well? Are you coming or not?"

I clutched the envelope in my hand as if protecting it with my life and walked behind her. Jim was stood next to a pile of hastily piled boxes. In amongst the shelves was an old-fashioned door that looked like it had come from a medieval castle. I tried the handle but it didn't budge.

"It's locked mate" said Jim as he pointed to the envelope in my hands. "But you have the key."

I don't know why but I felt like I had to tear the envelope open and pull out whatever was inside. The paper tore with a satisfying sound and I pulled out a beautiful and expensive looking white card.

"It's a card" I said puzzled. All it had on the card were the words 'it's time' and a black circle next to them. I had a strange compulsion to place my thumb there.

Rhea looked at me and nodded as if giving me permission. Within a split second of placing my thumb on the black circle, a sharp prick of my finger shocked me in to dropping the card. A slow trickle of blood started to run down my thumb. Before I could say anything, Jim had taken my hand and placed it on the handle of the door. It opened smoothly revealing a flight of jet-black stairs.

"Well, down we go mate. Quick sharp."

"And then, you will get your answers Naz" said Rhea as her and Jim started to walk down the stairs. I looked back to see the door had already shut behind me so clearly my decision had been made for me.

Chapter Four

Aithling stood outside and looked at the rain lashing down and swore to herself under her breath. She'd not been in the coffee shop for that long yet the heavens had opened, drenching everything and everyone in what looked like a vain effort to clean the streets of the filth that had long taken over them.

After taking a sip of the coffee she'd bought, a disgusted grimace crossed her face and she threw the cardboard cup in the nearest bin before pushing her hands as deep in to her pockets as she possibly could.

"Did the coffee not meet your high standards Aithling?"

"I honestly don't know how that shit hole is still open. They may as well just crap in a cheap cardboard cup, give it a fancy name and charge you too much for the fucking privilege."

"Who says they don't?"

Aithling looked at the man in front of her. He was completely nonplussed by the horrendous weather soaking them both to the skin. In fact, he managed to look effortlessly suave just brushing his dripping wet hair away from his eyes. She supposed it was easy to look suave when your coat cost more than her rent for this month.

"Ever the comedian aren't you Trent?"

Despite her distaste for his extravagant clothes and air of arrogance, Aithling couldn't help but smile at the way he smirked instead of answering her. It was the sort of smirk that could make the iciest of hearts melt and you'd wake up the next morning hung over and full of regret in an empty hotel room with hotel temperature champagne left in a bucket of melted ice.

"So, how did it go?"

The way he asked such a simple question yet made it sound loaded like a gun in a game of Russian roulette was not lost on her. She was more than aware of the plan and how it should work. In fact, *she* was the one that had come up with the plan to begin with.

"Don't worry, he saw me. I made sure of that."

"And I'm sure you gave him a shot of your charm too?"

"You know I did Trent. Charm all the way."

He chuckled to himself knowing the depth of her people skills or lack thereof only too well after being on the end of that attitude more than once.

"Enough of this then, we have an interview to get to."

After an eye roll and a sigh that even the moodiest of teenagers would have been jealous of, she pulled the collar of her coat up and made her way towards his car. Yet another show of wealth, the car looked brand new and spotlessly clean.

"I don't even see the point of doing these bloody things you know."

Trent's mood changed in a split second and he slammed his hand against the car door, preventing her from opening it. Aithling took a step back but not from fear, just from instinct. She knew full well that she could handle herself and this little twerp easily if it came down to it. Slowly but impatiently, he drummed his fingers on the car door.

"What's the point in having written a book if nobody knows the thing exists or even buys the fucking thing? What's the point in that Aithling? It's the perfect cover story. You do the interviews, the book signings and all that bullshit. Promote this book you've written and make sure it sells for us."

She shuddered a little at the way he said *us* and took a deep breath, safe in the knowledge that one day she was going to rip his head off and spit down the hole but sadly, that day wasn't today. For now, she needed this idiot, his money and his connections to set the plan in to motion. It's true that he was good looking but it was also true that he was a damned idiot.

"OK, I get it. Let's get this crap over and done with."

"Good girl" he said with that smirk on his face again. Always with the fucking smirk.

Trent let go of the door and moved around to the driver's side but a lot quicker than was needed. The glare on Aithling's face told him that he was now number one on her shit list. A loud bang signalling the passenger door being closed confirmed that theory so he decided asking her to not slam the door of his car was a very bad idea.

Driving through the city reinforced the feeling that this place was little more than a ghost town. Boarded up windows. The homeless asking for change while teenagers mocked them. People so drunk that they were passed out on benches and in shop doorways. It had always struck him as a truly pathetic place to be and one that he couldn't wait to leave. There was one thing that struck him as weird. Out of all the cities in the world, why did the Family choose this dump? It was a question that he knew he would never get the answer to, it was 'above his pay grade' as his father would have said.

Trent stole a glance at Aithling. She was staring angrily out of the window of the car at the surroundings passing by. He knew she hated these interviews. After all, each one was nearly exactly the same as the last. He got that but it needed to be done. He'd worked in promotions for nearly five years, hadn't failed yet and didn't intend to start now, especially not on a project this important. It was a smart idea. Write a book, pique the interest of people that were different. Mother then sends out the signal and it would tell them where to find more people like themselves. It was a great idea plus, nobody would suspect such a simple thing like a book being used as a call to arms.

"Trent?"

He looked up surprised that Aithling wanted to talk to him.

"If you ever call me a good girl again, I will slice your fucking throat from ear to ear and use the bleeding hole to store my pens."

***

I wasn't sure where I was any more or even where I was going. All I knew was that I felt strangely safer walking down these steps with Rhea and Jim than I had felt at my own mother's funeral. It seemed strangely calm and serene down here. The rhythmic dripping of water and the steady echo of our footsteps had put me at ease. It was Jim that broke the silence first.

"Is he ready for this?"

Despite his attempt to whisper the question under his breath, I still heard every word. It was a strange feeling. I had no idea what was going on, who any of these people were or even where I was going yet Jim asking if I was ready offended me somehow.

Seriously? Christ almighty Naz, grow up.

Rhea didn't answer but I knew that she was probably shooting that impatient glare at him. If anything, it seemed to be the default setting for her face, which I found weirdly endearing. What I didn't find endearing was the return of *that* voice.

Surprise cupcake. I'm back!

We finally reached the last of the stairs and stopped for a moment and I felt Rhea's hand reassuringly on my arm. Had she noticed I'd been holding my breath to try to make the voice in my head stop?

"Naz, you're going to see and hear some things that are going to sound unbelievable, fantastical in fact. Please, don't freak out. It's important you see this through and make your mind up for yourself."

I tilted my head and looked at her in the faint light coming from a tiny lantern that had been hastily drilled to the wall.

"What do you mean? Like why me? Like why am I down here? What the fuck is going on? Seriously, can somebody tell me what is going on?"

"Mate, that's a lot of questions all at once" Jim said as he scratched his head.

"It's probably better if we just show you and then if you want to go back to your old way of living then that's fine but you need to know" said Rhea kindly.

I was still confused but I couldn't help but want to go with them, especially with Rhea. I felt like if I left now I'd disappoint her somehow.

Jesus Naz, you're so desperate to be liked that you've followed two strangers in to a dark, wet tunnel.

The voice had a point. I didn't know who these people were. Why the hell am I following them in to a bloody tunnel? Are they going to murder me? Rob me?

Probably.

We turned the corner and suddenly, the whole tunnel was awash with sparkling lights. The tunnel actually looked like it was populated with hundreds of fireflies all with different colours that sparkled and lit up the darkness. I felt transfixed by just how many colours there were in the tunnel when one of the creatures flew right up to my face. I couldn't help but gasp at how beautiful the tiny figure in front of me was. A smiling face, translucent wings and a powdery sparkle of colour following them as they gracefully flew in tight formations through the tunnel.

"There are pixies here?" I asked out loud.

One of the creatures stopped in front of my face and hovered there but with an angry look on its face and arms folded against its chest.

"I'm a fairy, not a pixie."

I looked at the fairy surprised. The sparkling colours around it had turned a deep scarlet red as it flew away staring at me all the way.

"Fucking racist."

Standing there with a shocked look on my face made both Jim and Rhea howl with laughter, the sound of it echoing off the walls. I felt myself going bright red as Jim looked at me.

"Well that's Brian in a bad mood for the rest of the day then."

We followed the lights the rest of the way in silence. I still had no idea what was going on but I felt like a little kid at Christmas seeing all these strange and wonderful creatures around me. On the walls were wonderfully detailed paintings showing scenes of battles, of fairies flying, of elves sat around fires. Each one told a different story and I wanted to know each and every one of them.

I've seen better.

While I was looking at the most detailed painting of them all showing an angel flying high above a group of people. Some were human, some had wings of their own, some had pointy ears. It was truly beautiful. I didn't know what was happening in the painting yet I couldn't take my eyes away from it.

You know they're going to lie to you don't you?

I rubbed at my temples and could feel the now familiar throbbing in my head. I knew that meant I was going to have another one of those visions soon.

None of this is happening Naz. You're going insane. That's all this is.

I refused to believe that all of this was because of some sort of mental health issue. That just couldn't be true. I hoped it wasn't at least.

Rhea touched my back gently and looked at me with a concerned look on her face.

"Is it happening again Naz?"

I nodded and carried on rubbing my temples again.

"What's happening to me? Am I dying?"

Before Rhea could answer me, I felt myself falling again. I tried to focus on all the beautiful lights that I'd seen but everything just faded away in to a silent oblivion.

Chapter Five

The channels on the television flicked by quickly until it stopped on a news forecast. The newsreader was sat in stereotypical prim and proper fashion and looking serious while talking about a series of murders that were gripping the country. It felt wrong for people to be talking about this place considering that before the murders, nobody cared. Not even the people that were unfortunate enough to live here. The newscast was so matter of fact that not even the brutal details of the murders seemed to be important.

"Are you ready Aithling? Ready to work your magic?" asked Trent while standing there managing to look even more smug than usual. This was just another pay day for him, that's all. He may have fooled himself in to thinking this was some big moral quest for him but it was just a pay day.

Aithling looked at him. If he wasn't such an arrogant idiot, she may have even felt partly sorry for him but he was just a means to an end. She was using him, the whole Family were, deep down she felt that Trent knew that. Either he hadn't worked it out yet or he just didn't care but soon, she would be rid of this smirking buffoon.

"I swear, if the DJ asks who my literary inspiration is then I'm going to kill him live on air."

"I'd rather you didn't, it might affect the sales of the book. Then again, everybody loves a bad guy right?"

She looked at him. Did this guy ever take anything seriously? She wished that she could just get rid of him now but orders were orders. The door opening made Aithling spin around in her chair. A lady with glasses and a clipboard asked her to come with her to the booth and smiled. As far as smiles go, it was a friendly one but it was clear to her that the lady was not a fan of her work.

"Here we go again" said Aithling to nobody in particular as she straightened down her top. "Let's sell some books to the unwashed masses shall we?"

Trent watched her leave through the door and nodded. Aithling was a dab hand at this sort of thing and would have it well in hand. He raised an eyebrow while looking in the tiny mirror hanging in the green room. His stomach rumbled as he rearranged his hair. Lunch time, definitely lunch time. Looking at his watch, a one off that probably cost more than all the radio girl in this one-man local radio station and nodded. Definitely time for lunch. Aithling would be gone a while, being interviewed by a fat, sweaty man making goo goo eyes at her while pretending to be interested in her book while his mind wandered, inventing fantasies involving her that would never happen.

He smiled at his own reflection. Yes, he'd leave Aithling to her interview, to her thoughts of superiority, to thinking she was in charge for now but right in this moment, it was time to feed and feed he would. There was an appointment to keep.

***

Mortality. Such a strong word for such a fragile thing. Life itself can mean a lot of different things to a lot of different people. Some are lucky. Some see life as this beautiful, long lasting journey full to the brim of memories, happiness and experiences that last for eternity. Others see it as one long battle after another until eventually they're so tired that they just lay down and let it come to an end while others pass them by. Guess which one of those I am?

I looked up from my writing pad at my scribbled words. Would they bring solace? Would they bring peace? Would they give a reason to why I did this?

Don't get me wrong. There have been some amazing moments in my life where for a split second my heart and mind combined to truly feel free enough to be able to fly higher than I'd ever managed before. Those times truly were magical. It's just that those times were so few and far between that they are lost beneath the mountains of shadows and darkness that seem to follow and envelope my life at every turn.

This is nobody's fault. Please don't try to place the blame on anyone other than me. I know the sayings, I know the advice, I know the words of warning that every well-wisher has ever said. Suicide doesn't end the pain, it merely passes it on to someone else. I know that, believe me I know that but I'm too far gone to stop now. I have to follow this through and I have to let it come to this ending. I'm sorry.

I put the pen down and looked at the paper. I supposed that in reality I should be feeling something right about now but the truth of the matter is, I don't. I just feel numb to all of it. Everyone gets to the point where they have just had enough of a beating and emotionally shut themselves off from the world. This is mine.

Opening the window to my penthouse, I stepped on to the ledge before taking a look behind me. The thought crossed my mind that I had no idea what would happen to all my stuff. I had no will, I'd seen no point in writing one. Oh well, where I was going, I wouldn't need any of it anyway so it won't be my problem for much longer.

I took one last look down. Somehow a crowd had begun to form below me, all of them looking up in the sky to where I was. Some expecting a morbid show of a life ending and some expecting some sort of rescue, the sort that you would see on the ten o'clock news. With a deep breath and a silent prayer of apology to my mother, I stepped off of the ledge and started my fall.

Life is so fragile yet mortality is such a strong word. That thought ran through my mind and strangely made me smile serenely until the pavement ended my descent with a sudden stop.

***

A scream erupted from my throat as I sat bolt upright with a crowd of people around me. There were sparkling colours floating around my head and then I saw Jim and Rhea looking at me with concern on both of their faces.

"It's happening again isn't it?"

I looked at Rhea, unsure what she meant. If she meant these weird visions then yes and they were getting more and more vivid with each one. The pain in my head was getting worse each time too.

They don't really care about you. Deep down, you know that.

The fairies flew in looped shapes around my head, the colours sparkling behind them, leaving patterns floating in the air. Particles that they left behind littered the floor as if pointing the way to go. Struggling to my feet, I managed to stand unsteadily while I could see that everyone was looking at me. It was the first time I'd noticed just how many people were here and how many tents, hammocks and more were dotted in every inch of space available. It was also the first time that I noticed not everyone was human. There were people with elf-like ears, people that looked like they were more tattoo than person. In the shadows there was a figure skulking around that looked like they had wings. Maybe it was a trick of the light, maybe it wasn't but I was sure that something weird was happening.

Once again, it was Jim that broke the near silence that surrounded us.

"Maybe we should take him to Sopor. Even if he's not ready, he still needs to know what is going on at least."

I noticed that Rhea nodded in agreement but without much conviction before looking at me.

"Follow us, you'll be safe. You have my word."

You won't. Their words don't mean shit here.

Strangely, I felt sure enough to take Rhea and Jim at their words so I followed a couple of paces behind. I still wanted to look around at the paintings, markings and graffiti on the walls to try to make sense of why we were all down here. Who this Sopor was, I had no idea but clearly this person was important to everyone down here. Looking over my shoulder, I could see that everyone was following us but at a respectful distance behind, as if in amazement that I was being taken to see this person despite being a complete stranger. Without even knowing, I knew this was a privilege and a rare one at that.

The tunnel tapered off until we reached another ornate door that looked very similar to the one that lead us all here. Unlike the door in the coffee shop, this one had two muscular men standing guard solemnly while looking at us with not a single hint of emotion crossing their faces.

If you go through that door Naz, everything will change.

Rhea raised her fist to her chest and then pointed it towards the guards with her hand opened and palm open in a welcoming gesture and they repeated it back to her.

Every single thing.

The door slowly opened and I was ushered in to a long room with what looked like a large throne at the end of it. There were two simple wooden doors on both the left and right walls, each guarded by another muscular person. I'd never seen a room that managed to look both simple but also regal. I'd also never seen a throne with vines and flowers adorning it either, although the only other one I'd seen had been at a museum when I was still at school.

Behind us, the door closed with a heavy thud and the lock clicked. There was certainly no going back now even if I had wanted to. As soon as the sound of the lock had dissipated, the door on the right-hand wall opened and a man wearing a white robe with golden stitching walked in. I could see he was wearing a pair of sandals with wings on and a golden headband with a wing each side of his brow. Held gently against his side was a beautiful horn that he rested on his lap as he sat on the throne.

As soon as he sat, the vines either side of the throne started to grow. Within moments, there was an inverted torch on the right-hand side and a branch that dripped water on the left. The man was looking at me with a smile as he saw me staring at the branch with a look that was a mixture of curiosity and confusion.

"I see you're admiring my handiwork young man. That is a branch that drips water from the river Lethe itself."

He could see that there was an expression of recognition on my face. All this made sense now or at least his appearance did. I should have worked it out before. I'd studied mythology at university and now his appearance and that of the things that surrounded him made sense. I just wasn't sure what this had to do with me or if any of it was even real. I'd seen enough to know that this wasn't some weird, fucked up prank but at the same time, I could have been dreaming it all myself.

"As you know the river Lethe is the river of forgetfulness that flows through the Underworld."

I nodded. Sopor was the god of sleep in Roman mythology but was this really an ancient Roman god or merely a crazy person pretending to be one. He definitely seemed charismatic enough to have all these people under his spell but how would that explain everything else? The fairies, the people with elf like ears? I suppose that could be special effects and make up but that would be a hell of a lot of trouble to go to in order to convince me that all of this existed. Also, why me? I'm not important in the slightest. Just a man plodding through life at a snail's pace until my time here ends.

"Sopor, my lord, this is Naz. He has come for answers."

Rhea seemed almost transfixed by Sopor and spoke to him in a tone of voice that I'd only ever heard in a confession booth at my local Catholic church.

"Indeed he has Rhea. Thank you."

Sopor tilted his head to look at me and I noticed the dark hazel colour of his eyes as they bored in to me.

"And what answers do you seek child? Have the dreams not revealed the truth to you yet?"

I knew that I should answer, that I *had* to answer but something was stopping me. What could I even say? I didn't even understand the dreams myself and they were *my* damned dreams so no, I hadn't had an answer of any kind. His voice was patient and almost fatherly so despite my lack of answer, I started to stammer an attempt at a coherent sentence of some sort.

"No they have not your honour."

Sopor laughed a friendly laugh, the sort of laugh that would make a whole dinner party look up and smile. It wasn't a mocking one at all. In fact, it made me want to take a couple of steps closer, which is exactly what I did despite a quiet gasp of disapproval from Rhea.

"I'm not a judge Naz and this" he said as he gestured around the room "is most certainly not a court of law. Not your laws anyway."

I don't know why but I felt a compulsion to kneel down in front of the throne and did, leaning my head forward to look at the floor in front of me.

"Have you noticed each vision, dream and nightmare involve you dying in various ways?"

My head nodded in reply. I didn't know why but I felt like I couldn't speak at all to Sopor yet it wasn't the normal voice that stopped me. I hadn't heard that since he'd appeared.

"Have you been hearing the voice too? The voice of your mother?"

Again I nodded. How did he know all of this?

"The voice will not come in this part of our inner sanctum. We are all protected for this is our sacred ground and has been for centuries. It is where we and people like us come for answers whenever we have been reborn in to our image. In fact, it holds the entire history of all our people."

Reborn? What was this guy going on about? I could feel myself starting to feel very uneasy about all of this. It was all starting to sound like one of those clichéd religious cults that you see on badly made American crime dramas that you see on television.

I looked at Rhea behind me with a look of doubt on my face. There was a sense of foreboding and even fear building in the pit of my stomach but I didn't want her to know that. That's when she stepped forward and knelt next to me before looking up at Sopor.

"My lord, I feel the search for the answers Naz seeks will be weighed down with fear if he were to go looking on his own. I request I join in him as guide and guide alone."

I looked at her. Guide? Why would I need a guide? Sopor looked at her with no emotion on his face. If he was surprised by this request then he surely wasn't showing any signs of it.

"Guide you say? Do you feel he would fail if I were to send him alone?"

Rhea stiffened her body and kept eye contact with him as if waiting for the right moment, the right word, the right gesture to use. It looked like a human game of chess between them both and neither were going to allow themselves to be a victim of check mate.

"Not at all, I just feel it's a better use of my abilities other than being used as little more than a postal worker when you need your little cards sent out."

Sopor looked squarely at me and laughed as the look of realisation swarmed over my face. So the card was from *him* after all. It didn't answer why I was here or what the hell was going on but at least it was a start of sorts.

"If Naz agrees to you being his guide or advocate then I will allow it to be so."

I don't know why but I raised my hand and waited for my turn to talk. I didn't know the rules here but I wasn't going to take a chance on offending anyone accidentally.

"Am I going somewhere?"

"A journey of sorts, one of discovery and truths, both whole and half."

The sound of Rhea's voice whispering in my ear felt soothing, almost calming with the soft tone that covered each word.

"It will make sense soon Naz. It won't be easy but it will make sense I promise you but at the end of the journey, you will need to make a decision."

I looked at her and it was clear to everyone in the room that I didn't understand. I didn't understand any of it at all.

Rhea took my hand and nodded at Sopor, who in turn blinked slowly at us both and raised his horn towards us with a smile.

"Good luck to both of you. Your bravery does you proud and I truly hope you find the answers you seek. If not, then I wish you safety on your journey from here to the other place."

All around us, the room began to hum. Each and every person, creature and shadow were all humming in perfect pitch and time. Sopor hummed as he raised the horn to his lips before closing his eyes and blowing. A beautiful, soothing and mellow note floated through the air, the sparkling colours of the fairies all started to spin and twist in to various shapes and I noticed Rhea's eyes starting to slowly close. I felt the urge to hold her, to protect her but I knew deep down it was going to be her protecting me and not the other way around. Catching a glimpse of my reflection, I saw that I was smiling contently my eyes started to close as well and the world started to fall away from us all as everyone around us merged in to the walls.

I didn't know what journey I was being sent on but I did know that I was going there now and I was going to have to prove myself with this being my only chance to do it.

Chapter Six

Shirley was truly unremarkable in every single way that a living, breathing person could possibly be. Her work as a personal assistant was equal parts stressful and interesting but she enjoyed it for the most part. It was true that the random hours played havoc with her social life but considering that none of her colleagues could get her name right despite her having worked there for five years, she didn't have much of a social life to begin with.

As she stood up and stretched behind her neatly organised desk, she couldn't help but smile at the myriad collection of photographs of her never ending collection of cats that she lived with, they were only separated by a glass bowl of ever changing varieties of sweets that were free to anyone that passed. Give every one a smile is what her father used to say before he passed way two years ago. Give everyone a reason to smile and their day will be that little bit brighter due to it. She liked to think her cheap sweets was her own little way of following his advice, after all, it was better to be known as the lady with the sweets than to not be known at all wasn't it? They may not know her name or even remember it when they did know it but they *all* knew where she was when you needed some candy to put a little pep in your step. That was another thing her father used to say. Put a little pep in a person's step. He was a clever man right up to the day he passed away. His dementia may have robbed him of some of his memories and of some of his dignity but he was always intelligent in his own little ways.

Catching her reflection in the shine of the chrome accents of on the wall, she sighed. Her thick rimmed glasses made her look a lot older than the forty five years she had actually spent on this Earth. The hand knitted cardigan with cat faces on probably didn't help either but she was who she was and it was far too late to change now. What use was changing herself anyway? She didn't have anyone to impress and nor would she want to change.

Grimacing slightly as she picked up her bulky handbag, she definitely felt ready for the weekend to start. She didn't have any plans, she never did unless you count the cup of tea and the cheap romance novel with the shirtless cowboy on the front that she'd treated herself to on her lunch break as plans. She let her mind wander slightly as she wondered what sort of saucy shenanigans would be revealed between the badly and cheaply designed covers and couldn't help but smile. It was a simple life she lead but it was hers.

Shirley looked at her desk before turning out the office lights and shutting the door for the last time this week. Putting up her umbrella, a bright pink one with cats on, she watched the rain lash down and smiled. She always loved this kind of weather and thought it to be rather relaxing. It was almost like it was the world's way of washing away the debris of that days hustle and bustle.

Walking through the rain, Shirley stopped to look in the window of her favourite pastry shop. She normally popped in to grab herself a treat each evening after work but tonight there was a closed sign on the door. Not like them to close early but times change. Oh well there is always tomorrow she thought and headed off towards her apartment. She'd managed to snag herself a nicely sized apartment in the middle of town yet it was always peaceful there, just how she liked it. There was also the fact that it was only a fifteen minute walk to work so that was a nice bonus.

A noise behind her made her jump. Turning her head to look, she noticed a grumpy looking wet stray cat running across the road and smiled. Cats had always been her favourite animal ever since she was little and had a tiny ginger one of her own called Mabel. She had loved that cat and it had been her best friend through some of her loneliest times. They were always so graceful, so full of life and so utterly different to her. Maybe that was why she surrounded herself with friends of the furry variety and not of the human variety. The highlight of her evenings were coming home to their little eager faces even if their eagerness was for their impending dinner and not the pleasure of her company but she'd take any type of eagerness she could these days. Still, she loved and cared for them as if they were her own children.

She turned on her heel and started to walk again but gasped when she came face to face with a figure with his hood pulled all the way up and over a large part of their face.

"Oops, sorry love didn't see you there" she said giving the figure her friendliest smile.

The figured just stared at her without moving. Shirley couldn't see the figures face at all but could feel the eyes shining out at her like beacons in the night. Despite their shine, the eyes had no life to them, only a strange feeling of dread emanating from them.

Shirley stepped around the figure and sped up a little but felt the eyes never leaving her. She looked over her shoulder and saw that the hooded figure was completely stationary.

It may have been raining but the evening was warm despite the encounter having left a chill running down her spine. She wanted to walk quicker but didn't want to raise suspicion so decided that as soon as she turned the corner, she would run as fast as she could to her front door and not look back.

After a quick run to her door, she felt out of breath but relieved as she fumbled in her handbag for her keys. Some day she would be more organised but today, she was just her normal forgetful self.

"As the darkness breeds the shadows, the shadows breed the fear and the fear gives birth to power."

The voice had taken her by surprise as she spun around with her keys held firmly in her hand with the pointed edges poking through her fingers. Just like her father had taught her. This may have been a quiet neighbourhood but you could never be too careful, especially these days.

Confusion mixed with fear as she looked, puzzled that there was nobody in front of her. Had she been hearing things? Maybe she should lay off those cheese toasties from the deli if they were going to make her paranoid like this. Looking up and down the street, she was sure that there was nobody there.

"The darkness can hide many things but pain and the finality of death is not one of them."

Her keys hitting the pavement sounded a lot louder than they should have done in the darkness as the pounding of her heart echoed in her ears creating a strange concert of sounds in her head. Her hands felt all around the pavement as she tried to find her keys.

"Marshall? If this is you Marshall then it's not funny. You're not funny. If it is you then HR will hearing about this first thing in the gosh darn morning."

"Are you ready Shirley? Are you ready to succumb to your act of redemption?"

Finally her cold, wet hands wrapped around her keys and relief started to inch its way in to her brain. Just get through the door and you're safe. That's all you have to do. Just get through that door and lock it behind you.

Looking over her shoulder she realised she was further than she thought from the door. It looked so full of the promise of safety yet so far away. Quickly she stood up and started to swing the keys in every direction she could in the hopes of either hitting something or scaring them away.

"I am nowhere. I am somewhere. I am everywhere."

All the feelings that had built up inside of her started to flood out of her as she began to cry. In reality, only a few seconds had passed but it had felt like a long, drawn out mental battle.

She knew that the sane thing to do would be to run through the door, slam it shut and let it lock. She'd be safe there. She'd be alone with her cats but she'd be safe. Despite knowing all of that, her feet simply wouldn't or couldn't move.

The shadows in front of her parted and the figure stepped out in front of her, holding his hands out towards her. It looks as if the figure was offering a gentle embrace but the gesture was full of menace and a calm, silent foreboding. Her mind started to clear as the voice slowly entered her mind. The fear started to fade and she wiped her eyes, looking up at the figure as the hood slumped down. She knew that face, she saw that face every day and his words took on an almost hypnotic calm.

"Are you ready for the redemption of your soul Shirley?"

Wiping the last tears from her eyes, she nodded as the rain mixed with the stains of her the cheap mascara she'd put on this morning.

"Then come to me my child. Come to me with the hope of redemption in your heart and offer your soul to me."

Shirley breathed in deeply and took a couple of hesitant but silent steps towards him. In a split second, his arms embraced her as if embracing a long lost lover. A sense of euphoria flowed through her like a tidal wave of happiness and love. The smile that reached across her face made her feel younger than she had ever felt before and she closed her eyes as her heart slowed to a full stop.

Laying her body down gently on the pavement, the man looked at her with adoration in his eyes. Lovingly, he laid her arms across her chest and closed her eyes with a deft touch of his hand. She had aged decades while in his embrace and to him, she had never looked more beautiful. Those that give their souls willingly to him were always the most memorable of them all. He did enjoy the thrill of the chase and the joy of catching his victims but moments like these were rare and he savoured every single second of them. She had been such a lovely, innocent soul and as such, the energy and life he had taken had been of the most succulent and refined tastes.

    A pure white rose dropped from his hand and delicately landed on her chest in the middle of her hands. He liked to say his goodbyes in style but knew he didn't have much time here. After kissing her forehead, he took one last look at her laid out on the pavement before picking up the novel that had fallen from Shirley's handbag and laughed. It looked so cheap, so trashy but it would be a great keepsake from this evening so he slid it carefully in to his coat pocket, having to bend it slightly to make it fit.

    Taking the time to glance quickly at his watch, he knew he had to get going. After all, he had to pick Aithling up from the radio station no matter how much he wanted to leave that arrogant bitch there. That's when Trent smiled. Tonight had been a good night. A very good night indeed.

Chapter Seven

Twee and shrill circus music played all through the blackness of the tunnel. I couldn't see a single thing but something was compelling me to walk towards the music. If there was one thing I hated almost as much as my mother, it was the stupid and annoying music they played at those cheap and tacky circus shows that randomly turned up in your town once or twice a year with little to no warning. Did anyone actually enjoy going to those things or was it little more than some sort of rite of passage of some sort?

I could hear the music, distant chattering, cheers and the echoes of my steps. It was disorientating and felt like it was trying to over ride all of my senses. My ears were hurting, my eyes were sore and some pungent and unpleasant smell was assaulting my nose.

"Naz, keep walking. It will all be OK."

Despite not being able to see Rhea, her voice in my head set me at ease almost instantly. Is this the journey that Sopor had said he was going to send me on or had he just dosed me up with something? Could this just be some sort of bad trip?

The closer I got to the music, the more I could recognise the sounds. If I wasn't mistaken, there was a crowd laughing and singing along to the music. There were horns and clapping. It felt like a show was going on.

I stopped in front of a pair of heavy red velvet curtains. Something told me that through these curtains, I would see what everyone was cheering about but there was the possibility of none of this being real at all and that I was merely going mad.

"Step through the curtain, I'll be with you I promise."

My hands shook as I took hold of the curtains and threw them open, finding myself in an old fashioned circus ring. There were people to the left of me dressed in clown and jester costumes but they had their backs to me. There were people dressed in leotards covered in feathers and sequins that sparkled under the circus lights to the right of me but they too had their backs to me. Feeling a wave of curiosity wash over me, I looked at the benches all arranged around the outside of the circle. I knew I'd heard cheering, clapping and singing but there was no audience. No a single seat was taken.

In front of me, there was a second set of curtains that were exactly the same as the ones I'd just walked through. Taking a step forward, I couldn't escape the feeling that this wasn't going to be as easy as it looked right now. I took another tentative step forwards then stopped as the clowns started to chant and turn to face me. Looking to my right, the gymnasts were doing the same but had been joined by a man in a Victorian style strong man costume.

Each and every person there, were missing their eyes and their mouths were just empty black holes. I felt like I was trapped in some low budget horror film made by someone that clearly had a fucked up view about what a circus was meant to be like. That or maybe, someone had seen too many Marilyn Manson music videos. Either way, I did not like this at all.

The chanting reached a crescendo and as their words all merged in to one cacophony of sound, they all started to clap but with each slap of their hands, a drop of blood dripped to the floor. After a couple of seconds, the chanting turned to screams as they raised their hands in to the air and a man dressed in a gaudy circus ringmaster walked out from behind them holding a cane in one hand and a bloody severed head in the other. As soon as he reached the middle of the ring, he stopped in a theatrical pose holding his cane aloft and the screaming stopped in that very instant. What little lighting there was, glinted off of the silver and gold accents on his black circus leader outfit.

"Roll up, roll up. Welcome one and all and an especially warm welcome to our esteemed guest, Naz."

The ringmaster pointed at me with his cane and a cheesy smile on his face as if posing for some unseen Hollywood director. The crowd of performers all started to do their clapping and screaming as if in some strange, blood covered moment of ecstasy before stopping as quickly as they'd begun.

"You will hear things you never thought you'd hear", the ringmaster spinning himself around as if performing for an invisible audience, "you won't believe what is in front of your very eyes. You will be shocked, you will be amazed and you may even survive."

I looked around once he'd finished his clearly well rehearsed sales patter and saw that the performers had taken a couple of steps towards me with their hands raised mid clap. I'd seen enough horror films in my spare time to more or less know where this was going to go.

"It's OK Naz, you can do this."

Rhea's voice echoed through my head, bringing a sense of confidence and ease with it. As far as I knew this was a dream so surely no matter what happened I could just wake up. That's how it works right? While I was lost in thought, the performers had taken the opportunity to take a couple more steps towards me and were now within arms length.

"And now on with the show!"

The ringmaster bowled melodramatically and backed away towards the second set of curtains, walking through them with a wave of his cane as the performers stopped and stared at me. It felt as if they were sizing me up and their eyes were little more than blades trying to cut through me. A large clown started to rub furiously at his face and the rest of the group copied him. Their hands thrashed around dropping pieces of flesh on to the sawdust covered floor as they pulled the strips of skin from their faces. The clowns would have looked comical with the remaining bits of skin still having smudged face paint still on them had it not been so horrific. I felt like I should be screaming but instead I felt strangely fascinated by what they were doing to themselves.

A movement to the side of me caught my eye. In the darkness near the seating area, an outline of the deer walked through the rows. I could hear the scraping sound of its guts across the wooden planks of the floor. Turning back to the group of performers, I was shocked to see they were all laying in a bloody heap on the floor.

"Told you that you'd be OK Naz."

Taking a deep breath, I started to step over each of the corpses. I didn't know what had happened to them nor did I want to know. A hand twitched and I screamed, kicking it away from me as hard as I could. I stopped by the second set of curtains, turning to looked at the corpses that were left at various abstract angles. A trapeze artist's foot here. A clowns face there. Something about it was grotesquely funny and I laughed. I laughed my deepest and loudest laugh and for a moment, I could have sworn that the deer in the dark was laughing and shaking its head wildly. Taking a deep breath, I pulled the curtains open and walked through to whatever the next part of this nightmarish journey was going to be. I could hear the voice of the ringmaster humming a happy little tune and a tapping noise that was in time with the highs and lows of the humming.

"This man will at least give you some of the answers that you seek, he is a friend of ours but he still can't be trusted. He's a trickster so don't believe everything you hear."

Nodding silently, the sound of my steps remained as steady as my heart beating in my chest. A noise on the sawdust floor made me turn around. Behind me was the deer, its guts were still dragging along the floor and had sawdust stuck to the blood that covered them. We both looked at one another, trying to wordlessly work out why we were both here.

"Your journey interests me Naz. You interest me."

My hand stroked his head gently. There was no reason for me to stroke him, I just felt compelled to do it but he didn't seem to mind.

"Come on then Rudolph. Let's see what this guy wants to tell me then."

"Rudolph?"

The deer tilted its head to look at me. I wasn't sure if he'd appreciated the attempt at humour or if he was trying to deliberate whether or not to hit me before deciding to shake its head instead. The deer then started nudging me slightly in the side. I may be depressed, I may be sarcastic but I certainly knew when to take a hint.

It had definitely been a steep learning curve on this journey. I now know I bloody hate clowns, the creepy little pricks. This half dead deer thing that was following me clearly didn't have a sense of humour or any patience either. Whether this was really happening or not, this was certainly becoming a stranger day by the minute.

One thing I hadn't learned however, was what exactly was going on. That one had eluded me thus far but I hoped I'd at least get some answers soon. If they will be from this psychotic ringmaster guy then so be it. I just hoped that there'd be no more clowns pulling faces off of themselves in front me. That kind of shit I could easily live without seeing ever again.

***

Trent had been sat in the waiting room for less than five minutes before Aithling had come back from her interview. She was none the wiser about his little journey nor did she need to be. He stole a quick glance at his reflection in the glass, noticed that his hair was still perfect despite the rain and smirked in an arrogant satisfaction.

"Well?" Aithling looked at him impatiently with her arms folded across her chest.

"Well what my little ray of sunshine?"

Aithling sighed and rolled her eyes, letting a quick flash of an image of her standing over him, with a bloodied blade in her hand and him in a pool of his own blood run through her mind. She would most definitely enjoy killing the arrogant bastard but she had to be patient. For now.

"The interview Trent."

Trent knew that tone in her voice. In fact, he knew she couldn't stand the sight of him and even knew that she most probably wanted to do him harm in as many different ways as possible. None of that phased him in the slightest. If anything, he revelled in the fact that he could get under a person's skin so readily. A vibration in his pocket stopped him from making a sarcastic answer as he pulled out his phone and looked at the screen, swearing quietly to himself.

"We've been summoned. They want us at the church in an hour."

All of the colour had drained from Trent's face in an instant. He knew that when you were summoned, it was rarely for a good reason. Did they know about his little hobby perhaps?

"What have you done this time Trent?"

The tone in her voice was unmistakable. Whatever the reason was for them being summoned by the Family, she was completely sure that it was his fault and that she would fully blame him in every way possible. Trent shot her a glance, the first time she'd seen him so worried. He was the sort of person that would take each moment as they came to him and improvise a solution seemingly out of mid air. This was different. He had no ideas, he had no solutions, he had nothing at all.

Without saying a word, he walked out of the studio and completely blanked everyone he walked past. Aithling rubbed her tired eyes with her hands and followed him, thanking the DJ and the receptionist as she passed them. By the time she caught up with Trent, he was leaning on the car with his head resting on his hands. It was in this moment that, for the first time, she saw him as who he truly was. A young man with nothing but arrogance in his heart merely acting as a mask for him, hiding that he was just lost. He truly had no idea of his place in the world.

Trent saw her looking at him with pity in her eyes and pulled the driver's door open angrily and got in, gesturing at her to hurry up. She took a quick look around the city and hoped, it wouldn't be the last time she saw it. For all its sins, she had grown rather fond of the place. It was just a shame that it had to be filled with humans.

Chapter Eight

Doctor Robert Martel had been the city's coroner for nearly fifteen years. It was a pretty quiet job if truth be told. There were hardly any mysterious deaths or even exciting ones. Normally it was an odd drink driving fatality, a hunting accident or merely dying of old age here. The most mysterious deaths until now had been drug overdoses whenever the students come from the bigger towns around to blow off some steam. That's all changed recently with the dead bodies that had been turning up recently. The story had been all over the news when they started to appear first and were even quicker to label them as vicious murders despite there being no proof. Well, they had copies to sell and lurid details like that sell with or without proof.

Martel looked at the body on his table and sighed. There were no wounds, no signs of foul play, nothing on the body that could even hint at a cause of death for the victim. He'd sent the fingerprints off to be checked as something wasn't right. The identification in her purse said she was in her forties yet the body looked more like it was in its nineties. He'd also sent the photographs of the body, hair and nail samples off to be tested and the x-rays had shown no abnormalities of the bones and even the UV light had shown no unexplained residue at all on the body. Now it was down to looking at the body internally to see if there were any hints at the possible cause of death.

Martel would have just chalked it up to a tragic case of dying from old age from the looks of the corpse alone on the table but something about the body was nagging at him. To the naked eye, it looked almost as if the body itself had been dried out somehow. Either that or the victim was just very old. Or worst case scenario, the victim was a mummy from ancient Egypt but that seemed very doubtful despite the weirdness happening around the city recently.

"Subject appears to have no identifying wounds anywhere on her body" he spoke in to the microphone, "instead it looks like she is merely sleeping."

He turned the microphone away, scratching his head. This was one of many bodies he'd had recently where the bodies didn't match the identification they carried with them. It didn't help that there was such a backlog at the lab that they still hadn't gotten the results through for the previous bodies yet alone this one. How could they tell who they truly were if they didn't have the fingerprint results back? How would their families get the closer that they so desperately wanted?

Looking at the tray of instruments, he picked the scalpel and looked at the body before taking a deep breath. Even as a coroner, he hated this part. It felt invasive, almost wrong to be cutting in to a body. They always seemed so helpless and he always felt like he was taking advantage of that vulnerability. He punctuated the first cut by silently mouthing a silent prayer to the body on the table almost as if asking the victim for forgiveness.

Trying to shake those thoughts from his head, the scalpel started on its journey of making the Y shaped incision before stopping. There was always so little blood when he started this part due to the obvious fact that the heart wasn't beating and nor was there the helpful hand of gravity helping the blood flow. Even with that scientific approach, it still made his skin crawl. The lack of blood always made him feel like it was some sort of beginning for a horror story but he had a job to do and he was nothing but professional.

Martel shook his head and cursed his shaking hands. He'd only been alcohol free for a couple of months but surely the hand shakes should have stopped by now. At least he'd been lucky and none of his colleagues had mentioned seeing them at all. Pushing a little harder on the scalpel, Martel restarted his Y incision, cutting an incision from each shoulder then curving under her breasts so that they met in the middle of the chest and then cut a longer stem line down to the body's public region. He nodded, almost in approval at the straightness of the lines and smile.

"Are you OK Doctor Martel?"

The voice came from his assistant, a young lady called Webber. Almost too eager to please but insanely intelligent, she had been a breath of fresh air to a place that had felt more like an old boys club than a pathology department.

"Yes, yes I'm fine thank you" he answered while holding his gloved hand out and waiting to be handed the pair of rib cutters. As soon as they touched his hand, he set to work cutting the ribs and cartilage with the prune like instrument in a precise and determined style. Maybe a look at the heart and lungs might give some sort of idea as to why the lady on his table had passed away.

"Doctor Martel, can I ask you something?

Martel smiled. This was one of the pleasures of working with Webber. She always seemed to pop up with a philosophical question or needing an opinion on some big mystery of the world.

"Shoot away."

Webber smiled back. Despite the age difference between them, it had always been easy to talk to Doctor Martel, even with some of the other interns saying that they felt he was colder than ice.

"What's the deal with all these bodies?"

"Well Webber, we are a team of coroners so bodies are relatively frequent visitors to us" Martel replied with a smirk as he removed the rib cage to get a closer look at the heart.

"You know what I meant."

A frown crossed his face. After examining the heart, he took a step back and looked at Webber. If he hadn't known better, he'd have thought the heart belonged to someone much younger than who was on the table. It had been the same with each of the previous bodies too but still no answers. Martel gestured at Webber to come closer.

"What do you make of this?"

She moved the heart around in her hands for a moment, checking every possible part of it and then checking it a second time to make sure.

"If I didn't know better, I'd say we have the wrong heart" she said with a sly smirk on her face.

"Exactly. Can you get on the phone and get them to get a rush on with the finger prints and the other results please? Something really isn't feeling right here at all."

He pulled his gloves off with a slap sound and threw them in to the bin with a frustrated sigh before walking over to his computer screen. Moving the cursor over the screen, he zoomed in on one of the x-ray pictures and tapped his fingers on the desk. No matter how closely he looked or whichever angle he chose to look from, the heart looked completely normal. There wasn't a single thing on that screen that could explain why there was a dead body on his desk. For all intensive purposes, she should still be alive and walking around as if nothing was wrong not laid out and getting poked, prodded and cut in an effort to find some thread of an idea as to what happened to her. A shadow crossed over part of the screen and Martel knew Webber would be looking over his shoulder like she always did. Her sense of curiosity was equal parts endearing and annoying, especially when he was trying to concentrate.

"This her x-ray?"

Martel nodded and rested his head on one of his hands.

"It's like she was in perfect health and her body just stopped for no reason. I can't explain it and she's not the first one like this either. Her death is definitely connected to the others, I just don't know how to explain that connection other than the simple fact that they all look like their bodies just stopped working one day. That's it. That's the only connection."

"No links between the victims then?"

"Not at all. They're all from different parts of the city, none of them are connected either socially or via their work. Different ages, different races, different gender and different sexual orientation. Not one is the same."

"Maybe the link is that there is *no* link. It would act as an MO of some kind surely?"

Martel looked at Webber with a look of realisation on his face. He may have been in his mid forties but he'd always looked younger. Today, he looked every single one of those years and then some.

"You could be right Webber but if that is the case, then how do we stop someone that has no rhyme or reason from committing murder? How do we stop these random deaths if it's something biological instead? There are so many variables that I get the feeling that a lot more people are going to end up here before we even come close to working out a fraction of what is really going on."

Webber rubbed his back in a vain effort to console him then felt her phone vibrate in her trouser pocket. Excusing herself for a moment, she stepped in to the corridor.

"Yes ma'am. She's here. No ma'am he has no truly no idea, if anything, he's more lost than he was with the others. Yes ma'am, I'll be there. Same time, at the church."

Webber hung up and looked at her reflection in the glass of the window and rearranged her hair over her pointed ears and smiled. Nobody knew who she truly was but they would although for now, she had to get out of here. She had an appointment to keep and the Family didn't like to be kept waiting.

Chapter Nine

When I woke up this morning, walking through a dark tunnel with a talking deer after seeing circus performers tearing their faces off in front of me was not how I imagined my day going. There was one silver lining however. However creepy and fucked up this dream was going to get, at least I wasn't hearing my mother's voice over and over again. That shrill, tainted voice that would tear my mind in to little pieces before shitting all over them. If not hearing that ever again was the upside of being in this half world, then I could gladly put up with all this crazy shit.

"That's quite a change for you Naz. I like it."

Rhea's voice was starting to feel like a comfort blanket for me but also was feeling like a crutch that was helping to build myself some confidence. I couldn't allow myself to get too ahead of ourselves though. I still had no clue what was going on. I still had no clue why I was being made to dream this and I still had no clue what I was meant to be doing other than walking down this tunnel with a dead deer with its guts making an annoying scraping sound as it walked. The feeling of frustration was really starting to make me feel impatient to get some answers then I could get the fuck out of here.

Turning to look at the deer, I couldn't help but feel that it looked almost curious. Its head tilted from side to side as if watching the walls while we walked, taking in each and every detail that it possibly could.

"Is there a reason you're staring at me Naz and not at where we are going?"

No matter how many times this creature spoke to me, it still sent shivers down my spine when it did. The voice had next to no emotion in it and when he talked, it echoed around the tunnel giving it a really creepy effect. After seeing those clowns, I don't think this day needed any other help in that area.

"Not every day you meet a talking deer with its guts hanging out is it?"

The deer looked between its legs and chuckled at the sight it saw.

"No I don't suppose it is."

I felt myself slam in to something cold and solid in the dark. Squinting my eyes as tightly as I could, I could make out a faint outline of a door cut in to the black stone but there was no handle. Both I and the deer looked at each other as if expecting one of us to have the answer. As soon our eyes met, we both started laughing, a laugh born of frustration that reverberated off of the walls. After a few seconds, we both took a deep breath and I started to feel my way around the outline of the door with my hands to see if there was some sort of catch or switch so we could continue on this journey. The deer sniffed at the door and took a couple of steps back from it looking slightly alarmed.

"There's someone behind that door. They're waiting for us."

I looked at the deer. This creature had always seemed so sure of itself each time we'd crossed paths but for some reason, there was a clear uneasiness in the air.

"Is that a good thing?"

The deer held my gaze with one of its own trying to will its voice in to my mind just to tell me that I'd asked a really stupid question.

"Should we go back?"

We looked at each other, both of us completely unsure what step to take next. On one hand, we had a door with no handle that we couldn't open with someone or something behind it waiting for us. On the other hand, if we turned back then we'd be going back to the circus performers that had ripped their own faces off with their bare hands. It didn't seem like much of a choice either way.

"Naz, perhaps you could try knocking on it?"

Rhea's voice smoothly flowed in to my mind once again. She said she'd be my guide so perhaps her idea wasn't such a bad one after all.

I raised my shaking hand to the door and tapped it three times with my knuckles and took a step back, standing next to the deer. I'm not sure what I expected by knocking on the stone but it was near silent for what seemed an entire life time before a high pitched scraping noise pierced our ears as the door slowly pushed open at a snail's pace. Despite having my hands clamped tightly over my ears, the noise still bored in to my head like a pneumatic drill.

A small albino man wearing miners overalls stood with his arms folded and looked us up and down. His eyes looked full of anger as if we were taking him away from some important task and wasting his time.

"Took your bloody time didn't you?"

I wasn't really sure how to answer so I just smiled and tried to look as confident as I possibly could while, next to me, the deer shuffled its hooves against the stone floor nervously.

"Dumb as well as bad at time keeping I see. Well, hurry up then. I've got much better things to do that babysit the pair of you so follow me. If you can't keep up then tough shit, I won't be coming back for you."

"People skills seem to be seriously lacking down here" I said, in what I thought was a whisper to the deer but the miner whipped his head around and shot me a glare. If looks could kill then I would have been a smouldering corpse after that look for sure.

The man sped forwards, only stopped momentarily to touch the walls and sniff his fingers before nodding and carrying on every now and then. My legs were starting to ache and cramp but I knew better than to ask him to stop. It felt like we had been walking for hours when the three of us reached another door. We stopped and as I looked around the tunnel, it seemed exactly the same as where we had left from. Even the door looked identical.

"Where are we?"

"Who says we went anywhere" the man said before disappearing before our very eyes. Before either of us could say anything, the door screeched open and once again, the very same man was in the door way.

"Took your bloody time didn't you?"

Rubbing my eyes, I couldn't help but stare at the man in front of me. Had he deliberately walked us around in a circle?

"Well? Are you coming or not?"

The deer nodded at me to lead the way so I took a couple of steps towards the man who had, once again, sped off in front of us. This time, I didn't rush. If this was going where I thought it was going then we were just going to end up back at the beginning again so why bust my arse trying to keep up?

By the time we'd gotten to the door, I was near certain that we hadn't moved anywhere. The man was stood in front of us, arms folded and sweat pouring down his face while he tapped his foot impatiently.

"For a person wanting to find a destination, you sure are slow finding it."

With a flick of his hand, he disappeared again and I rolled my eyes. This was getting boring. What kind of spiritual or mental journey am I meant to be on if this man won't stop walking me in circles like I'm some kind of pet dog? Looking at the deer, if I didn't know better then I could have sworn that he was smiling at me.

"I swear, if that little shit comes back and walks us in circles again, I'm punching him in the god damn bollocks."

I felt a hand stroke my cheek and despite there being nobody there, I knew in an instant that it was Rhea. Her touch felt like a spark inside me and I knew what I had to do. Knocking on the door again, I steeled myself for the reappearance of the man but he never came. Instead the door opened slowly and there was a gaudily lit room in front of us. Something in my head was telling me to go in so I tentatively took a couple of steps before looking behind me. The door had closed silently behind me and no matter how much I pushed, it wasn't moving at all.

"Welcome back my dear although I must say, I'm the sort of fellow that doesn't like to be kept waiting Naz and kept waiting I have most certainly been."

I turned to face where the voice was coming from and I recognised him straight away. It was the ringmaster from earlier only this time he wasn't dressed in his circus attire. That was hanging neatly on an antique looking coat rack that stood next to me, taking pride of place amongst all the finery that adorned the shelves on the walls. There were old books of all shapes and sizes, jewellery, hats and anything that a person's heart could desire. It felt like a veritable treasure trove in here.

The ringmaster in here was wearing a garish robe with feathers around the neck and the cuffs, knee high boots with the tops of his fishnets poking out unevenly and what skin of his I could see was covered with various tattoos and piercings.

"I hear my darling that you are in search of answers."

His voice was smooth as silk and definitely showed while he would be the ringleader of a group of circus performers. The charisma literally dripped off of him as he spoke, a mesmerising sound that fuelled the heart and the senses. All I could do was nod at him in a meek attempt at answering his question.

"Then answers my darling you shall get."

He reached over to one of his shelves, pulling down a dusty but ornate book. The writing on the spine immediately looked familiar as I started to remember the card that had started me on this strange and twisted journey. The book had my name written on it in the same, swirly writing as that card.

"Are you saying you summoned me here?"

The ringmaster laughed a delicate laugh that seemed at odds with the serious look on his face.

"Summoned my dear? No, no, definitely not summoned. Where would my manners be if I summoned you here like some common house servant. No, no that just wouldn't do. I merely invited you here for a little chat."

I got the strange feeling that I had offended him deeply with my question but I wasn't really sure what else I could have said.

"I suppose you would like me to start at the very beginning, like all good stories should?"

There was something so strange about his voice. Whenever he spoke, I couldn't take my eyes off of him. I couldn't hear or feel Rhea reassuring me, I couldn't see or hear the deer creature that had been following me through the tunnels either. Strangely neither of those things mattered as long as I could hear his voice telling me the answers I wanted to hear.

He opened the book with a theatrical flourish but then placed his hand on it gently and thoughtfully. His eyes met mine with a friendly but curious glint.

"Before I begin my dear boy, would I be right in having heard that the woman you call your mother is dead?"

The question took me by surprise. I mean, he wasn't wrong, she *was* dead but it seemed weird someone else saying it, like it made it even more final. I nodded again and sat down in a wooden chair trying to not look so awkwardly out of place.

"Oh good, I hated her so much that I wouldn't have pissed on her if she was on fire. Well, unless I could have pissed gasoline then perhaps I *would* have pissed on her. Oh do pardon my language, that truly was rather vulgar wasn't it?"

I couldn't help but smile. Earlier, at the circus, he seemed angry and almost bitter but here, he seemed serene and content in talking to me. The whole thing earlier seemed merely like a show put forth to see if I would make it to this point. Maybe I was wrong but it had seemed rather staged for my benefit although I still would not want to see them do that to their faces again regardless if all of this was a dream or not. Also it was quite nice to know that somebody else hated her as much as I had but it did make me wonder how he had known her. Perhaps that was a different question for a different time.

"You Naz are different but you've always known that haven't you?"

My body shifted uncomfortably in the chair that left me feeling like a little boy sat in the headmaster's office awaiting punishment for some infraction of the school rules.

"Well, what you didn't know is *how* different you are so with that in mind my dear, let's begin the long story of *who* and *what* you are."

Chapter Ten

The church had seen much better days. Where beautiful stained glass windows had once stood overlooking the city were now just empty holes in the wall. They'd long since been smashed to pieces by anyone with a relatively good throwing arm. Only one window out of the many had survived and stood strangely untouched. The scene on it wasn't at all remarkable. It certainly hadn't been anywhere near the most beautiful or even memorable yet this window with a simplistic image of a snake wrapping itself around an apple tree was the only one to have survived.

For the first time in decades, the pews were all full to the point where people were having to stand anywhere they could find space and jostling amongst themselves to be able to see.

The pulpit on the right hand side had been hastily repaired in an effort to bring some sort of pride to proceedings. There had once been been a golden cross next to it, an overbearing symbol of wealth meeting religion, but that had long since disappeared. Instead there was a makeshift wooden stand and an old looking microphone that wouldn't have looked out of place at an Elvis Presley concert. People busied themselves with the wires and making sure that the cheap sound system worked while others talked amongst themselves. Each distinctive voice trying to find out who knew why they had all been summoned here like cattle to the slaughterhouse.

Aithling walked through the open wooden doors alongside Trent and looked around the busy scene in front of them. This was the first time that they could both remember where everyone was here at the same time. Some lived in this very city and others had clearly travelled a long distance from the looks of their dishevelled clothing.

Both Aithling and Trent looked at the crowd itself with curiosity etched on their faces. There were some people they recognised but not many so clearly something big was happening. Near the back of the church, an ancient looking clock chimed, the noise flowing through the building and the crowd was instantly silenced. No matter how many times they had seen the effect the clock had on people, it still impressed them. How people could have such a feeling of respect towards an inanimate object yet still do horrendous things to one another confused Aithling but it was still an impressive sight to behold.

A rather rotund man with thinning, greasy looking hair and a Charlie Chaplin style moustache stood at the microphone and cleared his throat loudly. Trent looked at Aithling and mouthed asking who the man is but she shrugged and carried on watching. Whoever he was, he looked very uneasy being in front of so many people as he stared at everyone before fiddling about with some badly unfolded pieces of paper.

Some mumbling started up in the pews as impatience grew amongst them and he started to fumble with the papers some more. Trent looked at the man with a look of pure annoyance and marched up the middle of the room, arms swinging and a smirk crossing his face more with each step. The mumbling turned to gasps and various members of the audience started to point accusingly at Trent. Murmurs of discontent rippled through the air as Trent stepped in front of the greasy man and took the microphone in his hand with a melodramatic flair.

"I'll take it from here mate. Go sit down, there's a good chap."

The man stuttered a feeble attempt at protest then hung his head before walking to the nearest available seat. It creaked almost comically as he sat making him blush even more with embarrassment.

"As you can see, there are a lot of us that have been summoned here with little to no explanation from anyone. We are in the middle of this attempt to swell our ranks and yet we're called away to sit in a cold, damp church awaiting for something, anything to happen."

It felt like a trigger had been pulled amongst the gathered crowd of people. Some were shouting their agreement. Some were telling Trent to sit down and others were asking how much longer they would have to wait. It seemed like a sea of noise was threatening to drown them all with it's ferocity.

"Someone, anyone needs to step up and take charge of you all, especially now that Mother is dead."

The wooden doors at the back of the church were thrown open with a loud thud and a woman dressed entirely head to toe in black stood with her hands on her hips. Her appearance sparked a full stop to all of the noise other than the quietest of voices. Every single set of eyes were completely locked on her as she slowly and deliberately took her veil off and handed it to the nearest person while smirking.

"As someone once said the reports of my death are greatly exaggerated my dear Trent so I would appreciate it if you sat down and allow the big boys and girls to talk. You'll get your chance when or if I allow it. Understand?"

Trent looked at Aithling for support but she had her arms folded firmly across her chest and shook her head. Seeing that nobody was going to stand behind him he walked back to where he had been, passing Mother on the way. She took her place behind the microphone and smiled at the crowd. It wasn't a smile of happiness but one with menace and most certainly a plan behind it.

"We have all been discarded like trash. Let's not mince our words. We have been discarded like trash and that has to stop. We need to stop hiding in the shadows like we should be ashamed."

"But then the humans will know that we exist and hunt us down like dogs. It will be the Salem witch hunts all over again for each and every one of us."

Mother didn't even bother looking at where the dissenting voice had come from, it's origin wasn't even remotely important. What *was* important were the words that had been spoken.

"Well, hear this. There are now more camera's in the world than there are people. Let that sink in. More camera's than people. Chances are we are known already. With that many ways to see, some of us will be collateral damage. We have to prepare for that, we have to know that and we have to accept that."

There was a murmur of dissent threading its way through the audience.

"I know, you all want to do this from afar. You all want to do this subtly and slowly before picking up the pieces at the end but we can't do that. Not any more."

"There are less than 10% of us left here. We are called The Family yet our ranks have been thinner than they have ever been. With all due respect, what can be done about that?"

Mother's eyes locked on to the man at the front that had asked. There was no malice on her face, instead she looked at him with pity.

"Since when have superior numbers equated to an automatic victory in what amounts to a war of attrition? You appear to have forgotten the aim of The Family" replied Mother as she reached out her hand towards him with a playful smile on her face. The words felt at odds with how she was looking at him until she rolled her eyes back until only the whites of her eyes were visible.

Suddenly his hands went around his throat as he gasped for breath. As he fell to his knees his folded wings unfurled and fluttered in a feeble attempt to create some space between him and the crowd. Mother walked calmly to where he had fallen and tilted her head towards him.

"Have you forgotten your place? You think that I am dead for what? A day and you lose your sense of where you are in all of this?"

His mouth open and closed pointlessly as words refused to come as he gasped for breath, his now bloodshot eyes starting to look more and more panicked the longer he couldn't get the air in to his now burning lungs. The pain running through his entire body was excruciating but still, he couldn't scream.

"Those that forget their place must be shown the error of their ways. Such consequence shall be so severe that it will never be forgotten, in this lifetime or any other."

Aithling took a step forward. "Mother, please. There's no need for this. Please, I implore you."

Trent was surprised by the amount of pleading in her voice but grabbed her arm quickly, pulling her close to his side and whispered to her to stay where she was.

"Now that the interruptions are over, your consequence will begin Michael."

Mother lifted the front of her dress and unsheathed a dagger that had been strapped to her leg, looking at it glint in the candle light and smiled before dropping to her knees. She grabbed one of his wings roughly as he looked over his shoulder with his eyes looking at her pleading for mercy. She had no mercy to give and let out a guttural roar as she used the gleaming knife to saw violently through the flesh and bone that connected his wing to his back. Her roared mixed with his screams of pain and the crying in the audience as she threw the first wing on to the concrete floor.

Michael started to weep as she set to work to cutting through the second wing, this time taking her time and she screamed to the heavens. The audience behind her started to push and surge forward, pairs of hands scrabbling to grab at the severed wing. Feathers started to float through the air as the hands ecstatically grabbed at the wing, tearing it in to tiny pieces in an orgasmic frenzy. With a cry of triumph, Mother ripped the second bleeding wing from Michael's back and threw it to the other side of the audience, the wing suffering the same fate as the first while she licked Michaels blood from the blade of the knife, her eyes rolling back in to her head.

Two of the audience members grabbed Michael by the arms as he sobbed and shook with blood pouring from the two raw stumps on his back where his once magnificent wings had been. Mother looked at them and smiled.

"Take the non believer outside."

One of the men cleared his throat.

"How do you want us to kill him Mother? Will he be our sacrifice this evening?"

Mother shook her head and looked at Michael, her face a mystery of hidden emotion. Her eyes met his and they looked at one another for a brief moment before she gestured at them to take Michael away.

"No, dump him in the trash where the broken things belong. He will forever know the great power that he lost here tonight. He is now one of them and a traitor to our kind. Now, if you could be so kind, get him out of my sight."

Michael was dragged violently out of the church, his face staring at the floor as he sobbed uncontrollably. As his body was dragged past Aithling and Trent, his eyes met hers before closing in resignation.

Aithling could feel her own tears welling up in her eyes but took a deep breath and steadied herself. She knew that tears would make her look weak in front of Mother and she couldn't allow that to happen. That would never happen. Aithling looked up and saw Mother was staring at her as she licked the blood from her fingers before dancing and twirling back to the microphone.

"Now. Where were we ladies and gentlemen?"

***

I couldn't help but stare at the book in the ringmasters hands. It truly was a thing of beauty and exquisitely created by the most talented of craftsmen. The ringmaster held it lovingly in his lap, smiling to himself absent mindedly.

"Now my dear, what I am about to tell you will do two things. It will explain a lot of what you need to know but will also leave you with more questions than you already have."

I was taken by surprise with the concerned tone in his voice. I wanted to tell him to hurry up and get to the point but I knew this had to be done at his pace and his pace alone.

"Your mother was not who you thought she was or even what you thought she was. She is the root of all of this and the cause of all that has happened to you Naz."

This was starting to sound like the sort of counselling session that I've been known to partake in more than once. If he started to point out I have mummy issues or mentions I'm embarking on a self fulfilling prophecy then I was out of here, answers or no answers.

"Your mother was Kybele, a diety who gave birth to gods and gave birth to more creatures on Heaven and Hell than you could possibly know. They saw her as the giver of life and when she linked to Iasion, we knew our line was secure. The bloodline of the gods, the blood time of all of us creatures under her care.

Yet she broke that bond and lay with a mortal, distorting the bloodline for all of eternity. That mortal was your father. He sadly is but a footnote in our history yet is with us always. Iasion murdered him when he discovered that he'd not only lain with his eternal partner but also left her with a baby inside her belly. It was a frightful and furiously jealous rage. He murdered him, leaving him cursed to wander the world's between life and death forever more."

I had so many questions running through my head but the look of sadness on his face broke my heart so much that I had no words to say. I gestured at him with my hand to carry on despite this sounding so fantastical and unreal.

"You are a half born. Born of a union between human and deity which offended the gods to their very souls. They cursed you to a thousand deaths and as you were born on the thirtieth day of March, each life would end before you reached the age of thirty."

Somehow, that made sense to me. Not in a melodramatic way but I'd always felt like my entire life had been nothing more than bouts of deja vu over and over again.

"With each passing death, she became more bitter, twisted and resentful. In time, she started to blame you for it and for her fall from the gods good graces. The thing you need to know Naz, is a god isn't truly immortal. They can reincarnate themselves in to whatever form they wish to take. However, if you remove their head and desecrate it, then they will die an eternal death. You however, can't change your form because you're a half born. The curse has seen to that."

He looked at me with a look of pure pity on his face. Something about that made my heart not only beat quicker but also scared me. Was this all really happening or was it all just in my mind?

I waited patiently for him to continue, wondering if this all of this could explain some of the weird shit that had happening around me.

" You come back each and every time as you because of the curse they placed on you. The best way to put it would be that you, my dear boy, are stuck in an eternal loop of repeated death. Yes, the methods may differ but the results the same. You've been murdered, there have been accidents, you've even committed suicide but nothing changes. You always end up here. It's why you have the visions. They're not actually visions, they're memories fighting your brain in to letting them be remembered but your brain is in a constant state of shock at being alive then dead then alive again that it struggles to know what is a memory and what isn't."

I leant forward with my head buried in to my hands. This sounded like some sort of bad dream. Surely that's all this could ever be. A bad dream, nothing more.

"That's when the split happened Naz."

"Split?" I looked up at him, only now realising that I had been crying quietly to myself while I listening to his voice tell me the story.

"We used to all live as one. Gods, dwarfs, fairies, elves and so many more of us. But Mother lost her mind, starting to believe that she could be the mistress of rebirth and the keeper of souls. She became obsessed with a little told story of an apparently cursed blade that could kill our kind, taking away their ability to be reborn. It changed her more and more until there was nothing but hatred and bitterness left in an empty shell of a woman."

I looked at him as if trying to keep track of everything he was saying to me. A cursed blade. A descent in to madness. It seemed like some kind of messed up version of a Shakespeare play.

"Some of us, followed her. She blamed the humans as well as you for having seduced her in to laying with him. That it was their fault that the curse was passed down. She was doomed to see each and every one of your deaths and that would make anyone go crazy but some of us, some of us sadly agreed with her that the humans were to blame. Agreed that they need to be ruled over like slaves and servants. The rest of us just wanted to live our lives like we'd always done and be one with nature, the world and the people inside."

"And which one are you?"

I was surprised at how accusing my question sounded as it left my lips. Part of me knew I shouldn't believe any of this. That I should stand up, turn around and walk away without looking back. I could have easily have done that but with all I've heard, all I've seen, something in my heart said this man was to be trusted more than anything else.

A movement caught my eye as the wall fluttered slightly like a curtain in a breeze and Rhea stepped forward, stopping in front of me to kneel down and take my hand. It was almost as if the wall wasn't solid at all yet when I touched it with my free hand, it felt as real as before.

"It's true Naz. All of it. It sounds like it shouldn't be possible but it is."

She stood to her feet and a pair of beautiful, translucent wings unfolded and an sparkling array of colours flowed through them like a waterfall.

"I'm a half born too. Part fairy and part human."

"And him?"

Rhea looked at the ringmaster and smiled.

"He took me in when I had nobody, when I was alone in this world and scared of what I was."

"That didn't answer any of my questions Rhea."

"I, my dear boy, am a siren" he said as he cradled the book to his chest.

"But I thought.." I said stumbling over my words.

"That sirens could only be female? Don't be such a cave man, adhering to your social constructs and misinformation. She has wings and you're more worried about me being male and not female?"

"No, I just.." I rubbed my temples gently with the palms of my hands. "Never mind. Who do you follow?"

"I follow nobody except my heart. I live how I want to live. Wear what I want to wear and love who I want to love, exactly how a life should be lived without fear of judgement or repercussions."

Strangely, I felt a surge of belonging coming from these people, these creatures. I'm stood with a fairy and a siren with a deer with its guts hanging out of its belly outside but I felt like I belonged with them. I also felt like this was the start of something major but I couldn't shake the feeling that not all of us would be here when it ended.

***

Mother looked at the now hushed audience. Smiling at them looking at her in reverence, she bowed like a performer during a curtain call.

"Now as you know, we've released a book out in to the world that will make more of our kind reveal themselves to us. Inside it are our legends, some of which are being told for the first time. Legends that only our kind will know to be true. Once people of our kind have had their senses heightened by these stories, they will hear my call clearer than ever before and they will come from far and wide. Our numbers will swell. Our powers will increase and then, we will begin our rule over those worthless humans."

A hand raised at the back of the church and Aithling turned to see who dared ask a question, especially after what had happened to Michael. Whoever it was, it was either a brave or a foolish move.

"What about the humans? Are we sure that they won't hear you too?"

The small, stout man stammered each and every word that came out of his mouth nervously as he asked the question.

"No Jacob. Only our bloodline can and will hear it, I can assure you of that much. We've had a couple of new members thus far but that will only increase. Then once we find that dagger, we'll keep the humans in line."

He sat down, dabbing at the beads of sweat dripping nervously from his forehead before letting out a sigh of relief. Mother gestured for everyone to stand up with her arms outstretched to her sides.

"Do it for blood. Do it for Family"

The whole church felt like it reverberated with everyone repeating the words passionately and furiously as Mother smiled at the crowd.

"I love you all my beautiful children."

Chapter Eleven

Martel shut the front door of his apartment behind him, leaning against it heavily and dropped his backpack to the floor in frustration. A small white pug came bounding over to him, tail wagging excitedly.

"Hey Barney, how you doing pal?"

The dog looked up at him happily before running in circles around his legs and rushing off to the living room to jump up on to the sofa to get comfortable. Martel knelt by his bag and pulled out a pile of files. He knew he could get in a lot of trouble for bringing these home with him but something about these cases just didn't feel right at all. How could people just die with no explanation? How could people that looked old enough to be over a hundred years old have hearts that seemed to belong to a much younger person? It just wasn't right.

Sticking the files under his arm, Martel walked in to the kitchen to put some food in Barney's bowl before starting on his own dinner. Looking at his watch, a gift from his father, he saw that he should have been home three hours ago so it was no wonder that Barney was greedily snuffling down the food in his bowl. Chuckling to himself at the realisation that might be the quickest he's ever seen his dog move, Martel fixed himself a simple dinner of beans on toast and brought it through to the living room.

Spreading out the files on his small coffee table, he took a bite of the toast and stared at the photographs. Every photograph was of a body on his autopsy table, lit by the harshness of the rooms lights. He couldn't help but think that each photograph would tell a story, he just had to work out how to find the beginning. If he did that, then the story would flow forth and give him all the information he needed.

Taking another bite of toast, he ran a finger over each of the pictures before leaning back in the chair with both his hands behind his head and stared at the ceiling. His apartment wasn't exactly a palace with its cracks in the ceiling and strange marks on the wall but it was his home and that was good enough for him. While counting the cracks, a thought popped in to his head. The corpses all looked dried out, almost mummified. Could they have been stolen from somewhere and dumped where they were found?

Martel jumped up from his chair and grabbed his phone from his jacket pocket and dialled the phone number for the lab. Webber answered and he creased his brow with confusion. What was she doing there so late?

"Webber, I've had an idea. Do you think that the bodies could have been dumped there after being taken from somewhere else? Maybe they were robbed from a graveyard perhaps or from a historical exhibit? They look old, almost mummified."

"I suppose they could have been yes but why?"

"I don't know yet but I will."

"And what about the hearts?"

"I don't know that yet either Webber but if we work out where the bodies have come from then surely that answer will come out of the darkness too?"

"Perhaps."

"Can you take another look at the results and see if there is anything that would point at that or something similar?"

"Sure thing but it'll cost you."

Martel chuckled with a fresh flush of confidence now he may have found a lead at long last.

"I'm sure it will Webber, I'm sure it will. I'll do some rooting around on the internet and see what I can rustle up too. Call me if you find anything."

Hanging up, Martel looked at himself in the screen of his laptop. He felt energised for the first time in years. He was sure that he was going to get to the bottom of this as his fingers danced over the keys, searching to see if any of the museums in the city had had break ins. Finding a news report for a nearby museum, he smiled as he dialled its number. Time for an educational trip.

***

Webber looked around the lab and smiled. She was definitely alone as she walked over to the desk and typed in the password on the computer screen. Martel was right, he always was. The bodies did look mummified and dried out but not for the reason he thought. The problem however was that he was getting close and that meant he was putting himself in danger.

She snatched the phone on the desk and waited as the ringing repeated. It clicked then a familiar voice.

"Yes?"

"Mother? It's me. Martel might be on to something with these bodies. It could be nothing but I'm concerned that it could lead somewhere."

"Well, if he has found something then he will need to be dealt with."

"I know Mother and he will be. Should I wait and see where he takes this?"

"Yes. Keep me informed."

The line clicked and went silent. Mother always was a woman of few words and this time was no different. If she was worried about this then she wasn't showing it.

Webber sighed and looked at the records on the screen. She could easily just delete them. It would only take a second. That's all. A couple of clicks and they'd be gone forever but she would be exposed and that couldn't happen. Not yet.

She ran her hands through her hair and over the tips of her pointed ears. Sometimes she wished she didn't have to hide who she was but it was for the best. Humans would never accept her or any of the others for who they truly are. That's why Mother is protecting them. It's why all of this had to be done. It was for their own good and for the humans own good too.

One of these days Trent was going to get caught and blow the whole plan. Murders this weird don't go away, they just end up on those cheesy unexplained mysteries television shows that channels show in the early hours of the morning. The sort of thing that conspiracy nuts watch with a near religious fervour that most priests could only dream of coming from their flock. That was dangerous. It would mean people would never stop trying to get answers.

The screen zoomed on the bodies. It was incredibly faint but it was definitely there. The outline of a hand. Trent just couldn't keep those hands of his to himself, even when he didn't need to feed, he was still leaving this desiccated bodies all over the city. He had to be clean and clinical about it. A body here, a body there. These days, he was just dumping them wherever they fell and damn the consequences. It was sloppy and it was going to get them caught but she couldn't say anything without putting Aithling in danger. She was his partner and as much as she wasn't fond of her sister, she didn't want to put her in Mother's firing line, especially after seeing what she did to Michael earlier.

Webber went back to looking at the screen. She was just going to have to fix this herself. It was lucky for Trent that she was so good at computers. She'd just put the picture in to one of her programmes, erase the outline and put it back. Easy. It would take some sort of miracle to see the outline but she wasn't prepared to risk it. Looking at the clock, she sighed. It was going to be a long night.

***

Martel knocked on the museum door and waited. The voice on the end of the phone really hadn't sounded happy about his intrusion but had agreed to meet him here regardless. He pulled his coat tighter around himself but it didn't do much in this weather. Making a note to himself to buy a new coat next time he was in town, Martel waited and considered knocking again.

Finding his hunch was right and there had been a break in at the museum had been a stroke of luck but the voice had seemed very coy on the end of the phone when he asked what had been taken. It had felt like they were trying to hide something but he wasn't sure what. Surely if something had been stolen from them, they would want it found?

It seemed a regular thing these days that there was always a voice at the back of his mind making him doubt people. He used to be able to trust people more but the bitterness of this city was definitely starting to seep in to him. Maybe he could use that to his advantage.

Knocking on the door again, Martel grumbled to himself. What was the point of saying to meet here but then no showing. Trying the door handle, he found it unlocked and slowly walked in. The alarm wasn't going off so he stepped inside and tried to take a look around before shutting the door behind him.

Darkness covered nearly every inch of the entrance area like a sheet but his eyes were drawn to some lights just ahead of him, the exhibit cases were still on. Either that was a stroke of luck or someone was playing games with him but he had to check. He couldn't shake the idea that this was somehow connected to the murders. The voice at the back of his head urged him on as he walked towards the cases.

The lights from the displays cases cast an eerie glow across the museum, abstract and elongated shadows criss crossed one another in stark patterns on the tiled floor. It was at times like these that he wished he'd bothered to purchase a flash light but it was too late to worry about that now. Looking around the displays, Martel took stock of the strange layout of the displays. There didn't seem to be any type of rhyme or reason to how they were put together. You had taxidermy birds in one case but then ceremonial swords in another. Yes it was a small building but this was ridiculous. None of it seemed to make any sense.

Turning his head, he noticed a door slightly ajar. The faded writing on it said Doctor Wallace Holden so he took a couple of slow and quiet steps over to it and knocked respectfully.

"Come in Dr Martel. I've been waiting for you."

The voice answering had surprised him. Why were all the lights turned off in the museum if you were working in the office? Tentatively, Martel stepped inside and was surprised to see a younger looking man sat behind the counter. He'd naturally assumed Holden was going to be older, especially with how the voice had sounded on the phone. Holden waved a hand at Martel as if offering him a chance to sit down in the well worn leather chair in front of him.

"Thank you for having me at such short notice Dr Holden."

Holden shuffled the papers on his desk to tidy them up and then looked at Martel with a curious look on his face. He stared for a few moments before speaking.

"You said on the phone you wanted to talk about the recent break in that we had although I don't know how you can help. We told everything that we knew to the police already but they didn't seem all that worried. Gave us the stereotypical run around saying they'd let us know if they found out anything or caught anyone but I'm going to guess that there's more chance of me dancing on the moon that there is of that happening."

Martel nodded with a slight smirk on his face. He couldn't fault Doctor Holden's pessimism there. It was true. The police here weren't exactly falling over themselves to solve any crimes in the city let alone a random break in at a dusty old museum. It was the sort of crime that didn't exactly rate highly on their list of priorities.

"Could you tell me exactly what was taken Doctor Holden?"

Holden pushed a newspaper clipping over the desk to Martel before leaning back in his chair.

"I can indeed Doctor Martel. So can the local rag you appear to call a newspaper. They seemed to have had the story before I could tell people what was going on myself. Not sure why it was so important that it needed front page reporting however. It was just an old ceremonial dagger that was taken. It wasn't even worth much if I'm honest so I doubt they'll get anything for it when they try to sell it on."

Martel deflated in his seat slightly. He hadn't read the newspaper report fully after being in such a rush to find a lead, any lead, to try to open up this case. Maybe if he'd concentrated more, he wouldn't have had a wasted journey.

"A dagger?"

"Yes Doctor Martel, a ceremonial dagger."

"And nothing else was taken at all?"

"That's what I've said and what I've told the police. The window was broken, that's where whoever did it in clearly came in, and the case unlocked."

"Wouldn't it have been quicker to just smash the case?"

"Well yes but they obviously knew where the keys were so why take the risk to do that when they could just unlock it instead?"

Martel stood up slowly and extended his hand out to Holden. He looked at the hand for a moment before shaking it and turning away from Martel slightly in his chair.

"Well, thank you very much Doctor Holden. I'll keep that in mind while I'm check other things out. I'm sure what or if it has any kind of a connection to what I'm working on but I'll let you know."

Holden stood up and crossed his arms behind his back, leaving him looking like a stern headmaster.

"Well forgive me if I believe that when I see it. One more question before you go if you'll permit me that luxury?"

"Of course."

"You're a coroner are you not?"

"Yes, I am. Have been for many years."

"So, why are you checking out a break in at a tiny city museum?"

"You know, I'm not sure. Just a hunch and sometimes, a hunch is all it takes."

With that, Martel walked from the office and back through the darkened museum. Looking around, he decided that he had most definitely had enough for the day and headed for home. A hot coffee and a shower seemed like a great idea right about now.

Back in the office, Holden sighed and cracked his knuckles.

"Well that was bloody pointless. He was no help at all."

He walked over to a large cupboard in the corner of the office and opened the doors with a flourish, letting a body fall to the floor in an unceremonious heap. Kneeling down next to it, he ran his hand through the corpse's hair.

The man looked at the corpse with a smirk as he took off the lanyard he was wearing and placed it around its neck.

"Well Doctor Holden. Thank you terribly for letting me permanently interrupt your evening and for those meticulous notes about the dagger being stolen. You have most certainly been incredibly helpful."

Standing up and seeing his reflection, he couldn't help but feel invigorated after that little bit of fun and games. His hands felt electrified as he rubbed them together.

"Well Trent my ol' boy. You are looking sharp tonight."

He ran a hand through his hair and pressed Aithling's name on his phone. She picked up almost immediately.

"Hello my dear woman, yes it's done. This Doctor Martel fellow could very well end up being a thorn in our side if he uncovers much more but right now, he's harmless. However the dagger has been stolen and not by one of ours either. Let Mother know. I'll be there as soon as possible and not a minute later."

Trent hung up without giving Aithling even the slightest chance to reply. There was no reason for it other than he knew fully well that it would piss her off. The clock chimed two o'clock at him. He had plenty of time so now that he'd fed, it was time to have some fun of the carnal kind.

***

Aithling shook her head behind the desk. She'd been sat here for ages signing books, sat in the most uncomfortable chair she'd ever sat in and still the queue was bigger than expected. She snapped out of her wandering thoughts when a copy of the book was placed in front of her.

"Who do you want it made it out?"

She wore her best and friendliest smile while she asked the same question she had been asking all evening.

"Do it for family" whispered the teenage boy in front of her. He surely didn't look the part with the torn Nirvana t-shirt, pink spiky hair and pierced eye brow but she knew better than to judge a book by its cover.

Smiling at him, she signed it for him and write the name of the church under it in the symbols and letters that only their kind would understand. He smiled back at her, allowing a closer look at his almost reptilian eyes before thanking her and walking off.

All of this was slow and grinding but even the smallest number of additions to their cause made it worth it. The next person to come to her table was an older lady who looked completely out of place in the queue as the rest of them all seemed to be wearing the alternative fashions and band shirts that seemed to be in fashion at the minute. It was currently cool to be different right now, which is why her book was proving so popular amongst the humans that felt out of place regardless of race, colour, gender as well as her own kind.

The woman smiled at her in the same way that a grandparent would smile at a small child before handing the book over. She talked for what seemed an eternity to Aithling, telling her that her book had inspired her to go back to school and gave her a hug before leaving.

She didn't know why but the whole, awkward interaction had gotten to her. As she watched the woman leave, she let her mind drift before looking at the next person in the queue that wanted their book signed.

Yes, not all humans were bad but this needed to be done. Didn't it?

Chapter Twelve

I couldn't help but look at the ringmaster with a look of both curiosity but also one of longing. He smiled at me, satisfied that he had told the story no doubt, and stood to his feet. Somehow I felt rather drawn to him, attracted to him almost.

"Now that you know the truth, you will have a decision to make when you leave here my sweet, innocent Naz."

He stroked my cheek while I looked at him and despite the chaos around us, I smiled and allowed my face to rest in the palm of his hand.

"Make sure you choose wisely, it's not a step to be taken lightly nor is it an excuse to over think. Let your heart pick the way you go. It is merely your job to follow it to the destination that it decides."

I put my hand on top of his and found myself stroking it with my thumb.

"Thank you."

I turned to Rhea and smiled. I felt rather strange inside. A lot of what I had been told made no sense. In fact, a lot of it had sounded like complete and utter bullshit to me yet it had taken a deep hold of me and was refusing to let go. I, for the first time in my life, felt content and happy. In fact, I could even say that I felt complete. I don't know if I'd ever felt that way before. There were still so many other questions but I knew that my time here was sadly at an end. The ringmaster gently put his hand on my lower back.

"Trust the deer. He knows more than he lets on. He's not a pretty thing to look at my darling but he knows. Trust him and trust Rhea. Everything else will fall in to place, of that I am certain."

With a twirl and a puff of smoke, both he and the room were gone, leaving us standing in complete and utter darkness. I couldn't shake the feeling that it wasn't just darkness, it was the complete absence of anything. No sounds. No heat or cold. Even the ground under our feet felt unreal. I didn't like the feel of this at all. It didn't feel right. It didn't feel good. It didn't feel safe.

The deer started to stamp his hooves on the ground silently. His nostrils were flaring angrily, his head shaking around. I stared at him for a moment not knowing what to do to help him, unsure of if he really was angry or if he was in some sort of pain. Flicking my head to my right, I saw Rhea kneeling on the floor with her hands over her ears. Her mouth was wide open as if she was screaming but there was no sound coming out. I tried to reach my hands out to them both but they looked right through me as if I didn't exist.

Panic started to grip my insides and it felt like it's jagged hands were trying to twist and pull my guts out from within me. My earlier confidence was completely gone, replaced with a growing sense of fear and foreboding brewing up in my stomach like bile waiting to be vomited on the floor.

Rhea was on her hands and knees, trying in vain to move towards me. The deer was to reach my hands with one of its hooves but no matter how hard and how far each of us stretched, we just couldn't reach. It felt like there was some force between the three of us stopping us from touching, from hearing and from helping one another.

Suddenly, everything turned a bright white and I tried to shield my stinging eyes with my hands but the light still managed to stream through the gaps in my fingers, hitting my eyes like red hot blades. A high pitched scream pierced my ears and my head started to throb.

Thought you could get rid of me did you, you ungrateful little shit?

No, no, no. Sopor said I was safe from this. He said I was safe from *her.* That she couldn't reach me where we were. The high pitched scream merged in to laughter in my head. *She* was laughing at me. *She* was mocking me. I squinted towards Rhea and mouthed help me at her but she was screaming too and rocking back and forth. I looked towards the deer, he was laying on the ground twitching in a series of fit like movements. I was alone. They weren't going to help me. They couldn't help me.

They don't even know I'm here you idiot but they will. I know what choice you are going to make and it won't end well for you. You have been deceived by their lies and their pretty words. Any one would be able to see that but you're so hungry, so desperate to be liked, that you have fallen for it oh so easily.

It felt like there was a huge weight on my body pushing me to the ground, trying to crush me in to it. Trying to crush me in to tiny particles of dust, ready for the wind to blow me away, never to be seen again. I wanted to scream out, to weep, to beg for this pain to end but I couldn't.

You can't win Naz. You're following myths and fallacies.

All of what the ringmaster said was starting to ring true. How could it not be? Someone, something was trying to kill me here and now. I could feel the pain building up inside my arms and legs as I tried to will myself to not crumple under the weight of whatever was pushing me down. I couldn't let it do this to me, to any of us.

It's all bullshit Naz. Follow us and I can stop this now.

Outlines of figures were coming slowly in to focus. I couldn't make out who they were or what they were but they were bringing fear with them. I could feel it like a beacon reaching out to me.

Naz, you need to make your choice else this will be messy. Fun for us, messy for you. I'll make sure it's painful too, especially for that pretty little thing behind you.

The pain coursing through my body was suddenly replaced by something else as I pushed myself to stand up. My breathing was getting heavier and heavier but I was slowly getting to my feet. I stole a glance at Rhea and then at the deer. They were both doing the same. The more upright I was managing to get, the more the rage and anger took over my movements.

Naz, this is a mistake. One, for which you will pay dearly. I'd rethink if I were you.

Finally, I was on my feet as the figures were getting closer and closer. I forced myself to open my eyes wider and to my surprise, it didn't hurt any more. I could make out more of the figures now. Some had wings, some had horns, some carried weapons of various kinds. I knew I'd been in fights before but I knew the odds weren't on my side here. However, I knew I had to fight. I couldn't just lay down and die. I couldn't just give up. I had to be strong. I had to be brave.

Rhea touched her hand to mine. The deer rested its head on my side, a slight trickle of blood dripping from his nostril but a steely eyed look of determined anger flashed from both their faces.

"I've made my choice. I made my decision. I'm making my stand."

As you wish.

The figures started to scream in unison as they rushed towards the three of us. Rhea's hand squeezed my shoulder but all I could think of was wanting to wake up. I was acutely aware that this was a dream world but something was telling me that if I die here then I would most certainly not be waking up.

My pocket felt heavier so I pushed my hand in it and felt my the handle of a gun in my hand. A look of surprise crossed my face as the ringmasters voice danced through my mind.

"Use it. It will buy you time. We're coming, just do what you need to do Naz. You have Rhea. She's your guide. She's your shadow. She's your way back."

I pulled the gun out of my pocket just as the first of the creatures neared me so I raised the gun, shut my eyes and pulled the trigger. A blood curdling cry of pain rang out and I looked to see a creature with wings and cloven legs twitching on the floor as scarlet red blood seeped from where its left eye once was.

You have chosen poorly like you always do.

In the blink of an eye, they were on us. I had no time to register what that bitter, twisted voice had said in my head. Hands and claws pulled at me. I could feel the wind from unseen wings flapping furiously around me. Rhea punched and kicked in every direction possible as a grunt of triumph echoed from the deer as he managed to spear a small bearded man with fangs jutting out of his mouth. We were standing our ground but I wasn't sure how long we could last through this bombardment.

I felt a sting in my arm as a blade sliced across it, making me drop the gun in the throng of creatures endlessly attacking us from every direction. The blood flowed freely from my wound and I found myself mesmerised by it as it started to drip from me on to the floor. Each splash of blood started to move and form letters.

We Are Here

Looking up, I saw blades glistening in the light, arrows thudding in to the creatures bodies around us. The sparkles of the fairies got brighter as they tried to blinded the creatures and clawed at their eyes. There was a storm of movement all around us, bodies falling left and right. Then I heard a familiar and very welcome voice.

"Hello my dears, did you miss me?"

The ringmaster ran through the middle of us, followed by his circus performers as they sliced, punched, bit and kicked their way through the mass of creatures. I felt my body start to falter and weaken. Rhea threw her arm around me while aiming a kick at the head of a man with a unicorn horn, snapping it in two.

Suddenly, the creatures that had attacked us started to fall back and retreat back in to the light, leaving their dead and dying behind.

This isn't over Naz.

I fell to the floor, exhausted. The deer lay next to me resting his nose on my side. He had a nasty cut to the side of his face but he was breathing. Rhea had what looked like a black eye and was holding her arm but we'd all survived. Looking up, I saw the ringmaster standing over me. He was covered in blood and breathing heavily but had an excitable grin on his face.

"It's you."

Those were the only words I could make come out of my mouth as I looked at him with exhaustion and worry in my eyes as I fell in to his arms.

"Would it be anybody else my darling boy?"

Letting go of me, he looked down at himself and frowned while pointing at the blood that covered him from head to toe. I looked with concern at just how covered his entire body was.

"Oh this? Don't worry my dear. It's not mine. Red is simply not my colour. Now if you don't mind. It's wake up time for you two and don't worry, I'll look after the deer."

He leaned his head back and sung the most beautiful notes I've ever heard in my life and the world around us started to fold in on itself like an envelope, dashes of colour sparking around like an electric rainbow bursting in to view.

I felt the ground beneath me suddenly before solid and I tried to stand up. I looked around me at the sea of people rushing towards me all muttering words of concern for how I and Rhea looked. Sopor strode towards me with his arms out wide, calling to me. A couple of feeble, clumsy steps later, I fell in to front of him as he knelt in front of me and whispered in my ear. His gentle voice told us that we were safe now, that we were home. For the first time in my life, I actually believed it. I really was home.

Sopor gestured at a couple of the guards and told them to get us to the healers so we could have our wounds dressed but then we would eat and tell all of our journey in to the dream world.

Chapter Thirteen

Aithling was still seething from the phone call she'd had taken from Trent while doing her latest book signing. She hated when he called, it always left her feeling angry and frustrated. He probably knew that too and was deliberately obtuse and short on the phone. It had been a draining couple of days and her head was all over the place. She knew she badly needed sleep, her whole body was demanding it but whenever she tried to close her eyes, all she saw was what Mother had done to Michael. It was following her and haunting her each and every chance it had.

The photograph on her bedsit table had stood there in its frame for what seemed forever, showing a scene of her and Michael from a much happier time. They'd managed to keep their relationship secret but now she was having to accept that Michael was probably dead. She had no idea where they had taken him after removing his wings and knew he was helpless without them. She couldn't even phone him as he didn't own a mobile phone, saying that it would be little more than a tool to enslave humans to being little more than simple minded sheep. Now, when he needed her and she needed him the most, she had no way to contact or find him.

She felt her eyes finally starting to close when the shrill, jarring ring of the phone jerked her out of her half sleep. Snatching the handset up, she put it to her mouth.

"Sorry, were you sleeping?"

Straight away she recognised her sisters voice. It had been a long time since Webber had spoken to her at all, even longer since she'd bother to phone her.

"Trying to" she replied sharply.

"How you are doing sis?"

Aithling bit her lip and rubbed her eyes with her free hand. She really didn't have the time nor the inclination to deal with her shit right now.

"Why do you care? Don't you have better things to do?"

The silence on the other end of the phone let her know that comment had hit its intended target. She had no idea why her sister was calling but she was sure that she wanted something. It was the fact that Webber had called her sis. She hadn't called her that in years. Not since they were kids.

"I'm sorry about Michael, I know how much he meant to you."

"How did you.."

Aithling didn't want to finish the sentence. As much as she wanted to know how her sister had known about their relationship, it would have meant having to talk to her for longer. Now for a pre-emptive strike. She wanted answers and she'd get them.

"Where is he? Where's Michael?"

"Aithling, I.."

"I said where is he?"

The ferocity in her voice even made her jolt a little but hopefully it had the right effect on her sister. She knew Webber was closer to Mother than she was. That mean she'd be more trusted so surely she'd know some details, even if they were only small ones. She needed to find Michael before it was too late. In the state he was left in, he wouldn't have long left without help.

Aithling was surprised by the long sigh at the end of the line. Clearly she either knew something and was feeling guilty. The idea that she actually was upset by what happened was laughable at best.

She'd known herself that she was shocked at the level of anger and hatred that Mother had shown Michael. He'd always been so loyal to her, had done everything that was ever asked of him yet she did that to him in front of an audience that were no better than a pack of rabid animals. They screamed for blood and she served it to them like a three course meal, leaving them to lap it up.

"They ripped his wings apart and held the remnants up like prizes Webber. That could happen to any of us. You know that."

"I do but I truly don't know where he is. All I know is they were told to throw him away."

She slammed her fist in to the pillow next to her head. They treated him like trash all because he asked the wrong question. Is this what The Family had become? A group of beings all living under the rule of do as I say and not as I do? When she joined them, they just all wanted to live together as one. They just wanted to be allowed to be who they truly were. When did that get perverted in this?

"I truly am sorry Aithling. I liked Michael a lot."

"Liked him? I loved him. LOVED. HIM."

Tears were flowing freely from her eyes now. She knew that Michael wouldn't want her to be sat here feeling useless, wouldn't want her crying. He'd always had faith in her. Always believed in her. Just because he was gone, that shouldn't change.

"I need your help."

There it was, the *real* reason she'd called. Aithling doubted that she even cared about what happened to Michael.

"And you can't tell anybody. Swear you won't tell anybody, especially not Mother. I don't want what happened to Michael to ever happen again."

"Don't you ever say his name again. Do you hear me? If his name ever crosses your lips again, you will be sorry."

"The murders. They're Trent."

The realisation hit Aithling like a gut punch. She knew he'd been up to something since they were paired on this book idea but didn't know what. The fact that she'd known next to nothing about him that been used to Trent's advantage. She could see that now.

"He's an incubus Aithling. Only Mother knows."

That explains the condition of the bodies then.

"Fuck."

"He drains them by touch. So far, I've kept ahead of Martel and got rid of anything pointing towards that but he knows something is wrong. He's not stupid."

"Fuck."

"Not helpful."

"Fuck you."

"Still not helpful."

Aithling looked at the photograph of her and Michael. It had been taken when they went to the beach for the first time as a couple. Despite all that was happening, she felt herself smile. It had been one of the best days of her life.

"Does anyone else know?"

"As of yet no but it's only a matter of time. He's sloppy and unrefined."

"Well, that I can agree with. His arrogance is going to be the undoing of us all. He's more concerned with how he looks than he is of anything else."

Her eyes hadn't left the photograph but she noticed that she had absent mindedly started to stroke Michaels face. Trent was alive. Michael is probably dead or dying in agony somewhere. How the hell is that even remotely fair?

"Has he left any evidence?"

"Only the feeding mark on their chests but it's faint and only noticeable if you zoom in on the photograph. I've doctored the files to erase that though."

"Are you sure you've managed to get to them all without anyone noticing you messing about with the files?"

"Of course but like I said earlier, it's only a matter of time."

Part of her wanted Trent to be caught. Part of her wanted to see him be punished by Mother. She was desperate to see that happen but for now that would have to wait. She had a book signing to attend to.

Book signings had become the bane of her existence. Line after line of people wanting her to speak ages signing her pen name and some pithy little one liner before talking about how much they loved the book. She knew full well that they would be selling the damn thing on some internet website before she'd even gotten in to bed.

There had, of course, been one or two that had revealed their nature to her but not many. She was starting to think that maybe, just maybe, there weren't as many of them left as they had originally thought. That wouldn't surprise her after the years and years of being hunted for sport, used as performers in freak shows and worse. She knew her mind kept going back to that thought but it always surprised her just how truly evil people can be if someone is different, truly different, like they were. Maybe Mother was right, the humans really had brought this on themselves.

With a sigh, she grabbed her bag and left. The sooner she got there, the sooner she could come back and shower the stench of the humans off of her skin.

***

The sun was shining through the window as Martel sat hunched over his laptop. None of this was making sense at all. Bodies that looked mummified. A break in at a museum but all that was taken was a near worthless ceremonial dagger. That in itself was strange as there were many more things there that were worth a lot of money.

He had searched every website he could find. He had fired off email after email, phone call after phone call but nobody knew of any links between the bodies and the crime scenes.

The lab results were thrown all over his desk and across some of the floor. The toxicology results showed no chemicals, drugs or anything else that would have caused either the deaths or the condition of the bodies. Yet another dead end. It was the finger prints that were the most surprising results and the one that he couldn't wrap his head around. All the finger prints matched those of people that had been reported missing, except for the most recent one. That would be a good thing normally. A nice easy identification like that doesn't normally happen but they turned out to be the biggest problem. The prints matched records of missing people that were much younger than the bodies in his morgue. The bodies looked old and dried out yet they hadn't been missing long enough to have ended up in such a way. Age wise, there were at least three to four decades difference in how old the bodies looked and the ages of the missing people. All of this seemed impossible yet it was right here in front of him.

Rubbing his eyes, Martel wondered if he was missing something really obvious. There must be a reason for the discrepancies in between the records and the conditions of the body. He picked up the office phone and dialled the number for the results lab.

"What you need?"

The voice on the end of the phone always made Martel smile. No matter what she was about to say, she always said it with a grin and a spark of life. Didn't matter if it was something happy or something horrendous, it was all the same. That spark was always there and he knew it always would be.

"Hi Margaret, it's Martel. I have a question about these results. Something isn't adding up."

"Sure thing. Ask away hun."

"The finger print analysis has matched the finger prints to a group of missing people."

"Sure has."

"But the bodies look like people that are late 70's-80's and the missing people are all 20-45."

"That *is* strange."

"Don't take this the wrong way but is there any possible way the results could have gotten mixed up and I've got the wrong ones?"

Martel braced himself. He knew that despite her sunny exterior, if there was one thing Margaret didn't like it was being asked if her team had made a mistake.

"Doctor Martel. I run a tight ship, you know that. The sun may shining outside but our minds, all of them, are inside working on these results so there is no chance of that happening."

"No, no. Quite right. Just wanted to double check."

"You're welcome."

The line went dead. Yes, she was definitely annoyed now but in her world that just meant he would be getting only one home made cupcake at lunch time instead of her normal two. On the plus side, his waist line might be grateful for that but he was sure his taste buds would disagree.

Looking back at the results, he was even more confused than before. How could the finger prints of the missing people match the corpses? No matter how much he tried to make sense of it all, it just kept going round in circles inside his brain.

The digital clock on his desk flashed 9:08 at him. Webber was late. She was never late so he pursed his lips together and considered calling her. He'd give her another ten minutes then he'd check in with her. Maybe she was just checking something out. It's the sort of thing that she would do. She was always working past the clock, always working on things on her own and was known for finding things that other assistants would have missed. It reminded him of Sherlock Holmes in the Basil Rathbone films that he used to watch with his father growing up. He had always admired her level of tenacity, even felt a bit jealous of it too. If he was honest with himself, he'd been the same when he first started working until the never ending run of violence and ugliness had worn him down.

Martel looking down at his notes and then at the picture of the stolen dagger that he'd been given. Something really didn't feel right about the burglary and if he was honest, something didn't feel right about Doctor Holden either. He knew that as a coroner he was here to speak for the dead bodies, not for a missing dagger, however he couldn't help but wonder why someone would take something like that. It wasn't even deemed important by the very museum that had displayed it.

Part of his mind wished that he could just write up these murders as unexplained and leave it at that but he knew his conscience wouldn't allow that to happen. He had to at least try to get to the bottom of all this or at the very least get some sort of reason to tell the families that would explain their deaths.

The clock carried on blinking its numbers at him. Time felt like it was standing still in his office despite it being early. A knock at the door brought him out of the myriad thoughts running through his mind. A young intern was stood by the door looking very nervous and holding a bit of paper. Martel had seen Stanley before, he was young and incredibly eager to please.

"Yes Stanley? What can I help you with?"

"Sorry to disturb you Doctor Martel, I was asked to give you this. Miss Webber said to come straight away and she'd meet you there" he said while handing him the handwritten note and rushing off again.

Martel looked at the note. Webber wanted to meet him at the museum. A body had been found there. His eyebrows creased in confusion as he grabbed his jacket and his equipment bag. It was definitely going to be a long and confusing day.

Chapter Fourteen

A beeping woke me from my slumber and I slowly opened my eyes to look around a dark, clinically clean looking room. I was in a bed with a machine beeping next to me as I rubbed my eyes.

With so many thoughts running through my head, I just didn't know which were memories and which had been dreams. I remembered Rhea and Jim. The circus ringleader. Sopor on his ornate throne. Fairies and elves. Creatures running towards us. Clowns and circus performers pulling their faces apart in front of us. It all sounded like some sort of weird television show that I had stumbled upon halfway through an episode.

A searing pain radiated from my arm and I looked at the tightly wound bandage wrapped around my forearm. A strange strain of a memory violently pushed its way in to my head. A glint of a blade, an angry set of eyes on something that looked like it was wearing an ill fitting Halloween costume. Had I been attacked?

About time you woke up.

That voice. That infernal voice.

You were lucky this time Naz.

Somewhere deep inside of me had known that she wasn't gone for good. I remembered hazily that the voice had stopped for a short time but couldn't remember why no matter how much I tried to force the memory to come.

Swinging my legs out of the bed, I let my bare feet touch the cold floor and tried to catch my bearings. I knew that I had been in a motel room and then I'd gone for a walk but after that was one long blur.

That mistake you made will bring you to your day of reckoning.

I had no idea what the voice was talking about as I wearily tried to shake the sluggishness that ran through me. Tiredness started to once again prick at the back of my mind as I felt my eyes closing. Lifting my legs back in to bed, I tried to get myself comfy. Exploring would have to wait for now. I was pretty sure I was in a hospital so I was clearly safe for now.

That optimism won't save you. Nothing will.

***

The ringmaster sat in his chair with a tired sigh. Naz had had a close call there and he dreaded to think what would have happened had he and his performers not gotten there in time. He was sure that somehow Naz was the key to all of this, they all were sure of that. What he didn't know was just what part Naz was going to play in all of this.

A great war was coming and many would not be left alive afterwards. There was still so much more to do to prepare yet not a lot of time to do it. Something needed to be done and done quickly to ensure the survival of as many of them as possible and of the humans too. This genocide of either of them couldn't be allowed to happen.

Opening his book, he leant back in his chair with a heavy heart and began to read. Naz had so many questions and rightfully so but he knew he wasn't the one to give them to him. Yes, he could answer some but others Naz had to find for himself as part of his journey. Only then, would Naz truly be able to make a decision that was pure of heart.

***

The room around me started to spin and explode in a mixture of so many colours that I felt like I was in the middle of a rainbow.

I wanted to open my eyes but something told me to keep them shut and to stay exactly where I was.

Wakey wakey Naz.

A hand stroked my cheek lightly and I felt my body tighten in response. A strange smell was making me want to gag.

Rise and shine.

Slowly I let my eyes open and immediately closed them again. An intense light was making my entire face feel like it was on fire. The smell was getting worse and I could feel the bile building up in the pit of my stomach.

Suddenly I felt like my entire body jerked and I was on my feet. Dizziness came at me from every direction and still my eyes stayed tightly shut. Everything felt like a horrible nightmare that I had no chance of waking up from any time soon.

You're not asleep so keeping your eyes shut is a futile gesture.

Fingers pried at my eye lids roughly forcing them open. Everything slowly started to come in to focus. I was standing in a dimly lit cave and a sensation of coldness made my bare feet hurt, sending my entire body in to a shivery spasm.

How very nice of you to pay attention finally.

A hand grabbed my face and squeezed. I could feel fingers digging in to my flesh and a trickle of something wet start to run down one of my cheeks. My mouth started to open and close but I couldn't hear the words coming out. Panic was starting to twist my already nauseous stomach as the smell around me was getting worse and worse.

Look around you Naz. This will be your home soon.

Turning my head, the horrific realisation of what was around me cleared in my mind. There were piles and piles of bodies all around me, all in varying states of decay. Maggots were everywhere. Flies were buzzing around the bodies. Vultures flew in and out of the smoke floating around the cave in wispy clouds in search of a good meal. Despite my better judgement I felt my feet taking me towards a pile of bodies. It was as if they were somehow calling to me.

Look at them Naz. What do you see?

Repulsion at what I was looking at washed over me but I couldn't look away. Each body on the pile was somebody I knew. Colleagues, friends, family members and some were people I half remembered from what I thought had been a dream. A woman called Rhea, Jim, Sopor and many more. A puddle of viscous liquid oozed from under the bodies. I wanted to scream but my body just tightened up instead, leaving me there to watch these bodies just slowly rot and decay in front of my very eyes.

I said what do you see?

I didn't want to but something made me take one more step closer to the grotesque pile. It seemed like some kind of nightmarish art gallery installation with the bodies were all hooked and curled around one another.

The feeling of the hand against my face disappeared and the nausea in the pit of my stomach started to burn as it made its way up to my throat. A taste of vomit permeated my mouth and I tried to swallow it back down. One of the corpses hands jerked and reached out to me. My eyes widened and I stumbled backwards, falling on to the floor. Scrambling backwards, I felt my back hit a pair of legs. Looking up, the figure had no face, just a black and emotionless hole. The figure pushed its hands down on to my shoulders to stop me from getting away and I stared in fear at the movement in the pile of bodies. They shook and juddered as if something was trying to burrow its way out.

One by one, the bodies fell away from the pile and on to the wet floor of the cave with an almost comical plop sound.

No answer? Well then, the answer shall come to you.

Corpses fell away from the pile at a much quicker pace now and a corpse with a greenish tinge and multiple cuts and bruises started to crouch with its hands moved in jerky, random movements.

"Please don't make me see this."

I was surprised at how feeble and pathetic my voice sounded in the silent cave. The slight echo in the air only served to amplify just how weak I had sounded.

This will be the consequence of your choice.

The corpse rose to its feet unsteadily as some of the viscous liquid dripped from it and I could see some of its bones were visible. I could see ribs, some of the leg. Flaps of skin hung from where its face had once been, leaving some of the skull visible but even in that state, I still knew it was the man I knew as Jim.

This will be one of many consequences.

Jim walked towards me in irregular, spasmodic movements. He looked like someone was awkwardly controlling him like a puppet. His mouth dropped open, closed then did it again. Jim was trying to say something to me. The smell of his decomposing body was so bad that the odour was strangling me and the bile spewed from my mouth.

His hands wrapped around my clothes and pulled me closer until my nose was almost touching the remains of his. I could hear a gargled mess of words coming from his throat. Tears streamed down my face as I stared at the eyes looking lifelessly at me. Something wet dripped from his face on to mine.

"We are ALL dead because of you. You will watch us rot and decay in front of your very eyes again and again until the end of all days."

The scream exploded from me and didn't stop.

Chapter Fifteen

Martel walked into the museum for the second time in two days but this time the place was illuminated on the outside by the lights of the police cars and inside by the various torches of the officers searching the place. He looked around and saw a young officer who looked a mixture of confused nerves. Showing his I.D. to the young officer, Martel smiled.

"Why are the lights not on? Surely that would make searching a lot easier than using torches."

The officer looked around, managing to look even more nervous than before and started to stammer before taking a deep breath and tried to compose himself. He scratched the back of his neck and tried to look around as if hoping to find the answer in a reflection or hopefully in the faces of his fellow colleagues but none were to be found. This officer was definitely some fresh meat from the academy and Martel would have been happy betting his life savings on the simple deduction that this was probably the young man's first crime scene. Not that he had any life savings to actually bet mind you.

"First one?"

Martel hoped that he'd tried to make that sounds as friendly and supportive as possible. People skills were not his strong point but this young police officer looked absolutely terrified as he nodded in answer to his question.

"I'd say it gets better but that would be a lie."

The officers eyes widened with absolute panic and he started to scratch at the back of his neck even more awkwardly.

"You just get better at handling it and then better at striking out on your own. You'll be fine. Honestly."

Martel heard his name called and looked at where he thought it had come from. Standing in the doorway was Webber and she waved at him to ask him to come in. He smiled kindly at the police officer and walked towards her. She looked more concerned the closer he got.

"There's a body inside, we think it's Doctor Holden."

"I only saw him yesterday and he seemed fine. Any idea on cause of death or have you not started yet?"

Webber shook her head and looked back over her shoulder in to the room where two other police officers and two scenes of crime techs were looking over the room, all with the same look of confusion on their faces.

"It's the same as the others. Same body condition, same mummified look. Just like the others."

Webber stood aside and let him in to the room, allowing him to march over to where Holden was laying on the floor. She was right, it was the same as all the others in his morgue. Holden looked dried out, looked like he wouldn't be out of place in an ancient Egyptian exhibition. Kneeling down next to the body, he tilted his head and checked the lanyard on the floor.

"Webber, is this the right lanyard?"

She looked at him puzzled and looked at the lanyard he was holding.

"Of course, we even doubled checked with the employee records. Why?"

"This isn't the man I came to see last night."

"Are you sure?"

"Positive. This is definitely not who I saw."

"Then who did you see?"

Martel shrugged and looked around the room again. It seemed to be exactly how he had seen it last night, even down to the files on the table. So many questions flew through his head that he couldn't pin any one particular down long enough to ask.

"Are you OK?"

He looked at Webber, who was looking at him concerned.

"I had an inkling that all of these was somehow connected. I didn't know how a stolen dagger, which is why I was here last night, connected to the strange conditions of the bodies but with us finding Doctor Holden here in the same way that proves it's connected. This is clearly the *real* Doctor Holden so who the hell is the guy that I spoke to and how is it connected to an apparently worthless dagger?"

"That's a lot of questions there Martel."

"Well, we're clearly due a lot of answers then."

***

Rhea stood by Naz's side while he screamed. Jim stood on the opposite side, holding his arm.

"What's happening to 'im?"

She shot him a glare that told him to shut up as she stroked Naz's back and whispered at him to come back to her as his body thrashed around and his screaming drilled itself through the air in the room. He'd tried to rip off the bandage on his forearm, scratched his face and even tried rip the gown off during the nightmare he was clearly having.

Sopor walked in to the room, his normally serene face looking concerned. He reached his arm out to comfort Naz but then pulled it back thinking better of it. They all looked at each other, unsure what the next step to take would be. Naz should have been out of the dream state by now. He should have been awake and helping with the plans but he was stuck wherever he was right now. He'd never seen this before.

Naz's body thrashed and struggled in the bed, throwing the covers in every direction despite Rhea's best attempts at calming him. Something was clearly attacking his mind but what? He sat bolt upright and Sopor stepped backwards from him. Naz's eyes were completely black. It was as if he were looking in to a never ending well of darkness. Despite his body twitching and vibrating, his unblinking eyes were staring a hole through Sopor.

Rhea looked at Sopor and saw the worry on his face. She'd never seen him like this, he was normally serene and calm but right now he was anything but that. Turning he grabbed his horn and blew it towards Naz in the hopes he could send him back in to the world of dreams but he just sat there twitching and staring. A smile crossed his face.

Such a futile gesture Sopor.

The echo of the horn hitting the floor reverberated around the small room like a gunshot. Sopor raised a hand to his mouth in shock. Jim stepped away from Naz with a look of fearful recognition on his face and Rhea stood silently just staring at him. That was not his voice.

Any more of your feeble magic tricks left?

All three of them looked at each other and breathed deeply, wondering who would be the first to break the silence.

Silence is a welcome change from your cheap parlour tricks and attempts at slight of hand or fucking with the minds of idiots.

All the colour had drained out of Jim's face and he looked like he was about to pass out.

"It's her. She's back. It's her Sopor, it's her."

Sopor looked at him and shook his head.

"It can't be, she's dead. It was witnessed and documented."

And yet, here I am.

The words were coming from Naz's mouth yet it was her voice.

I have him. He is mine. He is ours. He will never be yours.

"Give him back to us. His soul is the one that decides, neither of us can decide for him."

Too late Sopor. Your group of rejects and failures have lived up to that reputation, to that self fulfilling prophecy.

Rhea looked at Sopor and stepped forward.

"Send me back in. I can bring him back. I know I can."

Oh yes, send the girl. Who could possibly ever defeat a little girl who is scared of her own shadow?

"You can insult me all you want, you're little more than a thought in his head right now. That's all."

Sopor started to shake his head but before he could answer, she'd lifted his horn and inhaled deeply before falling to the floor fast asleep.

***

The rotting body started to shake in front of me and opened what was left of his mouth. He looked like he was trying to say something before falling in a heap in front of me. As the body twitched, a gargling sound erupted from deep in his throat before his skin started to slide off of his body.

My stomach couldn't take any more of this and I lunged forward vomiting next to the body.

No respect for the dead Naz.

A tiny pin prick of light started to float behind the ruined pile of bodies and moved in erratic patterns like a confused fly. As bile dribbled down my chin and my hands dug in to the wet floor, my eyes followed every movement of the light.

Listen to me Naz. If we leave now, all of this can be avoided.

I looked at the dark figure then at the light and struggled to stand before wiping my chin with the back of my hand. The movement of the light was getting more and more erratic with every second that I looked at it. It started to flicker quickly as it came to towards me but dodged to the left as the dark figure behind me tried to grab at it angrily.

Ignore that annoying little nuisance.

The light dodged in a loop, flew close to my face then back to where the bodies were. Bodies started to move, a leg here and an arm there as they tried to get to their feet. Bodily fluids dripped from their rotting lumps of flesh.

The choice is already made. You are mine, you are ours, you are here.

Something at the back of my mind was telling me that all of this wasn't real, that I wasn't really trapped in some dank cave with a faceless creature. I'd seen a lot in the last couple of days that would have driven anyone insane no matter how strong they were mentally but I knew I could stop this. I knew I could get out and that I should listen to the voice at the back of my mind telling to follow the light, not the voice that belonged to my mother.

The figures hand was still tightly holding on to my shoulder but I'd gotten to my feet as the bodies did the same. I don't know how I knew but something in my head was telling me that if those things got to the light before I did then I would never get out of here. Throwing my fist as hard as I could in to the stomach of the creature that had been holding me in place, I ran as fast as I could, leaving it howling behind me. Chancing a look over my shoulder, I saw it standing there with a hole in its stomach where I had hit it but the hole was filling up as if being recreated by smoke. Vultures dived at my face, the bodies lumbered nearer but still the light bobbed around as if willing me on.

A decaying hand grabbed at my shoulder but I somehow managed to dodge and it slammed clumsily in to the wall, slumping down in to a puddle of viscera, blood and rotting flesh falling from its bones. The bodies started to slam in to one another in an effort to get to me, some even trying to climb over each other.

Shining ahead of me, the light blinked and darted off towards the opening of the cave and I tried to will my legs to move faster. My lungs felt like they were burning, my throat still stinging after throwing up but I got to the light, looked behind me and shook in fear as the bodies and the dark creature all roared in anger before I ran down the tunnel.

Chapter Sixteen

Michael opened his eyes and grimaced as the pain in his back shocked him in to being wide awake. Reaching his hand as far up his back as he could, his fingers traced the scabbed over wounds where his once elegant wings used to be. He felt nothing but anger towards Mother for having robbed him of the one thing that made him truly unique. There was no time for pity, he had to get out of here before someone found him. He may have lost his wings but he hadn't lost his pride.

Resting his hand on the side of the dumpster that he had been thrown next to, he looked to make sure nobody was around. There was a rusted fire escape above his head and he wondered if it would hold his weight. At least if he was able to get up there, he'd have a good vantage point over the city and would be able to work out where the hell he was.

Climbing on to the bottom step of the ladder, he slipped slightly as his body juddered with the pain in his back. This was going to be a lot harder without his wings than he thought. Pulling himself up, he managed three of the rungs before having to stop again and swore to himself. Mother was going to pay for this and she was going to suffer. He would make sure of that.

Resting his head on a rung, Aithling's face appeared in his mind and a smile crossed his face. Revenge couldn't be his only motivation, Aithling needed him and he needed her. Closing his eyes, he could hear her voice talking to him, telling him that no matter what, they would be safe if they had one another. He'd even promised her that and no matter what he'd done in his life, he was a man that never broke a promise.

Michael had a good view of the city from half way up the fire escape and watched people just walk about minding their own business. He almost felt sorry for the poor humans as they were completely and utterly ignorant of what awaited them. As a species, humans had to be the most hateful, selfish and apathetic of them all. They waged wars in the names of various bastardised versions of their religious texts. They separated and segregated each other based on their race, their sexuality, their gender. How these things had existed for so long was beyond him. Maybe if they knew respect, intelligence and understanding instead of worshipping the next reality television star then maybe, just maybe none of this would have needed to happen. Maybe then, they wouldn't need to rule over these unimportant insects.

Finally, he reached the roof of the building and fell to his knees praying to the gods above him. He was no longer sure if they listened to him or any of the other members of The Family but sometimes, belief is all you had in this world and the next. Part of him naively thought that if he prayed that Aithling might hear him and know he was alive.

Looking down at his clothes, he looked exactly how he felt. Like he'd crawled through a pile of garbage. He'd stand out like a sore thumb if he went down there looking like this but where would be able to grab clothes? It was a catch 22. If he didn't get changed then he'd be noticed but if he went to get clothes then he would be noticed. Time wasn't on his side. He had to stop Mother before she led The Family in to disaster and wiped them all out in front of their very eyes. A smirk stretched its way across his dirty face as a plan formulated in his mind. Before he did anything, he had to find that coffee shop Rhea's human friend ran. That would set the cogs moving and soon, there'd be nothing left.

***

The light looped around my head then hovered slightly above the floor before going out. Looking at where it had been, I could hear the sound of foot steps coming towards me. They sounded like they were running fast but I had nowhere to go. If I went back the way I came, I'd be confronted by the rotting corpses, that dark figure and more. If I stayed here, then I'd be confronted by whatever was running towards me.

I didn't have time to decide as a body slammed in to me, knocking me to the floor painfully and forcing the breath from my lungs. My panting to regain my breath were mixing with the attempts to breath by who ever or whatever had slammed in to me.

A hand grabbed mine gently and I scrambled back slightly.

"Naz, Naz, it's me. Rhea. You need to wake up. None of this is real. We need you back. Wake up, please just wake up."

I could feel tears welling up in my eyes as I shook my head knowing I couldn't wake up. It wasn't *that* easy. If it was, I'd have done it way before now.

"You're only here because *she* is keeping you here. Defy her and you'll wake up."

"I can't. I can't."

My voice still sounded so pathetically childish that I couldn't stop the tears from coming and Rhea wrapped her arms around me, holding me close to her.

"We don't have much time Naz. Wake up and we can tell you everything you need to know. You only have friends there, we will protect you but you need to be strong. You need to be brave. You need to wake up."

A memory came to the front of my mind. I'd almost woken up when the blade had cut into my arm. Maybe that was the answer. Seeing a rock near me, I placed my hand on to the cold floor and counted to three before slamming it down on to my little finger and letting the pain explode in my hand.

***

Rhea was to the left of me and Jim was to the right with Sopor staring at me with his hand over his mouth. Clutching my wrist I looked at my hand. The little finger was pointing in an abstract angle, almost making it look liked it was pointing backwards before I could say anything, I blacked out for a moment, oblivious to my three friends pushing my finger back in to place.

Chapter Seventeen

Mother screamed and threw the brass bowl at the wall, watching it impact and then land on the floor, spilling the contents in to a soggy pattern on the floor. She'd used it to mix up the herbs and various other ingredients for the concoction that enabled her to force her way in to Naz's dream state but it hadn't worked. They'd clearly underestimated his power and the level of faith he had in his new found friends.

Aithling stood on the other side of the door to Mother's room. She could hear her shouting and cursing in there and didn't really want to intrude. The anger in her heart was still burning bright but she had to be smart about this. Whatever had made Mother angry was definitely something to be feared besides if she believed in such a thing, she'd have thought that karma was playing a trick on Mother.

Taking a deep sigh, she knocked on the door and waited. Another crash echoed as Mother threw a vase against the wall. At this rate, she wouldn't have anything left in the room. She knocked again, this time a little harder but didn't bother waiting. Opening the door, she slid in to the room slowly and a book thudded heavily against the wall next to her face making her jolt a little.

"Mother? Is this a bad time?"

Mother whipped her head around to look at Aithling. She could see the sheer fired up anger in Mother's eyes as she glared at her, sending a shiver of hesitation down her back.

"I had that little shit. I fucking had him. That little fairy got him away as I had my hands on him."

A roar escaped Mother's throat as she punched the wall, leaving a graze on her knuckles.

"I fucking hate half breed fairies."

Aithling sighed. For someone that wanted to bring all the creatures and species in line with her to rule the humans, Mother was merely a being full of bitterness and anger aimed at anyone and anything that got in her way. It didn't matter if it was the humans, her own people in The Family or the ones that didn't follow her teachings. She saw them as little more than traitors and cowards. Her heart beat with the hatred of them all. As Mother took a deep breath, Aithling could see that she was slowly calming down.

"I've always believed in you Aithling. You've always given me the faith that I'm not surrounded by complete and utter idiots."

She nodded at Mother. That was true, she had always had faith in her abilities, even going so far as to put her in charge of keeping the notoriously difficult Trent in line but that was not going as well as she had hoped for. Mother obviously didn't know but she would have to deal with that in a moment.

"Thank you Mother" she said as she knelt on one knee in a sign of respect.

She stroked Aithling's cheek and look her in the eyes.

"My child, I've always known I can count on you, even in the hardest of times."

Aithling nodded as Mother sighed.

"Is there any news on the dagger?"

When Mother looked at her again, Aithling could see she was tired. Breaking in to Naz's dream had taken its toll on her and drained her, leaving her skin looking alabaster white and the lines under her eyes darker.

"No Mother." Aithling didn't get a chance to finish as Mother slammed her to the floor, kneeling on her chest with one knee to force the air out of her lungs.

"What do you mean no Aithling?"

The question dripped with venomous menace as she hissed it in to her face as her hand grabbed roughly at her throat.

"And before you answer, choose your words wisely. I may have faith in you but it doesn't mean I won't choke the life out of you if I have to."

Scrabbling at Mother's hands with her own, Aithling felt her eyes bulge as she tried to speak.

"The dagger was gone from the museum by the time we got there. Holden was dead and the police are there now looking around but they won't find anything other than his body."

The words were a struggle to get out but she kept her eyes fixed on Mother, trying to show as little fear as possible. She knew that the woman fed on fear and enjoyed it and there was no way in hell that she was going to allow herself to be her next snack.

Mother let go of her neck, standing up besides her as she gasped for breath, holding out her manicured hand for Aithling to take. She ignored the gesture and got back up to one knee. Thoughts of killing Mother right then and there ran through her head. She could easily get revenge for what happened to Michael. She wouldn't get out the church alive but at least she'd have had her revenge.

"Too many of you have failed me. The Family needs to be together for us to make our plans a reality. You know that more than anyone Aithling. Your kind and all the others have been hunted all through the centuries by these humans with no rhyme or reason as to why they want to wipe us out. They destroy their own cities, fight wars that can't be won, turn brother against brother, enact the most disgustingly evil acts against one another. Giving them free will was the cruellest of jokes the Gods ever played on such a monosyllabic species. That is why we need to rule them, to get them in line and if they don't follow then they will be broken. Do you understand?"

Aithling nodded silently. Yes her kind had been hounded by the humans and even members of her own family had been used as sideshow attractions but why was Mother so enamoured with the idea of ruling this creatures? After seeing what Mother had done to Michael, she was starting to have her doubts but for now she would be patient and see where this plan was going to take her and the others. There would be time for revenge soon enough.

"I want you to go find Snow. See if she knows anything. Try to find out what that coroner knows too. Webber appears to be less than forthcoming in that department. Understand?"

"As you wish Mother."

Aithling walked through the door and left it to shut behind her as she moved quickly down the corridor. Mother turned her head and gestured with her hand. Two shadowy creatures in hoods floated purposefully towards her with their heads lowered and their hands together in a prayer position. Their movements were so graceful and considered that it always made Mother smile.

"I want one of you to follow her and see what she's up to. There's something not right about her and I don't like it and you" she pointed to the other figure "I want you to find what the ringmaster knows."

They left the room silently and Mother watching contented. Aithling was smart, very smart in fact but she knew when something wasn't right. How else would she have survived this far if she didn't trust her instincts?

Mother opened the door nearest to her and the warmth of the room made her smile. The door was a richly black marble with veins of charcoal grey running through it. Easily her favourite room in the whole of the building, one she had insisted on when they moved their base of operations here. In the middle of the room was a white porcelain bath tub with gold wolf paw shaped feet. Walking over to the tub, she was pleased to find that one of her ladies in waiting had already filled it with sacrificial blood in preparation for her arrival and traced a pattern in it with her finger.

"Is it to your liking Mother?"

The lady in waiting was knelt on one knee respectfully holding one of the jugs that she had poured the blood from. Dressed in a long plain gown, a sleeveless tunic and a wimple for her hair, she looked like she belonged in the middle ages but the choice of clothes was by decree from Mother for her ladies in waiting as it reminded her of the past when things were much simpler.

"Yes, it's rather exquisite thank you. You may go but I'm to not be disturbed until I summon your return."

"Yes ma'am."

She stood slowly, curtsied and left the room, closing the door behind her. Mother sighed and watched the flicker of the candles that were illuminating her bathing room. This was her sanctum and she'd decorated it as such. A minimal amount of furniture, just the bath and a chair, with an old stone fireplace and candles. Her one vice in the entire room was a hand cast, gold mirror hanging on the wall. Looking in to it, she noticed how tired she looked. Using her power to force in to the mind of Naz himself always drained her but it was a small price to pay for such a power.

Undressing slowly, she folded each item of clothing neatly before placing it on to the chair. Taking one last look at the bright scarlet shade of the blood, she lowered herself in to the bath and laid back gracefully. Allowing herself to relax, Mother felt her breathing slow and she drifted off to dream of simpler times.

***

Webber answered her phone and was surprised to Aithling on the other end of the line.

"Yes?"

She could hear breathing on the other end then Aithling started to whisper.

"I think Mother knows. She's asked me to check what you're doing and if you have any answers."

Webber couldn't help herself and gasped. If it was true and Mother did know that she was hiding something then she was sure that she would suffer a similar fate to Michael.

"What does she know? Does she know about Trent?"

"I don't think so but she knows something is wrong and Mother is never wrong on that front. We need to be careful."

She looked at her clock, she'd need to get back to work soon. The last thing she needed was for Martel to be suspicious as well.

"Thank you Aithling."

She heard a heavy sigh through the phones speaker.

"I'm not doing it for you. I'm doing it for Michael. We need to find him and soon. Make that happen."

Aithling hung up and Webber looked at the phone in her hands. There was a time when they were incredibly close as sisters, at least in her eyes, but now they could barely stand to talk to each other for more than a couple of minutes at a time. That, however, was another problem for another time. She had more than enough problems to try to solve. Martel, Michael, Trent. All needed solving and soon before Mother found what they were up to but right now, she needed to get her arse to work.

***

Trent watched as Webber left her apartment, walking towards the lab. A smirk crossed his face as she walked out of sight around the corner. Poor little Webber. She knew nothing. She always knew nothing yet everyone placed so much faith in her. Nobody knew that her one and only skill was bluffing to everyone that she was important to the cause. A valuable talent but one that was going to get her in to more trouble than she would be able to handle. She was already in way above her head and soon she'd drown.

Chapter Eighteen

Rhea sat next to my bed with her head in her hands sleeping fitfully while I looked out of the window from where I was sat. My mind felt hazy but I knew I was somewhere safe at least.

The door opened slowly and Jim walked in with a man behind him carrying a tray with a breakfast of toast, juice and some chunks of cheese on. My stomach growled at the sight of the food as if shouting joyfully at the prospect of feeling full for the first time in what felt like forever.

Jim looked at me relieved as he nudged the tray towards me.

"Morning lad, ya gave us quite the scare for a minute or two there."

I looked down at my hand. There was a bandage on my forearm and my little finger was held in place with a medical splint and I shrugged, trying to look confident and play off the confusion I was feeling.

"Gave myself one too."

Jim looked at Rhea with genuine affection on his face, which gave me the feeling that he was rather protective of her. Crouching next to her, he shook her shoulder as gently as possible and she sleepily opened her eyes. Taking a second to let everything come in to focus, Rhea looked at everyone and smiled as Jim stroked her arm.

"Welcome back little one."

Rhea smiled at Jim and threw her arms around him, giving him the tight kind of hug that made you feel that everything was going to be better in the end.

"This stubborn little one is the reason you made it back to us Naz. She used Sopor's flute on herself and came back to get you."

"Which was either brave or rather foolish my darling."

That voice was so warm, so familiar that it was like putting on your favourite pair of slippers after a long day at work.

"A little from column a and a little from column b I think" said Rhea with a cheeky smirk before looking back at Jim "is Sopor mad?"

"Well darling, he's not going to be throwing you a soiree any time soon that's for sure."

"A soiree? You know you're not in the eighties any more right?"

"More's the pity."

The man stepped out from behind Jim, taking a slice of toast from the tray and then bowing ceremoniously at me.

"Welcome back my dear boy."

It was the ringmaster. He was real, a fact he laughed at heartily when I pointed it out to him.

"I am indeed or at least I was the last time I looked in the mirror."

The door flew open violently and we all jumped back. An out of breath fairy was floating in mid air looking at us worried. The sparkling outline around it blinking in time with its heavy breathing.

Rhea rushed over to the fairy and took him in her hand, stroking his hair softly to try to calm him. She could feel the pounding of his heart vibrate on the palm of her hand.

"Outside. Outside. Family"

The fairy was only able to get the three words out before passing out in her hand. Laying the fairy on the bed, Rhea was looking at Jim. He'd already ran towards the door.

"I'll check it out. You all stay here. Satara, you know what to do"

The ringmaster bowed and took off his jacket, revealing his myriad of tattoos and piercings.

"I do indeed my dear. I've not failed at it yet and I don't intend to start now."

Jim slammed the door shut behind him while Satara busied himself with the blades that he had in sheaths attached to a holster like belt over his shoulders. He span them in his hands and flicked them in and out, testing the weight of the blades themselves. Sliding them back in to their sheaths with their brightly embroidered circus tent designs, Satara looked at me with a cheeky smirk.

"Why do so many of you have knives?"

"Because my dear boy, guns are so barbarically simple. There's just no style or class to them is there?

"And those" I asked as I looked in awe at the blades themselves.

"Beautiful aren't they? Rhea here made them for me after I saved her life once. They go everywhere with me and have done ever since."

Rhea looked almost embarrassed but the distraction took her mind away from the fact that none of us knew what was happening. The fairy slowly sat up on bed and looked around.

"Why is he here? Why is Michael here?"

Satara opened his eyes wide in shock at the mention of Michaels name and I stared at him, puzzled by the reaction.

"Who's Michael?"

Satara pointed to a jagged scar above his hip and a series of scars that criss crossed the entire top half of his body.

"He's the arsehole that gave me this while working for The Family, a group of creatures like us that want to rule over the humans instead of living in peace. If he comes anywhere near me, I'm giving him a receipt for what he did to me."

Anger flashed across his face. It was the first time I'd ever seen him angry either in this world or when I met him in the dream world. In a split second, the anger disappeared to be replaced by a determined yet almost playful smirk.

"But hey, we can't all be happy little bundles of joy can we my dear?"

***

Aithling walked in to a part of town that she hadn't visited for years. It was known to the locals as Hollow Town and for very good reasons. This was where people came when their hopes and dreams died. When their lives crashed and burned in to a million burning flames. The homeless were everywhere here, just trying their very best to stay alive despite all the odds being so heavily stacked against them. There were no jobs, no legal ones anyway and drugs ruled over every aspect of the lives in this town.

A scream screeched through the air and cut in to her. Her eyes darted around but she couldn't see where it had come from so she took a deep breath and carried on walking down the street. Part of her was accustomed to coming to places such as these, the sorts of places where the police force themselves feared to show their faces. A place where even the shadows were fearful and hesitant. The scream stayed stuck in her mind but there was nothing she could do, nothing she should do. It wasn't her problem anyway, she was just here to do one simple job then to get the hell out of here and not look back.

She stopped for a moment and looked at the wall of the abandoned building next to her and looked through the peeling posters of missing people. Some children, some adults. The weird thing was, some of the adults looked a bit like the children. Could they have been the grieving parents trying to find out what had happened to their offspring, ending up as missing themselves? It didn't bare thinking about. The sheer amount of wasted time, of broken lives in this part of the city could cut a person in two without a second thought. It honestly seem that this shell of a city had been bought on top of the broken souls that lived here, only to add more with each moment the place existed.

A strange clicking made Aithling look up from the posters and she sighed. She knew it wouldn't be long until she found trouble or in this case, until trouble found her. The one solitary street light that hadn't been smashed cast a dismal been across the pavement, illuminating the source of the noise. Cutters. A self appointed name for these creatures, these strange hybrid creations of a messed up mind. Part human, part mechanical they clicked everywhere they went due to the blades they had for hands. Their minds were as broken as their bodies and they had nothing to lose, making them more dangerous than anything else in this part of town. Dozens of them would allow themselves to be mown down, in order for one single Cutter to get to their chosen victim. Aithling looked at the six in front of her, a mere few paces away. One stepped forward and tilted its head towards her and stared before licking its dry and cracked licks. Scars criss crossed its face and one eye was half closed, giving it the look of a grotesque wink of sorts.

"We are hungry."

The voice had a rough robotic sound to it making the words sound stunted as it pointed the blades towards her and the Cutters behind it copied the movement in a near perfect synchronised unison.

"We are hungry."

Aithling looked at them, feeling a surge of pity towards the poor creatures. It's true that they were murderous and vicious without a hint of remorse for their actions but that was due to having no mind of their own. How they could exist in such a way was a mystery to her but she couldn't help them. Nobody could.

"You will feed us."

This time they were all talking to her at the same time. It created an eerie background noise to what Aithling knew had to be done. She didn't want to do it to them, after all it wasn't their fault they were like this. It wasn't their fault that the only thing their fractured minds could fathom was to kill to survive and nothing else. She stepped towards them and opened her jacket showing her whips, both of which she unhooked with a deft flick of her hands. The whips unfurled and the blades on the end of each, echoed as they hit the pavement.

"Feed us."

"We are hungry."

"Live within us forever."

"Be one of us."

She shuddered at the monotone nature of the metallic words coming from their mouths. Each movement a mirror of each other. She'd always known that the Cutters had a hive mentality but to actually see it in person was creeping her out.

"I don't want to have to do this."

Aithling cracked one of her whips to emphasise her point to them. Deep down she knew it wouldn't work but she wanted to at least give them a chance, a sort of warning shot.

Guttural screams erupted from the things in front of her and they started to walk stiffly towards her, blades gleaming and clicking all the way. Many of them had dried blood and stains on their clothes and faces from their previous attacks.

"Well, don't say I didn't warn you."

She took a step back and flicked both whips out, the left piercing one of the eyes the nearest Cutter bringing it crashing down to the floor with a thud, the right whip slicing the throat of another. A mixture of oil and blood slashed across the floor as she retracted the whips, eager to take another shot. The remaining Cutters seemed unaffected by the loss of two of their number and carried on towards Aithling with their hollow eyes staring straight at her.

"We are hungry, we will feed."

Still the four remaining creatures were advancing and still they were chanting the words at her in that nightmarish monotone collection of voices. Flicking her right whip, it hit lower than she'd aimed for, slicing across the thigh of her target. It jolted on the spot for a moment then continued towards her as she aimed the left whip, slicing through the exposed chest of one of them and smiled as it fell forward in a shower of oil, blood and skin. One of the creatures seemed to be holding back slightly, surveying the violent scene in front of them.

"We are hungry. We are hungry. We. Are. Hungry."

The monotone voices seemed to be getting more and more staggered, as if losing three of their group had diminished their ability to stay in unison. They weren't backing down however as she cracked the whips and prepared to strike at them again. This time she wouldn't miss, she'd make sure of that.

She started to flick and spin her whips around her head like a cowboys lasso with a sly smirk on her face before aiming them directly at the Cutters advancing towards her and releasing them towards the creatures. The blades sliced through their necks as the whips cracked with the intensity of a thunder crack and they too landed lifeless on the floor. The remaining creature looked at her intently, baring its jagged and dirty teeth at her as she steadied herself for one last attack.

"We are hungry. We are one."

As she attacked, it grabbed the ends of both whips and pulled them out of her hands with ease, dropping them to the floor. Aithling blinked and backed up slightly. Nobody had ever survived her whips. Nobody had ever managed to take them from her before. Her eyes darted around her, looking for something else she could use as a weapon against this inhuman thing. The pity she had felt for them had quickly dissipated, replaced with a feeling of indecision building inside her. She knew she could run but it wouldn't stop. Once a Cutter had chosen you as its next meal, they either eviscerated you or you stopped them yourself. There was no middle ground. They didn't stop, they didn't tire. The chase would go on until someone was dead, if these things could even be thought of as alive to begin with.

Saying a quick prayer to any person or deity that would listen, she launched herself as the Cutter, gracefully avoiding its lunges at her with the blades it had instead of hands. She could grab the whips but they'd be useless with how easily this one had disarmed her. The clicking of the blades intensified as it swiped and stabbed at her. The whole thing made Aithling think that the creature was toying with her, almost inviting her in to some sort of grotesque dance of life or death.

The Cutter dove at her legs clumsily and she kicked it's hand away from her then looked repulsed by the fact that it had started to smile, its rotten teeth being worn as a badge of honour. The distraction proved effective as the back of her heel hit the outstretched arm of one of the death creatures and she tumbled to the floor. She tried to roll backwards but found one of the creatures blades had somehow become entangled on the leg of her trousers. This things were a lot heavier than they looked but somehow the one coming towards her seemed quicker, almost graceful in comparison to the others.

She tried to kick out at it with her free leg, hitting it in the stomach. The Cutter staggered backwards slightly and looked at her with an amused look on its face, as if daring her to do it again. Trying to sit up, Aithling knew this was the end but if she was going to go down then she sure as hell was going to go down fighting. Clenching her fists, she prepared herself for its next attempt as it looked at her quizzically. Baring its teeth one more time, it raised the blades above its head.

"We are hungry. We will be fed."

A loud bang deafened Aithling and she covered her ears as she saw a large, bloody hole appear in the middle of the creature in front of her. It fell to its back with its arms still raised, landing with a tinny echo.

"Sorry fucker, the kitchens closed."

The feminine voice sounded almost amused with the quip it had just made as it walked towards the remains with a smoking, ancient looking musket rifle held in one hand by her side and she knelt down to survey her handiwork before walking over to Aithling. From the look of her elegant dress and expensive looking heeled boots, she didn't even need to look up to know who saved her life.

"Hello Snow."

Chapter Nineteen

Webber sat at her desk and leant back in the chair. Aithling knew about Trent and there was a good chance that Mother knew she was hiding something too. She was on a slippery slope and trying her best to keep all of this under wraps. If Trent could have just kept control over his urges then none of this would be happening. She had to tell someone before it got out of hand.

The door opened and Martel walked in holding a file, stopping to put it on to her desk.

"Have a look at this file Webber and tell me what you see."

She flicked it open and saw pictures of all of the bodies, including the one of Doctor Holden. Breathing in deeply, she looked at Martel and tried to work out just how much he knew from how he was looking at her. All she saw on his face was a look of excitement. He seemed almost like he had been completely re-energised by whatever it was that he found in this file.

"They're just the autopsy photographs. The bodies are all dried out, they look mummified and they've all been examined. Am I missing something?"

"Look closer."

Webber leant over her desk and took a closer look before raising her hand to her mouth. The newest corpse, that of Doctor Holden, had the faint outline of the hand print that the others had before she'd doctored the photographs. How had she missed this one?

"Do you see it? Do you? There's a hand print on Holden."

"There is, it's very faint. How did you find that?"

Martel chuckled and smiled at her. She'd always found that smile warm and welcoming but right now, it worried her. She didn't know how much he knew or if he knew she was involved so she'd have to play it cool.

"Honestly, by accident. I was looking at the photographs and zoomed in on a bruise on the latest victims shoulder. When looking at that, I noticed a very faint outline near it. When I looked closer, it made the shape of a hand."

She looked at Martel. He knew, he had to know.

"And do the others have the same mark?"

She studied his face to see if there was any hint at all but other than that smile, he was completely stone faced.

"That's just the thing. The mark wasn't on the others but something just felt off about the pictures themselves so I got one of the techs to look. They'd been doctored Webber."

"And who would do such a thing? How would you even know how to?"

"I don't know yet but I will. The tech is trying to find the raw file as we speak and when he does, he'll be able to show me the original photograph."

Martel put his hand on her shoulder and smiled kindly.

"We'll have them Webber, we will and then we'll find who is behind these deaths. I promise you."

***

Jim stood at the door of the coffee house out of breath. He didn't know how Michael knew where they were but he did know that they were safe. He couldn't possibly know where the others where. You had to walk through a tunnel and many different doors before you got to the safe house itself so there was no possible way he knew that they were there.

The blind was down on the door saying that the place was closed so Michael couldn't see him which gave him a chance to collect his thoughts. He had to be quick otherwise Michael being there would attract a crowd and that was the last thing they needed right now.

After taking a deep breath, he opened the door and jumped back as Michael fell in to the coffee house in a heap. He didn't look good at all with his pale face covered in sweat, eyes rolled back in to his head and mumbling the word Mother over and over. Jim looked out of the door quickly and dragged the body in before closing the door and locking it, making sure the blind was down and the windows covered before sitting Michael up against the wall.

Part of him wanted to leave Michael there to succumb to whatever had put him in such a condition but he knew he couldn't do that. It was against his nature. He remembered the rule he had been taught at medical school.

Primum non nocere.

First, do no harm.

Hearing footsteps, he looked over to the door of the stockroom. Rhea walked in and put her hand over her mouth.

"He's hurt or sick, I'm not sure which yet."

Rhea looked at Jim then at Michael and ran her hands through her hair and tried to decide what to do.

"We need to tell Sopor before we do anything Jim."

"And let him suffer while we debate for hours on end?"

Jim had a point and she knew that he was talking from his years of medical training. His priority was always to make sure people were safe and were well. That's why he was such an important part of their group, of their lives here.

"My dears, give me five minutes with him and he won't be a problem any more, I can assure you all of that."

They looked at Satara standing in the doorway. He already had two of his blades in his hands and was twirling both of them menacingly, his eyes not leaving Michael. Jim stood up and pointed at him.

"Put those away, there will be no blood spilled in here tonight."

Rhea looked at them all. Tensions were running high. Michael had once tried to kill Satara, leaving him with wounds that he had been lucky to recover from and he'd never forgiven nor forgotten that. One of his tattoos even framed one of the scars as an ornate badge of honour of sorts. Jim turned his back to them both and started to look over Michael. His pulse was erratic and he was hot to the touch. Something was very, very wrong.

"We're going to have to take him downstairs. I think he's dying."

"Good, let him."

Both Jim and Satara locked eyes fiercely with neither one backing down. Rhea had had enough of this.

"Both of you. Stop acting like damned children."

Michael slumped forward and Jim swore at the sight of Michaels butchered back. The wounds were still bloody but were leaking yellow puss down the back of a dirty white shirt where his wings had once been. To take a person's wings was the biggest punishment you could give to a being like Michael and their body always rejected and fought against such a barbaric punishment. In fact it was nearly always a death sentence.

Jim looked at Rhea. There were tears in her tears at seeing such a thing. Regardless of what Michael had done in his life or had done while under the control of Mother, he didn't deserve this. Nobody did.

"Let him die. He showed none of us mercy so why should we show him any?"

It was Rhea that was the first to answer, her face a picture of sadness and concern.

"Because Satara, if we don't show mercy then it makes us little more than clones of them. It doesn't just make us as bad as them, it makes us a lot worse because we have the want and the need to show mercy and compassion. They don't. We can't and won't live that way. That would be poison to us all if we did."

Satara put his blades in the sheaths but the look on his face told them all that this wasn't over. Not by a long margin. Unlocking the door, he stared at the three of them.

"Well my dears, I hope you know what you're doing. I am having no part of it. I have my own affairs to attend to and none of them involve trying to save the life of the thing that tried to kill me."

Without giving them a chance to answer, he slammed the door shut and walked away. Jim glared at where Satara had been. He had always known that Satara had a temper but he'd come around eventually. He always did. He told Rhea to lock the door then called down to the people in the tunnel.

"I'm going to need some help up here. We have an injury and we need to dress the wounds."

While Jim and Rhea were busying themselves in preparation to take Michael down, he opened his eyes slightly and smiled. It was a close call with Satara, he definitely had unfinished business with him to take care of, but the plan was working exactly how he'd expected. This was going to be a lot easier than he had imagined it would be. With a deep breath, he allowed himself to fall to the side and drunk a quick sip from the tiny glass vial he'd hidden in his hand before smashing it behind him. Feeling the concoction start to work, he hid the tiny pieces of the vial underneath him and closed his eyes as he fell in to a deep, artificial sleep.

Chapter Twenty

Mother felt her breathing deeply and evenly match the beat of her heart. The blood around her clung to her protectively and she let it wash over her body. All her senses were firing off as the bath weaved its magic through her and energised her more than anything else ever has. She'd been thankful for learning from a countess about the secret healing properties of virginal blood and had used it ever since. It was a real shame what happened to the poor woman in the end, all because of a simple misunderstanding about the use of the dead and mutilated bodies that were found in her castle in the Carpathians. Such a shame how she died alone and confined to a windowless room. So disgusting to think that just because a woman wanted to stay looking youthful, people would let her rot away in such an inhuman punishment.

Waving her hands through the blood, Mother had always loved the way it moved over her hands and through her fingers. It made her think of easier times, of her life in her simple but homely place in the courtyard in Greece while she readied herself for the linking ceremony with Iasion. Things seemed so much simpler then. Humans were still an apathetic species, ultimately selfish at heart, but at least they knew how to worship their deities in a respectful manner. Gifts, sacrifices, prayers, all to the deities that they loved and feared in equal measure.

Mother felt her mind begin to wander as she began to doze again. When her mind wandered, it was the only truly authentic time that she ever felt free of the confines of the human world. She could see the world for what it truly was. She could see the humans for what they truly are. It also gave her a chance to keep track of that boy that seemed so close yet had been so far out of her reach. Arching her back, she let her soul lift through her and closed her eyes.

***

I fell to my knees hard, feeling both ecstasy and fear. My breathing quickened and my chest tightened as my mind began to spin and explode in a maelstrom of thoughts.

Visions of a courtyard were slamming in to my mind as if being forcibly placed in to my memories. Thoughts of a ceremony, visions of flowers in a temple and of a woman with her back to me, dressed in a simple gown that fluttered in the light breeze.

A temple rose up in my memories giving me a feeling of love and worship that ran throughout my body and I felt the cold hard floor against my back. I wanted to scream out in pain, I wanted to scream for help but my mind was telling me that only I would understand this.

It's time for the ceremony.

That voice. It was *her* again. Invading my mind at every opportunity.

You need to see this.

The world around me burst forth in a series of colours and shapes before I felt myself standing in a courtyard as people rushed past me. There were so many people carrying vases of flowers, jugs of wine, carrying huge piles of food through to the temple.

A woman stopped in front of me, attaching a small red flower to the front of my tunic before smiling and walking towards the temple with my hand in hers. Struggling to keep up with her, I felt an urge in my heart to see what she was so clearly desperate to show me.

***

Trent walked along the carpeted corridor with a sense of purpose written all over his face. Each person he passed seemed surprised to see him here but he just looked and smiled at each and every one of them. He had as much of a right to be here, perhaps even more so.

Seeing the maiden outside the shut door of a room told him he had the right place so he straightened his expensive suit jacket, took a deep breath and walked towards her, prepared to charm her out of his way.

***

Mother smiled as the blood washed over her face, feeling like an electrical charge running across each and every part of her body. Voices ran through her mind as memories chased them. Thoughts of flowers and ceremonies span in circles as one of her hands gripped the side of the bath.

***

I followed the woman holding my hand in to the temple and the beauty of the paintings that adorned the walls took my breath away. Each small painting felt connected to the next until when I looked up I saw a painting that spanned the entire ceiling. A painting of a woman giving birth with angels, fairies and so many more creatures holding each of the babies and feeding them. The woman had geometric designs all over her body, making them look a bit like scales that added to the beauty of the image.

Not exactly true to my likeness but I always liked it.

I could make out some curved and highly detailed words spelt in letters from the Eucleidean alphabet. My eyes followed each and every curve and turn of the letters as I tried to decipher the words.

It says mother of the gods.

***

Trent walked over to the maiden and gave her his most charming smile and leant with his hand on the wall next to her.

"She is to not be disturbed under any circumstances."

The maiden looked Trent up and down, allowing herself a slight smirk to dance across her face.

"Not even by you."

Trent ran a finger playfully across the maidens wimple that covered her hair. They'd always fascinated him because your mind always wants what it can't see.

"See? Now I'm offended. How could anyone not want to be disturbed by me? I'm a delightful kind of guy to be disturbed by."

He ran his finger down her cheek and traced a circle over her skin.

"I could always pass the time with you if you'd like?"

The maiden looked at him, her smirk now replaced with a stern and deadly serious look that was going to take a lot of charm and persistence to change. He placed his finger under her chin and gently pushed it so she looked him in the eyes. The mistrust that was living in her eyes made him think that luck might be needed as well. A lot of luck.

***

A moan escaped Mother's lips as she once again arched her back and ran her free hand through her hair that had fanned out in the blood. She could feel parts of her soul flying free, her memories entwining with the memories of someone else and it felt exquisite.

***

The words ran over my tongue and I felt myself saying mother of the gods over and over as I was ushered in to a brightly lit room adorned with flowers and paintings of the same woman in various different ways.

People were sat on cushions in every available space in the room. Some were standing, some were crouching or sitting and some were even pressing themselves against the walls in order to just fit in to the room and watch the ceremony. Ladies were rushing around at the front, rearranging the flower displays and the offerings of fruit and various wines.

I trust you will bow your head in respectful reverence when the time comes?

No matter how hard I tried to distract myself with what was going on around me, that voice was still finding its way inside my mind and worming its way in to my sanity.

What there is left of it.

A pair of hands grabbed me and roughly span me around. I found myself facing a large bearded man in a tunic grinning wildly at me before he kissed both my cheeks with such force that I stumbled backwards a step.

"Such a joyous day for a linking ceremony. Such a beautiful, joyous day indeed."

I agreed with him that yes it was indeed a joyous day for such an event in the hopes that he would go away but to no avail.

"Our very own beautiful Kybele being chosen to link with Iasion."

Once again I agreed with the overly friendly man but still he didn't leave me alone, if anything, agreeing with him was just making him talk more.

"Yes, it is a day of happiness."

"Happiness? What do gods need of happiness?"

Now I looked at him with a puzzled expression on my face. Did he just say gods? As in heaven above and hells very own brimstone style gods? The sort you pray to out of habit, not out of reverence or duty?

"Gods need no happiness. They need no such Earthly emotions. That is why they are to be revered young man. Have they not taught you such things before sending you out in the great wide world?"

If I was completely honest with myself, I wasn't all that sure if I had offended the man or if he was merely interested in my stance on organised religion but this really didn't seem the time nor the place to be having such a discussion, especially not in a temple of all places.

Oh how you disappoint me Naz.

A blinding pain in my head forced me to shut my eyes and when I opened them again, flowers were being thrown towards a couple at the front of the temple as, what I assumed was a priest of some sort, held his arms out and said that their union was now as one.

And now for the rebirth.

The what?

The crowd surged forward towards the couple and started to pull at them roughly. They didn't fight back no matter how much I tried to yell at them to defend themselves as their clothes ripped and hands clawed at their bare skin.

Watch carefully Naz, you may finally learn something.

Both their skins started to rip and bleed under the force of the assault from the oncoming mob of once happy onlookers. Their skin was being pulled off in ragged strips of bloody flesh and the rabid audience ate each piece in front of my very eyes. No matter how much I moved, I couldn't see the either of the couples faces as they fell under the never ending onslaught. A sea of blood was running down the aisle as they were devoured.

***

Mother started to breathe heavier and heaver with each memory bombarding her mind. Virgin blood splashed over the side of the bath and on to the floor. A noise started to bubble up from her throat and she roared like a caged beast.

***

Trent looked at the maiden then at his watch and sighed. He really didn't have time for this. Normally he loved the thrill of the chase but this one really wasn't worth the time.

He placed his hand on her chest, just above her heart and she opened her mouth to protest but the searing pain silenced her.

"Now you can let me in or I can leech the entirety of your life from your very heart as you watch. It's entirely your call. Either way, I'm going in there to talk to her."

In the few seconds that he'd had his hand on her, the maiden had started to gasp for air as her skin started to dry out and her heart started to slow. She gestured at the door.

"Thank you."

Trent released her from his grip and she fell to the floor gasping and coughing as he stepped over her.

"Much obliged my dear, much obliged indeed."

***

I looked at the bloody pile of flesh that used to be the couple that we were here to celebrate. The bodies had almost been picked clean and left in a puddle of blood and more.

The room erupted with euphoric singing. As I looked around, I saw the audience that were once watching respectfully as two people were linked to one another and now were covered in blood, chunks of flesh and singing like a Sunday church choir with the notes reverberating around the temple.

There was an air of worship, happiness and respect that seemed to clash with the violence that I'd just witnessed. It felt like two world's colliding and I was stuck in the aftermath of it all. I didn't feel scared any more, merely confused.

I hope you're paying attention, this is the best part.

The priest returned with a carved, wooden bowl, stopping to kneel by the remains and started to run his fingers through the blood. He scratched two words into the sticky liquid.

Surrecturus Sit.

Arise.

Chapter Twenty One

Satara walked angrily down the street, away from the coffee shop. How could they be so stupid as to let Michael in to their safe house? They knew what that creature had done to them, to *him*, but it looked like that didn't matter to them. Why were they showing him mercy when they wouldn't even remotely considering showing them mercy if the roles were reversed?

Absent mindedly he touched his side where the biggest scar was. He remembered that day as if it were yesterday. Yes that was a cliché but it was also true. Each slice of the knife, each moment of the blade being forced in to his skin. Every single second of pain, every facial expression as Michael looked at him. It was still as clear and raw in his memories as ever. Five years had passed but his mind seemed to have missed that passage of time.

The nightmares about that night were still coursing through his sleep each and every night. He'd never told the others about that. The surface of his life may be smiles, jokes and colourful things but beneath that it was chaos. He had an analogy about feeling like a duck and being calm on the surface but unseen under the water, were his feet flicking furiously to keep moving. Nobody seemed to like that analogy but he used it anyway.

Making his way to the tattoo parlour that he called home, he wondered if he'd get any customers in this evening. He found the art of etching his art on to the skin of people that would stay forever, incredibly relaxing and calming down was something he definitely needed. He'd done most of the tattoos on his skin himself. The ones on his back had been inked when he was much younger and a member of a punk band. Oh the years of a misspent youth. Despite everything going on, he couldn't help but smile. His youth was definitely misspent but it was fun for sure.

Looking through the window of his tattoo parlour, he saw the familiar furnishings inside. A real mix and match session of pretty much anything that took his eye and his admittedly short attention span. Kitsch palm tree statues stood shoulder to shoulder with steam punk style skulls with golden cogs and screws all over them. It felt like home to him each time he walked through the door. It always had and he doubted that would ever change. Looking at his watch, he saw he had just about enough time to make a cup of tea and, if he was feeling a bit more decadent than normal, even enough time to grab a chocolate biscuit too.

Unlocking the door and walking in, he paused to looked around the room. It was just him working tonight, something that he enjoyed immensely. Taking off his knife belt, he folded it under the desk and out of sight, sighing. As much as he liked the young lady that he had employed recently, he really did enjoy the time to just sit quietly and enjoy his own company. The young lady could give him a run for his money in the number of tattoos and piercings stakes, that's one of the things that drew him to her, especially considering that she too had drawn them on to herself too.

The bell tinkled as the first customer came through the door.

"I'll be with you in just a moment my lovely, just making a cuppa."

The silence in lieu of a reply made him feel immediately uneasy. This city may have some horrible bastards living here but it was almost like this place was a sanctuary away from all of that. People felt safe here and because of that normally felt like they could talk the night away.

Coming back through with his steaming mug of herbal tea, he looked around. The place was completely deserted and nothing had been stolen so that couldn't have been their aim. Maybe it was just people messing about to try to spook him out, children did seem to look doing that when left to their own devices.

Putting the mug down, he opened his sketch pad and began to draw the image in his head. A dagger, a simple ceremonial dagger. Nothing fancy, nothing too ornate. Just a simple dagger.

"Well that looks familiar."

The voice made Satara drop his pencil on the floor as he turned round to find a hooded figure standing behind him.

"Satara I presume?"

A gravely voice coming from the hooded figure seemed rather apt because it sounded neither male nor female, it just sounded like the owner had a major smoking habit to try to fight.

"Who's asking darling?"

"I am."

"A comedian I see."

Satara was grabbed roughly by the neck and slammed against one of the shelving units, knocking some of the tiny trinkets to the floor. The hand lifted him off of the floor and held him there while looking over its shoulder.

"What do you want done with him?"

Two men stepped out of the shadows, one holding a flute.

"Take him out the back, we'll get what we need from him."

Satara didn't fight back. He wasn't afraid or even surprised. There had been something in the air recently and Michaels appearance at the safe house had compounded that.

Being dragged roughly across the floor, he tried to get a good look at the faces of the men that had interrupted his evening. None of them looked familiar but the creature holding him had a brand of two horns on its hand. A money for hire mercenary with blood on its hands and a soul that was up for sale to the highest bidder. The question running through is mind was who had hired him?

Hearing the door lock behind them all, he realised this was going to be a very long night.

***

Aithling looked around the room she was in. She'd not been here in many years but it was exactly how she had remembered it. Running a hand through her hair, she looked at her reflection in the mirror that was hanging next to a grand looking clock. She looked a mess, with oil and blood all over her face but she smiled. She'd survived the Cutters, albeit with some help. Snow walked in carrying two bottles of beer and handed one to Aithling.

"So, is there a reason you're here or did you just miss my pretty face?"

She looked at Snow. Clearly, she hadn't changed at all. Just like the room they were in, she seemed stuck in a moment of time that she thought had been left behind many years ago.

"Mother sent me."

The mere mention of Mother made Snow's face screw up in disappointment.

"I thought she was dead?"

Aithling shook her head and took a swig of the beer, grimacing as the sour taste hit the back of her throat. She couldn't believe that Snow still drank this crap considering how much she prided herself on good appearances and such.

"No, she's still very much alive."

"More's the pity. So, what is it you want exactly? I'm rather busy."

Taking another look around the room, she was still surprised by how little the place had changed. There were antique weapons all over the walls from crossbows through to shotguns and everything in between. Each and every one of them had been passed down to Snow from her relatives. Seeing her look at the weapons, Snow smiled.

"Each one works you know, as you've seen tonight. I like to keep them ready. You know, just in case.

"Just in case of what?"

"Mother related attacks"

Snow had a point. Aithling knew that Snow hadn't left The Family in a good way. In fact, there had been a price on her head for years but nobody was either brave enough or talented enough to bring Mother her head despite a few close calls. They both spent the next few minutes in silence as Snow cleaned the musket, looking at it as if it were one of her own children before putting it back up on the wall.

"I knew you were coming you know."

Aithling looked at her surprised and put the bottle down on the edge of Snow's desk.

"You also haven't come alone."

Rubbing her eyes, Aithling sighed. She'd had a feeling she was being followed on the way here but chalked it up to her being nervous. She'd always hated being in this part of the city but that had clearly clouded her judgement.

"Who?"

Snow shrugged before dumping a severed head in front of her and turned her back to her as she looked out at the large window at all the tables below her office. You could see her entire operation from here. Herbs, spices, strange looking plants. All being worked on by the children that she had taken under her care. It was a good business. None of the plants were illegal but they all had varying degrees of effect on their kind. Some were simple cure alls and others allowed them to slip away from a wave of euphoria if they should wish to. Just because they were of a special bloodline, it didn't mean they were exempt from the hard, unfeeling nature of the world around them.

"Mother is a creature of habit, you know that. It's probably one of her little pets in the hooded cloaks or at least it was."

"The daemons?"

"Most probably. They won't kill you unless commanded so you would have been safe. It's single minded at best, dumb as a rock at worst so I couldn't take the risk."

Snow allowed herself to smile at the children going about their various jobs below. She'd said they could go eat until she needed them but they were still working away. Not because they had to but out of gratitude for her having taken them in. In a way, she loved each one of the seven children she cared for but she still had to keep a tight ship as it was, after all, a business. A very profitable one too.

"I suppose you're here about the blade."

Aithling was well aware that Snow probably already knew the reason for her visit and so wasn't surprised. Instead, she walked over to the wall and looked at the blade itself. It didn't look special or worth fighting over so why would Mother want it?

"I found out about it being in the museum by chance. An article in the local newspaper had a picture of Doctor Holden standing in front of a display and there it was. Strange really considering I've spent the last ten years looking for it and all of a sudden, there it was."

Snow's face had come alive with a look of passion and wonder while talking about the blade. It clearly meant a lot to her to have it back in her possession as Aithling watched her run her fingers over the handle gracefully.

"My family have sent many of our enemies to the afterlife with that blade and with it, we carry their souls and therefore, it is cursed with their deaths."

Now it all made sense. It was all starting to connect in her mind as to why Mother wanted this blade so much. Her power came from the souls of the various lives she had led. A blade that had so many souls attached to it, that would make her near unstoppable.

"If Mother wants it, she will have to come and get it herself. I'm not just going to hand it over merely because you've asked nicely."

Aithling nodded and had to admit to herself that she'd have given the exact same answer had the positions been reversed. One thing was bothering her about the whole thing. How had that knife magically turned up at a local museum after being missing for so long?

Chapter Twenty Two

The three men stood in the corner of the room talking amongst themselves. Satara couldn't hear what they were saying but he was pretty sure that it wasn't going to be anything pleasant judging from the glances they kept shooting his way.

Looking up, he saw that his hands were tied tightly with a hook protruding from the wall that was holding the knot securely in place. He'd meant to take that hook out of the wall when he moved in to the premises a few months back but hadn't found the time. The taller of the three walked over to him with a smirk on his face.

"Whatever happens here is going to be painful. Really painful to be honest. How much of it being really painful is going to be entirely up to you and the decision you are about to make. It's a simple choice. In fact, it can be summed up in a yes or a no answer. We are here at the request of our employer who would like us to find the location of a certain item. Thanks to some loose lips, we have found some information that you are the man to ask about said item."

"Is there one of those moments where the villain explains their entire plan to the hero before he then valiantly escapes and ends up winning? If so, I've seen that story way too many times my darling."

A fist slammed in to the side of his face and he grimaced slightly while the man rubbed his now red knuckles.

"Well, if I'd have known I was in for some kinky action, I'd have dressed for the occasion."

A second fist slammed in to face again, this time harder.

"Are you done with the innuendo Mr Satara?"

Satara chuckled.

"In your endo."

A quick one two punch to his stomach winded him and the man laughed, nodding at his two colleagues before gesturing at the hooded figure.

"Your turn."

As the hooded figure stood over Satara, he could feel his breath wash over him, the stench of decaying meat and rotten teeth made him gag. He had no time for a quip as the figures hands grabbed at his throat and squeezed, driving all the air out of him in an instant. Panic ran across his face as he tried to pull the hands away from him, as he tried to kick his legs out at the figure.

The taller man clicked his fingers and the hooded figure released his grip, leaving him gasping before stepping forward, resting his finger on Satara's chin and pushing up slightly so he looked at his face.

"Lets start again shall we?"

***

Martel looked at the photographs that the tech had given him. Leaning over them, he stared with a smile on his face. Each body had the same hand imprint on them. Finally there was a link between them although he was still unsure how the hand print had caused their deaths. It was a start at least and more than they'd had before.

He turned to look out of his office window and saw Webber standing in the corridor. She'd stepped out to make a call while he'd been looking at the pictures. Her face looked worried but he wouldn't push her to tell him, he knew she was a private person despite her easy going mask she sometimes wore.

They were going to solve this, no matter how long it took.

***

Webber tapped her free hand against her leg nervously while listening to the voice on the other end of the call.

"No I don't know how he knows, I just know he's seen the print that Trent leaves behind after he's fed" Webber said with a hint of exasperation in her voice. She'd gone over this three times now during this phone call, all while trying to look calm and make sure nobody would walk past while she was talking. She could have gone to her own office but didn't want to take her eyes away from Martel in case he found anything else.

Even whispering her answers, she couldn't help but be paranoid that she was going to be overheard. Her eyes darted around the empty corridor but caught Martel looking at her. He looked concerned.

"I've got to go. He's getting suspicious."

"As you've failed at dealing with this, we'll deal with it ourselves."

The line went dead and she clutched the phone tightly in her hand sighing heavily. This was meant to have been a simple job. It was meant to have been little more than her babysitting Martel and steering him away from anything he wasn't meant to see. The problem had been simple. She'd gotten lazy because she'd grown fond of him as a friend and a colleague. She'd let her guard down and it had lead to this.

Looking at Martel, she tried to smile at him. Was it to reassure herself or him? She wasn't sure. The one thing she was sure of was that she'd just thrown him to the wolves and he was about to be eaten alive without him even knowing it was coming.

Chapter Twenty Three

I looked at the priest as he knelt by the remains, with the blood still flowing down his fingers. He stared straight in to my direction as he licked them and smiled. The way he was looking at me sent a million shivers up my spine yet I couldn't take my eyes away from him.

Something at the back of my head told me to back away so I slowly took a step backwards, hoping to go back the way I'd come.

A low, rumbling voice started to talk in a serious, monotone style while reciting the same the same two words over and over. Each word was punctuated with the priest moving his fingers in time with the rhythm of the words.

Surrecturus Sit.

Surrecturus Sit

Surrecturus Sit

Trying to take a step backwards, I felt my body bump up against something. I turned sharply, coming face to face with the deer. A feeling of relief washed over me.

"You don't need to see this Naz."

Surrecturus Sit

Surrecturus Sit

Surrecturus Sit

The priests voice was getting louder and angrier with each repetition of the words. Bubbles started to appear in the blood, bursting with a high pitched pop as fingers starting to form and point in the viscous mess on the floor.

***

Mother floated under the blood and held her breath. The memories were dancing around her head and could feel the presence of someone watching the memories themselves. Not watching her in person but as if someone was in her mind and watching each thought individually.

Her body tingled as though a low current of electricity were passing through it. Even under the blood, the tiny hairs on her arms prickled and stood up slightly.

Sitting up in the bath, with the blood running down her face, she caught her reflection in the mirror. Even without cleaning the blood off, she could see that her face looked younger already.

***

Backing away, with the deer nudging people to clear a path for me, I found that I couldn't take my eyes from the priest and the things forming from the mess on the ground.

Surrecturus Sit

Surrecturus Sit

Surrecturus Sit

I could now see the naked torsos of a man and a woman rising up, pushing themselves from the pools of blood on the floor with their backs to me. Their muscles flexed and moved as they formed bit by bit while the priest chanted those two words again and again. Even now, his eyes never left mine.

"Naz, we need to go. If they see you, they will know you're here."

A pair of banshee like screams pierced the air and I froze to the spot. The deer nudged me over and over but, no matter how much I wanted to, I just couldn't move my feet. The deer pulled at my clothes, pushed me in every direction that he could but still, I couldn't or wouldn't move.

The priest stretched his hands out to me with the palms face up. I could make out a tattoo of a snake eating its own tail on both hands. Either side of him, the pair of bodies stood up with their backs to me.

Nos Fieri

Nos Fieri

Nos Fieri

He was repeating 'become us' over and over. Everything felt so out of place. Violence in the temple, a place of worship. Bodies rising up from the pools of blood and remains of torn apart victims. Latin being spoken in Ancient Greece. Nothing felt right at all. It was as if this dream, this memory, were all mixed up with other ones.

The bodies turned around with their hands outstretched in the same pose as the priest and somehow started to chant while their mouth less faces moved and formed. Their features slowly came in to focus and my eyes went wide with fear and recognition.

"Mother?"

Chapter Twenty Four

Snow walked down the stairs with Aithling slightly behind her, leading the way through a door and past a series of tables. Each one was covered with piles of various herbs, spices and liquids of many different colours. All were arranged neatly in uniform rows with handwritten labels on each and every one. The tidiness of the tables surprised Aithling but also impressed her. Snow definitely ran a tight ship here business wise and the impressive thing was that nobody could march in and stop anyone due to the simple fact that none of the mixtures were illegal. A human could take the concoctions and have no highs or side effects. Someone from the ancient bloodline however, they could have many different effects. She couldn't help but chuckle.

Counting the tables, Aithling noticed there were only seven workstations. That seemed strange considering how busy they were, considering how big the operation was. As if sensing the forthcoming question, Snow turned and smiled at her.

"I keep my circle small. Seven is an easy number to trust, to keep an eye on and to allow freedom to. Obviously you've seen the posters outside. All the missing children. I can't do much to keep them safe but I can do this. Sometimes I have to replace them when they too go missing but needs must."

"Sounds like you treat these kids more like a factory worker treats their machines then a person treating them as kids."

"I have to. It's a kill or be killed life here. The police don't care. The Family don't care. Nobody cares except for us so yes, I do treat them as machines of a kind. It prevents me from going insane from grief when any are taken from me."

Snow had a point. She had to keep herself closed off. You had the Cutters, those mechanical abominations. You had a corrupted police force letting the people here rule themselves. You had drug dealers, murderers and more destroying the city one crime at a time.

"You can have lunch but you're not taking the blade. Not while I'm alive anyway."

"Ever the hostess."

Walking through another door, the pair looked at a makeshift table covered in plates of food with the seven children all sat down, waiting and looking at both of them expectantly. The oldest of the seven stood up with her hands together in prayer.

"We have blessed the food ma'am."

Snow gestured at Aithling to sit down and then did the same herself.

"Thank you. Then let us begin."

As they all ate, Aithling couldn't help but wonder if she was doing the right thing. Snow was showing the children such kindness and safety but at what price? They worked for her, they delivered the packages and more while she protected them as best as she could with her arsenal of ancient weapons. Not that long ago, someone of the ancient bloodline wouldn't be seen caring for human children but times change. That left Aithling with one question that seemed to be insistently forcing itself in to her head.

Was Mother doing the right thing?

***

Satara hung limply from the hook with his eyes closed and his breathing shallow. Every single part of his body hurt but they hadn't broken him yet. He wasn't sure how much longer he'd last but he knew they would have to kill him before he even came close to breaking.

The three figures were stood quietly in the corner, the smartest dressed of the three rubbing his now sore knuckles.

"He's tougher than he looks."

"Well we knew that already, we just might have to change our style a bit."

"I could just kill him."

Two of the trio looked at the hooded figure with equal parts exasperation and annoyance.

"That's your bloody answer for everything."

A slow humming disturbed them from their conversation. Satara was trying to sing as the well dressed man walked towards him.

"That won't work you know, your siren tricks have no sway over us."

Satara looked at him and carried on humming a low pitched hum and the man could feel the tingle of the sirens song trying to creep in to his mind so he gestured at the younger man with the flute in his hand.

Lifting the flute to his lips, he blew a slow tune in to the air and Satara grimaced in pain.

"You may be a siren but this man here is a pied piper of sorts. His tune will burn in to your brain, rendering your song forever useless. It will, of course, be incredibly painful for you. Entertaining for us to watch but painful for you."

Satara forced himself to smirk at the man in the suit despite the searing pain he was feeling in his brain.

"Does he take requests darling?"

"As you wish" the man looked at the piper and smiled. "Burn the song from his mind but slowly, I want to hear him scream."

The tune started to play faster and higher leaving Satara grunting and breathing heavily in pain, a dribble of blood slowly running from his left ear. The suited man pulled a chair close to him and sat down, resting his hands with the bloody knuckles on to his lap with a grin as he watched Satara jerk in pain.

"Oh I'm going to enjoy this."

***

Mother gracefully got out of the bath and ran her hands through her hair, smiling to herself. The blood bath had done well this time, removing all traces of the ordeal of her earlier death.

"Hello Trent."

He stepped forward out of the shadows and looked her up and down approvingly.

"The bath was a success I see."

Mother turned around to face him and held her hand out to him. The tattoo of the snake eating its own tail was more detailed and vivid on the palm of her hand than it had been for a very long time.

"Indeed it was. I was just thinking of you. In fact, I was thinking of our rebirth ceremony but something strange happened."

Trent walked towards her, raising his tattooed hand to her blood covered face and stroked her cheek softly while looking intently at her.

"And that strange thing was?"

Leaning her face in to his hand, Mother allowed herself to sigh contently, safe in the knowledge that their bond as the linked bloodline was as strong as it had ever been.

"I'm not sure how to explain it. I was day dreaming about the ceremony itself, the beautiful moment when we were torn asunder only to be reborn in to our new image when I felt someone else watching my memory. It was *Him* Trent, it was Naz watching our rebirth."

"Your son watched your rebirth?"

"Yes, he was there with that infernal half dead deer creature. That means he must be near. We need to be prepared."

Mother looked Trent up and down before unbuttoning his suit jacket, letting it drop to the floor. Leaning forward she kissed him, feeling his power run through her veins. She could feel the lives that he had taken, the souls that he had stolen and it felt good. It made her feel alive as their souls danced across both their lips.

"But first, we play."

She ripped his shirt open and bit his chest hard as his eyes glimmered with a hint of his strength and the souls of his victims.

"And play we shall."

Trent kissed her deeply and picked her up in his arms to carry her to the bed chamber.

"You, clean that mess up and find me a new shirt then kindly piss off, we have more mess to make."

The maid walked quickly grabbing as much as she could before leaving the room.

"Shame, she could have joined in Trent" said Mother before pulling the curtains around the bed closed and howling in ecstasy.

Chapter Twenty Five

I could hear a lot of movement and sounds coming from the corridor outside of my room. There were hushed but worried voices going past, one of which I instantly recognised as Jim. I felt like I should go out and see what was happening but something in the back of my mind told me to stay in the room for a little longer.

Sitting down on the bed, I looked at the sparse decoration in the room. It was clear that everyone here lived really simple and clean lives, or at least as simple and clean as they could while living under a coffee shop. My bag was next to me, despite it having been in the motel room. Rummaging through it, I found some new clothes and changed out of these sweaty and smelly ones. It felt nice to let the clean clothes slide across my skin and I relaxed for the first time since all of this started.

Looking at myself in the mirror, it was clear that all of this was starting to take its toll on me. I looked haggard, almost like I hadn't slept in days, which was partly true thanks to the visions and the nightmares. What little hair I did have was sticking up in every direction possible so I looked a complete and utter mess.

A rainbow effect of colours swirled in the mirror, distorting my reflection in its glass. The colours were hypnotic in their movements and I found myself unable to take my eyes from the various shapes and patterns that were being created before my very eyes.

Slowly each colour came together to form an outline. Piece by piece, they joined together to create the visage of the deer from my visions. Its mouth was moving silently while I stood and stared. Each time its mouth moved, more colours joined the pattern making it look like a classical work of art that had come alive.

Stepping closer to the mirror, I tried to force myself to concentrate on the movement of the mouth of the deer. It was clearly trying to share some kind of message but still I couldn't hear anything. Its rainbow coloured eyes were full of frustration as it moved its head from side to side, trying to communicate just what it wanted from me.

My head started to spin quickly and I found myself surrounded by the clashing of the colours, leaving me staring at the multi-coloured version of the deer, complete with grotesquely colourful trailing guts. It felt like some gaudy, fucked up joke.

"Satara. Save Satara, he's the key."

I reached out to touch his face and my fingers went through it as if touching water, creating a weird rippling effect before coming back together and reforming.

"He's the key to all of this."

The deer tilted its head to look at me and moved towards me so that its nose was nearly touching mine.

"Go and go now before time runs out. I can't hold my soul together like this for much longer."

With a thud, I fell to the floor in the room and got to my heads and knees, staring at the mirror. It was back to completely normal and all I could see was myself and the rest of the room reflected back at me.

I knew what I had to do. Dust myself off, get out there and find Satara. It was important we find him and despite not knowing why, I knew if I failed we would all be in a whole world of trouble.

***

Martel had seen a lot of horrific things during his time as the coroner for the city. So many acts of violence and of the disgusting lack of respect for the human life itself. He'd even seen a lot of things that he couldn't explain but this was different. This was something that he had not only never seen before but was also something that wasn't even close to making sense.

How could a murderer leave an outline of a hand on a victim that looks like every ounce of moisture has been drained out of them? It felt like a low budget horror flick that you'd find late at night while channel surfing.

His fingers whizzed over the keyboard as he tried to search the internet to find some sort of reasoning behind the hand prints. There were so many search results as he scrolled down them all that he just clicked on a random one. A page came up with a whole list of myths and legends, with descriptions of strange creatures, illustrations of things people have seen in the dead of night and more. It was a conspiracy theorists dream.

The sound of something smashing made him look up from a poorly written article about a pair of creatures, one called an incubus and one called a succubus. Leaving the computer on the page he was reading, he poked his head around the door.

"Hello? Webber is that you?"

The silence sent shivers of trepidation down his spine so he grabbed the nearest thing to hand. A letter opener his mother had given him when he graduated from university.

"Webber?"

Walking down the short corridor to the lab, Martel looked around. Nearly all the lights were off except for one solitary one near the computers.

The lab had never been the best or happiest of places to be in, even when having to be there for work, but it seemed all the more creepier tonight. Silence crept around the room while Martel tried to focus on the one light that was glaring through the darkness. A deep breath later, he flicked the light switches on and the entire room burst in to the harsh lighting thanks to the old-fashioned fluorescent lights hanging on the oddly stained ceiling.

Despite how bright the room was, he couldn't see where the sound had come from. He wouldn't be surprised if it had been a rat or something of that ilk. It had happened before and no doubt it would happen again thanks to the wonder of their budget being cut yet again.

Working his way around to the lamp that had been on, he checked the desk. Nothing seemed out of place and was as tidy as Webber had left it. That was one of her quirks that he admired. She would never leave to go home until her desk was neat and tidy.

A hissing sound made Martel spin around holding the letter opener. There was nothing there again. This was starting to feel like a really bad prank of some sort. One that was mean spirited and not at all funny in the slightest.

Another hissing sound made him spin around again, this time with him swinging the letter opener in an effort to look heroic but instead making him look like a child playing pirates. As he bumped his hip on the corner of the table, he stumbled as something cold and clammy grabbed his wrist.

"Doctor Martel we presume?"

The voice hissed his name with a layer of contempt as if asking the question had caused it actual, physical pain. Its grip tightened on his wrist with each syllable of the words causing him to grimace in pain as something wet ran down his wrist and hand. He wanted to try to pull whatever it was off of him but something in the back of his mind told him to stay as calm as possible.

"You presume correctly but is there any need to grab me like this?"

The calmness in his own voice surprised him. He had no idea who this was but he did know that he needed to get away as quickly as possible.

"This is for your own good."

That voice again, that snake like voice, felt like it was trying to claw its way in to his brain.

"The process will hurt but I shall try to be quick."

Suddenly a sense of fear gripped him and refused to let go as something wet wrapped itself around his throat and face. With his mouth covered, Martel couldn't scream as a sharp sheering pain exploded in the front of his head and he started to cry.

Chapter Twenty Six

Sopor was sat at the end of the table with his head resting on his tented hands. Not once did his eyes stray away from looking at Jim and Rhea.

"So, let me get this straight and correct in my head. You have brought Michael, a member of The Family, in to our space?"

Rhea looked at Jim while he sat returning Sopors gaze.

"Yes Sopor, he was badly injured."

"So was Satara when he attacked him or had that slipped your mind?"

"Of course not."

"Then why bring him here?"

Jim looked flustered at the anger residing in the questioning from Sopor. He wasn't even remotely trying to hide the disgust in the tone of his voice or the way he was throwing questions at him.

"He looked like his wings were literally torn from his body."

"And? That's karma and nothing else."

Rhea put her hand on Jim's arm and raised her hand to get Sopor's attention.

"Sir, isn't our credo that we want to just live together in peace? Surely that should extend to everyone, not just the people that you like or have little history with."

They could both see that the words had hit home when Sopor leant back in his chair and sighed before taking a drink from the glass of wine in front of him.

"Get him out of here as soon as you can. If any trouble heads our way then it's on both of you. Do you understand?"

As soon as the last word had escaped from his lips, Sopor had stood up and stormed out of the room in a rage that neither of them had ever seen before. The slam of the door made them both flinch as it echoed around them yet the guards didn't budge an inch.

"He's got a point."

His voice, normally so full of confidence and sense, was shaky and unsure of itself. Covering his mouth with his hands, Jim looked at Rhea with a look of worry in his eyes.

"Have I done the right thing Rhea or have I doomed us all by bringing him here?"

"Jim, you are one of the kindest people I know. You've brought him here to help heal him, to maybe even save his life. You've done it with nothing but the best intentions."

"You know what they say though Rhea, the road to hell is paved with the remnants of good intentions."

***

Snow stood on the gantry above the workstations and stared at the empty spaces where the children normally were. A mixture of emotions ran through her in the silence. On one hand, it felt so serene and nice and on the other, it felt like little more than a ghost town.

She had spent a very long time building up this place, sacrificing many things along the way. She'd never had a family of her own but liked to think that the children here thought of her as family or at the very least thought of her as safety in a world so dangerous.

While she thought fondly of the children she had here with her, her mind kept coming back to one thing. What did Mother want with a simple ceremonial blade? It had been a one in a million shot that Snow had finally found it after years of looking, in fact, it felt rather coincidental. While the saying is true that it's a small world, it did seem rather strange that it suddenly turned up in a local museum after she had travelled around the world to find it.

Running her hands through her hair, Snow wondered if it had truly been so convenient that the blade had been found, mere luck or someone was trying to lure her in to being involved in whatever the Family were involved in right now.

She understood the simple fact that no matter how the blade had been found, no matter why it had turned up in the museum, she just could not be involved in any of it.

All she had ever wanted was to have the blade back. It was part of heritage, part of her lineage, part of her life. Yes it had spilled much blood, yes it was at the hands of her ancestors, but she was a largely peaceful person. She only fought when it was absolutely necessary and if the children needed protecting.

She also understood the loyalties of the ones that followed Mother. It was totally understandable in a way. Mother had earned their trust, earned their hearts and earned their unwavering devotion. Snow had never been one herself to blindly follow someone in that way, that way of thinking was far too dangerous. In reality she'd always been her own person but it was the idea of safety in numbers that really spoke to her as a sensible one.

Hell, she was doing similar here with the children. She just wanted to keep them safe, keep them healthy. She just wanted to give them somewhere to lay their heads in the evenings to have a full nights sleep without the fear of not knowing if they'd wake up again in the morning.

Snow walked back to her office slowly, the last thing she wanted to do was to wake anyone at this late hour, before closing the door behind her. Knowing that the world was full of hard decisions, this was going to be one of the hardest that she could possibly make. If she was to be completely honest with herself, there were only two choices and both had very different outcomes. The first, she could hand over the blade and let Mother do whatever she needed to do with it and just stay out of the way of whatever came of that plan. Maybe, just maybe, that would keep the children the safest. The second was that she refused. Flat out refused. The blade was hers and hers alone and it was going to stay here. The consequence of that would be the very real chance they would indeed come and try to take it from her themselves. What would happen then? Would the children be safe?

She felt her hands turn cold. The mere thought of putting those innocent lives in danger felt like an ice cold dagger being plunged in to her heart but there was the very real possibility that letting them have the blade could lead to an even worse result, possibly for all of them and not just the children themselves.

Turning to look at the blade, she swore under her breath. There was a gap on the wall with a hastily written note taped where the blade had once hung as pride of place in her collection.

I know that you are going to be mad at me but I'm doing this with the best intentions possible. I want to keep you and the children safe. I may not agree with you on everything you say and do but you are using your heart to protect these children and the least I can do is to try to protect you for doing so. That is why I've taken the blade. Not to give to Mother. Not to give to anyone. They will know I have it and chase me, not you. You once saved my life when we were younger and I've wasted nearly all of it since. This is my selfish chance of not only redemption for that but for also showing you the gratitude I should have shown you years ago. Be safe, be kind. Always. Aithling.

***

Aithling and Snow had always been inseparable. It had started at school when Aithling had been getting bullied by some of the girls in her class for the simple reason that she wasn't as well off as they were and therefore had to wear hand me down clothes to school. Some of that resentment had even bled through to the teachers who just saw her as a student there to make up the class numbers and little else.

That was when Snow started at the same school. She had an effortless sense of coolness about her that almost bordered on the apathetic. Nothing ever seemed to phase her in the slightest and she had a sharp tongue on her too, always ready with a quick retort or comeback no matter what someone had said to her first.

They'd never spoken before that afternoon but Aithling had definitely noticed and admired her from afar. After being shoved in to the lockers one too many times, Aithling hit back and slapped the ringleader of the girls. That was a big mistake. They all set on her like a pack of hyenas with kicks, punches, insults and even bites when all of a sudden they parted and landed in every direction possible.

Aithling looked up and tried to blink the blood and tears away from her eyes as she looked up at the person in front of her. Snow was crouched protectively in front of her, fists tightly clenched.

"Are you done? Six of you against one girl. Is that what being cool looks like to you?"

They all scrambled away from Snow, the looks in their eyes was one of absolute fear as she glared them down.

"If I see or hear of any of you touching her again, you'll get more than a bloody nose. Do I make myself clear ladies?"

Snow kept her voice calm and collected but something in the tone of her words made the girls realise that this was no a fight that they should follow through with.

A few weeks passed after the incident and the school felt like a different place entirely. The girls had been expelled and the teachers were nearly falling over themselves to make sure Aithling had every single thing she needed to go as far as her smart mind would take her. She never asked how Snow had managed such a change, if she had at all, but she was by Aithling's side every step of the way.

Of course there were rumours about them both. It was a small town after all and that sort of thing was second nature to the inhabitants but there was nothing to it all. Aithling saw Snow as a sister and vice versa, a rarity in the world that they were in. A world known for its selfishness and hardness but together they would take it on and together they would win, no matter how long it took.

***

Snow held the note close to her chest. She'd always loved Aithling through everything. She'd always been there for her through her issues with addiction, through one disastrous relationship after another and tried her best to lead her to find her own happiness above all else.

This was just like her though, taking the whole of the world on her shoulders and running away with it before anyone could help her but what will become of her?

She was right, The Family would indeed go after her, especially after seeing this as the highest betrayal imaginable. In fact, she'd be a dead woman walking. There was no doubt of that nor of the fact that Mother would make the worst kind of example of her possible, maybe even worse than she had done to Michael. Snow had heard about that through the grapevine, through one of her many eyes and ears in the city. Something that vicious, that horrific wouldn't go unnoticed for long.

Aithling would need help, that much she was sure of. The decision had been made for her. Snow would have to be involved in all of this. The only thing still undecided was which side her allegiance would fall on but for now that would have to wait. She had the feeling that the decision would be made for her very soon.

Chapter Twenty Seven

Something deep inside of me was telling me to hurry. I knew that I had to find Satara as quickly as I possibly could but I didn't know why, I just knew that he was in some sort of trouble.

The further up the stairs I got, the more my head started to buzz. It felt like a swarm of bees had somehow forced themselves in to my brain and were trying to find a way out. Each step made the sound louder and the pain inside my head more intense.

I couldn't let it stop me, I knew I had to get out of here and to Satara. A sense of foreboding swam all around me but I knew that no matter what, I had to make sure he was okay.

Pushing the door open, I forced myself in to the coffee shop and fell clumsily to my knees with my hands on my head. My entire brain felt like it wanted to explode.

Welcome back Naz. Bet you thought you'd gotten rid of me didn't you?

It all came rushing back. Sopor had told me that *she* couldn't reach me down there, that their space was protected from any of their powers or manipulations. Unfortunately, I wasn't in their space any more and that meant my mind was left unshielded, meaning *she* had found a way in to my head.

Had enough of their lies yet?

No, no no, I couldn't let her take me over like this. I had somewhere to be. I had someone to see.

Or have you been stupid enough to believe them?

Forcing myself to my feet, I stumbled towards the door. The little droplets of blood from Jim and Rhea helping Michael in were still there, making the wooden flooring look like a dot to dot puzzle.

Let's be honest Naz, you're not exactly smart enough to work out what is going on are you?

My entire body felt like I was being weighed down, making each and every step a battle in itself. A battle that I had to win yet I didn't know why.

A movement caught my attention out of the corner of my left eye and I slowly turned to look, seeing the deer standing amongst the tables. He was translucent, giving the place a strange and eerie feel.

Taking in strays as pets now are they? First you and now that thing?

The deer moved his mouth silently, forming the name Satara over and over again like some kind of sacred mantra. Slowly it walked over to me and gestured towards the door with his nose.

You're weak Naz. You always were and always will be.

My hand shook as I forced my fingers to wrap themselves around the door handle. Her voice had always been present in my life, echoing around in my mind, but this seemed different. It seemed stronger, it seemed to be trying to control my movements and even my mind itself.

They don't know it yet but you'll fail them like you failed everybody else.

Finally my managed to get a firm grip on the handle itself and turned out, leaving the door to open slowly as I crawled through it on my hands and knees.

Go then. Have your adventure but hear this one thing.

I could feel the grip on my mind loosening slightly as I looked up to the sky and tried to focus on the clouds above in an effort to ground myself and calm my beating heart.

Unlike your fantasy books you love to read so much, there will not be a happy ending for you, for any of you.

***

Mother looked at Trent with a look of impressed annoyance on her face.

"He's getting stronger. I don't know how but he's getting stronger."

She traced her finger down his chest and couldn't help but smirk. This had been a rather unexpected development but one that could prove to add a whole new layer of fun to all of this.

Trent looked unimpressed as he laid back on the bed staring up at the covering above their heads, his concentration lost as his eyes followed the gold coloured patterns.

It's them."

Mother turned to look at him with a quizzical look on her face. "I do agree with you Trent but how?"

"I don't know yet but there must be something. He's gone from being little more than a bumbling fool to being someone that can deflect our attempts at controlling him."

Mother nodded. Trent wasn't wrong. Whatever they had said or done to Naz was definitely working on him and that was dangerous to them and to their plan.

"Maybe it's time to start proceedings earlier than we originally planned."

Trent smirked at Mother's suggestion. It wasn't like her to suggest such a thing, in fact quite the opposite. She was the sort of woman that would plan religiously and then stick to that plan until the very end but this was different. Naz could easily throw a massive curve ball in to this so they needed to strike before he did.

Mother looked at her phone and looked up at him with a smile.

"Let's call The Family together. It's time. Blade or no blade, we need to move before they do. Make the arrangements."

***

Satara slouched over as much as the chains would allow him to. They were cutting in to his wrists and each sway of his body made it worse. It was as if every nerve in his body were competing for his attention, shooting waves and jabs of pain all through him.

The man with the pipe lowered it and looked at the swaying body in front of him. A trickle of blood was still running from his ears and from his left nostril yet he hadn't told them a thing. Looking at the well dressed man for instruction, he felt his fingers move over the pipe as if caressing a lover.

Stepping forward until he was next to the piper, the nameless man in the suit ran his hand across Satara's cheek gently.

"Wake up Mr Satara. You can sleep soon but not yet."

His voice was softer now, in complete contrast to the violence of the beating he gave Satara a mere few minutes earlier.

"Please don't ignore me Mr Satara, that is the epitome of bad manners and we all know how much I abhor bad manners."

A smirk crossed Satara's face and he couldn't help but chuckle to himself.

"Bugger, I thought I'd tricked you in to thinking I was having a nice nap my dear but clearly my acting isn't as good as I had hoped. Any chance of a nice cup of tea while we continue this lovely chat?"

The expression on the man's face remained blank.

"Sarcasm is the lowest form of wit so let us not stoop to that level shall we?"

"But what if I say please?"

A sharp knee to Satara's midsection took him by surprise and drove the air from his lungs in a loud raspy sound.

"How about pretty please then my dear?"

A stiff forearm shot to the side of his face quickly followed, leaving him swaying from his chains.

"Let's start again shall we?"

The piper stepped forward with the pipe already to his lips in readiness.

"I shall ask you where the blade is and you will answer. It's that simple. Mess me around at all then my friend here will play and it will be more than blood coming from your ears this time."

"Does he take requests at all because I'd love some Cole Porter tunes while I converse with you handsome gentlemen."

With a sigh, he raised his hand and the piper began to play once again, this time more furiously than before. Leaving the piper to play, he walked away from the two of them and stood next the hooded man while Satara started to moan in pain.

"I'm starting to think our friend either doesn't know or is too stupid to know that it would be beneficial to his health if he told us."

The hooded figure grunted in agreement.

"Either way, we're wasting our time here so let's leave those two to their play date and tell Mother."

With a nod of his hooded head, the two men walked out of the tattoo parlour as the high pitched tune coming from the pipe mixed with the desperate screams coming from Satara as he swayed back and forth from the chains.

Chapter Twenty Eight

Aithling stood in the darkened alleyway with her back resting against the wall. Breathing heavily and feeling the cold air bite through her, she watched as her breath came together in little clouds in front of her.

The weight to the dagger under her jacket felt reassuring but she knew she couldn't stay in this place for long, especially not with the cutters still embarking on their grotesque and murderous attempts at patrolling the streets in the hopes of finding a quick and easy meal.

Leaning her head against the damp wall, one thing struck her. She had no idea what she was doing or where she was going. That wasn't a new sensation to her, she always prided herself on living in the moment. The problem with not knowing on this occasion was the simple fact that this time, people were going to be coming after her. People that didn't particularly have a reputation for being kind towards people that didn't follow their ideals or their ways.

This had been a long time coming. That was the one thing out of all of this that she was sure of. She'd never been one for following rules blindly but somehow, she had fallen for the flawed rhetoric that Mother and The Family sprouted about the world, making her think that this place owed her something. She had believed that it was better to be the one above another than truly trying to just live her own life. It had given her an over inflated sense of worth, of importance amongst them all.

Mother had seen that, she had seen the growing confidence that was flowing from her and twisted that in to hatred, mistrust and bitterness towards anyone different from her. She had forged that in to a weapon, one she needed to fulfil her plan to make our kind the ones that rule over everything and everyone.

Aithling knew she wasn't perfect or even innocent in anything of this. She knew what she was doing, she knew what she was involved it but it's been taken too far. Yes the human kind had to be punished for what they have done over the centuries and even continue to do so now. Of course they do. Her kind had been hunted, shown off, punished just for being different but to destroy everything just to rule over them made them just as bad as the humans themselves didn't it?

A little girl tapped her leg, making her look down in to a dirty and hungry looking face.

"I'm sorry, I don't have any change or any food."

The girl continued to stare at her with cold and lifeless eyes.

"You're going to die soon."

Aithling shuffled a couple of steps away from the girl without taking her eyes away from her.

"Excuse me?"

She raised her little hands to her face and started to claw at her dirty skin as little spots of blood started to appear near her fingers. Aithling reached in to her jacket and cursed. She'd left her whips at Snow's place.

The girl took a step towards her with the bloodied remnants in her left hand. A smile had crossed the bloody and fleshy mess that had been left behind. The lumps of muscle and viscera were moving and pulsating with each movement she made.

"I said you're going to die soon."

A laugh escaped from the hole where the little girls mouth had once been. It sounded raspy and wet as her tongue rolled around in her mouth.

"And it's going to be painful, so divinely painful."

Aithling fell backwards as the girl dove at her, wrapping her little hands around her throat and squeezing tightly.

"You are going to pay for what you have done."

She tried in vain to pull the hands away from her throat as she gasped desperately to force any oxygen in to her lungs as the grip tightened. Blood and spit dripped from the little girls face on to hers.

Without warning, the face split in half revealing a skull with a long, forked tongue that flicked towards Aithling's face. A loud squeal erupted through the air and it tried to force its tongue in to Aithling's mouth. She tried punching the little girl but it had no effect, it didn't even acknowledge the force of the impact in to its side.

Gunshots echoed through the alleyway and the body of what used to be the little girl rolled off of Aithling with a heavy thud before a familiar voice spoke to her.

"That thing won't stay down for long, we need to hurry."

Snow holstered her gun and put her hand out, almost smiling when Aithling took hold of it and pulled her up.

"You look a mess."

Aithling couldn't help but smirk slightly.

"Thanks, can always count on you to help me with my self image."

"And clearly for saving your ass too."

The body on the floor started to jerk in strange movements, leaving its arms and legs at near obscene angles.

"We're too late, clearly they've already put their plan in to action."

This had been the first time that Aithling had ever seen Snow worried. The look on her face was one of anguish and fear, leaving a feeling of anger welling up inside of Aithling's gut. Reaching for the blade, she felt her fingers tighten around the handle.

That horrendous squeal erupted from the body again as it jerked to its feet and reached a blood soaked hand to both of them.

"You are both doomed to eternal damnation for your betrayal. You will be doomed to serve under us like a mere human."

Aithling lunged at the creature, plunging the blade in to its chest before it pushed her backwards. A wisp of smoke started to rise from the wound as its flesh started to flake from her body, landing in an ash like pile at her feet. The squeal came forth once more but was quickly silenced as dropped in to a pile of bones on the wet alley floor before melting in front of their eyes.

"Well, that answers why Mother wanted the blade then."

Snow looked at Aithling with the sorrow that had once been in her eyes replaced with fury.

"Does it Aithling? It means the stories are true. That there is a cursed blade that will bring about the end of our coexistence with the humans. If she gets told of it, then there will be nothing anyone can do to stop The Family. That's even if it's not too late already."

"So what do we do?"

"We run Aithling, we run and get as far away from this shit storm as possible, tuck our heads in and pray to whatever deity we can think of in the hopes that we get through of all this."

"And if that doesn't work?"

"Then we're fucked."

***

Webber sat on the edge of her bed. Files from work had been flung haphazardly around her leaving their contents to spill out on to her blanket. Autopsy photos of the victims that Trent had fed from looked at her from random angles as if accusing her of the crimes themselves. Even with the window open, sweat ran down her back making her feel even more uncomfortable.

A nervous and guilty energy ran through her making her both anxious and energetic at the same time. Her fingers tapped a steady beat on her legs as she waited for the inevitable phone call.

The phone lay on top of one of the photographs making it look like an oversized prop for the corpse. A quick glance showed Webber that nobody had called her yet.

She couldn't help but have second thoughts about all of this. Martel had been nothing but supportive and kind to her ever since we started working with him. It had even grown in to a friendship of sorts yet as soon as she had to, she'd thrown him under the bus without question. The guilt running through her was making her twitch. What were they going to have done to him?

Mother had sent the signal. All the pieces on the puzzle board were in play and the game had started. She knew that was going to mean that there would certainly be collateral damage on both sides but she had been naive. Stupidly, the idea of the man she was spying on being taken care of was one that she had been sure wouldn't affect her yet, here she was, feeling guilty about all of it.

There was no doubt about it being the *right* thing to do, after all Mother did know best, but she was unsure that it had been the right thing for *her* to do. That was a dangerous way of thinking, she'd seen what had been done to Michael when he showed his doubts but surely The Family would have understood her position in all of this. She was only young after all.

The sound of her bedroom door opening jarred her away from the jumbled up thoughts running through her mind. *They* were here.

"Was it quick?"

A naive question to start, she knew that but she needed to know. Part of her knew already that it wouldn't have been quick. Part of her already knew that it would have been painful. What she didn't know was had he called out for her? Had he called out for anyone?

Hissing flowed through the room feeling her with a sense of fear and foreboding.

"Sweet child, it was most definitely not quick. I saw to that. It was however, a lot of fun for me. His mind tasted exquisite on my tongue."

Webber shook and found herself biting her lip. This creature always gave her the creeps. The sooner this was over then the sooner she could get away from it, never to have to deal with it again. Silently, her brain was counting down the days until that would happen.

"What did he know?"

Her voice shook and cracked sadly. She was sure he had suffered dreadfully at the hands, or rather tongue, of this creature.

"Absolutely nothing but his memories were sweeter than the most splendid nectar of the Gods."

"And where is he now?"

"Switch on the news and see."

Silently, the creature was gone. She hated it when he did that. The fact that he could just appear and disappear at will made him the most convenient of assassins when needed.

Feeling around for the remote, she felt her fingers touch the on button and the television set sparked in to life. Flicking to the news channel, she felt her heart leap in to her throat as the reporter looked in to the camera. It felt like she was staring right at Webber and it unnerved her. She recognised the building behind her instantly. It was the complex where Martel lived.

"Earlier today, tragedy struck as Doctor Robert Martel was found dead in his apartment. Police were called anonymously to the scene, finding Martel with a gun like head wound. A note was found next to the body itself, allegedly written by the Doctor himself but the contents of the note haven't been revealed to us at this time but all signs are pointing at a tragic and suicidal end to one of the city's most beloved employees."

Webber turned the television off and stared at the blank screen. The creature had been smart, leaving the body in the apartment and not in the lab itself. That would have raised a lot more questions than answers but why had they had to go down the suicide route?

She sighed, knowing full well that they would have used the note as an excuse for a character assassination on Martel. That way, if any of them had been implicated in any way, it would have put his work in doubt. Webber truly felt bad for that. Work was all Webber had left other than his dog and he'd put his heart and soul in to trying to keep the city safe and protected.

Now was not the time for guilt and nerves to take over though. Now was the time to make sure that her kind and the followers of The Family, were given their chance to rule over this poor excuse of a city and then, to rule everywhere else and show the humankind that their time of reckoning was upon them.

Chapter Twenty Nine

Trent looked at Mother. Her eyes had rolled back in to her head and her entire body was vibrating. It was like her whole body was emitting pulses of energy all around her. He'd always loved watching her signal to the others, to The Family.

Her lips moved silently as she uttered the chants to call to them, to set the plan in motion. She swayed gently as the words floated in the air. Candles flickered in to life, the mirror started to shift and change colour.

The surface of the mirror started to flow and reach out to her. Random shapes moved across it and joined together to create a face that looked at Mother.

Suddenly her eyes opened and a smile crossed over her face as she stood before dropping to one knee. Slowly and respectfully she reached out to the face with her palms face up and smiled. Trent knelt down next to her and did the same.

Taking one of her hands in his, she continued to silently chant towards the face forming in front of her. It was slowly and awkwardly taking shape before their very eyes. As Mother threw her head back in ecstasy, the face roared before plunging back in to the mirror itself and reverting back to its normal surface as if nothing had happened.

She looked at Trent, noticing he had an arrogant smile ruling over his face. Standing up, she gestured to him before wrapping her arms around him in an embrace and kissed him passionately.

"And so it begins" she whispered as her eyes burned a fiery red.

***

Rhea tilted her head and watched Michael sleeping for a moment. He seemed at peace now that Jim had treated his wounds with the various salves and herbs that he always seemed to have at his disposal. She'd always been surprised at how easy Jim seemed to take everything in his stride, at how easy he always appeared to know how to heal any wound, any illness, any malady.

Sighing, she walked over to the wooden chair near the cabinet. Jim was sleeping silently after having watched over Michael since his arrival. She crouched in front him and looked up at him fondly. If she was completely honest with herself, she'd always been a bit taken with him. He may not have been the most handsome man she'd ever seen or even the funniest but there just seemed to be a kindness in his heart under all of the gruff exterior that he portrayed to everybody.

Her hand stroked over his and he mumbled lightly in his sleep before she stood up and left the room, shutting the door gently. Stopping to look up and down the makeshift corridor, Rhea sighed and closed her eyes.

"Are you all right Rhea?"

The voice mixed with the slight sounds of his wings made Rhea open her eyes.

"Is Sopor around?"

The fairy pointed down the corridor before lightly kissing her cheek and flying away, leaving a subtle sparkle in the air. She walked down the corridor and only stopped when she saw Sopor sitting at his table. He looked serious and withdrawn as Rhea walked in and shut the door behind her, leaving them alone in the room.

***

Jim opened his eyes and yawned. He'd been watching over Michael since he got here and it had certainly taken its toll on him. The sleep had been fitful at best because he knew, he just knew, that something wasn't quite right about Michael being here. Not because of the history between them, he knew that Michael was certainly not a good person. It's just that it seemed so rather convenient that he turn up here.

This place had always been protected by Sopor and his magic. Jim had never known how it worked or how it had managed to keep out Mother and her kind but he just knew that it always had.

Looking around the room, he breathed in and smiled. He had felt lost for years before finding Rhea and taking her under his wing. She'd been living on the streets with nobody to care for her and something just drew him to her. It wasn't that he wanted to help her, he did, but it was that he felt that he had to. He felt that it was up to him to do so and when he did, it felt like he had finally found a purpose and a reason for living instead of just tumbling through each and every day.

He was proud of Rhea in more ways than he could possibly know. She had grown up to be a proud, intelligent and beautiful young lady who not only had a handle on her abilities but always did so with purpose.

Looking in to the mirror, Jim saw his reflection staring back at him. He looked a lot older than his years thanks to the toll his life had taken on him. Drinking, drugs, it had all aged him beyond his years but he knew that as long as he was here, everything would be all right. Sopor had helped to get him clean, had helped to heal his scars and much more. In fact, he owed everything to that man and knew that no matter how much he did for them, he could never repay their kindness.

Suddenly, something in the reflection caught his eye and he span round to look. The bed was empty and Michael was gone.

Chapter Thirty

Opening my eyes, I found that I had been kneeling down in the middle of the street holding my hands out so the palms were facing upwards. People walked past me with a mixture of facial expressions. Some looked concerned, some absently dropped change towards me, some looked angry and others, well others just completely ignored my very existence.

I got to my feet and rubbed my temples to try to quell the pain I was feeling in my head. Each and every time that woman forced herself in to my mind, it felt like I was being beaten relentlessly with a sledgehammer.

Looking around I saw that everyone was going about their business. They say that ignorance is bliss and from the looks on their faces, that saying couldn't be more true. Part of me wondered just how many of these people were like me. How many of them had found that the world itself wasn't as it seemed?

Over the other side of the road, the deer stood looking at it. Despite the translucent nature of his body, little clouds of condensation were raising from its nostrils while it stared at me. Every now and then, it shimmied on the spot and looked towards a thin alleyway.

I stared at the deer and nodded. It was clearly telling me where I needed to go.

It's mouth opened and closing silently, once again repeating Satara's name. I knew I had to get to wherever he was but that left one question burning in my head. What was I going to find when I got there?

I couldn't help but feel that old familiar sense of foreboding running through me yet I knew that I couldn't let that stop me. No matter what I found, no matter who I saw, I would get to Satara and do whatever needed to be done. Looking up, I could have sworn that the deer was smiling at me. It gave me a sense of self pride and even strength.

As I crossed the road, a vision danced before my eyes and stopped me mid stride. It was a vision of Satara's body swaying from what looked like a hook with his wrists bound by chains. I could feel the pain of the clasps cutting in to my own wrists, the pain of cuts and bruises all over my body. Stumbling the next couple of steps, I steadied myself with my hand on a nearby post box.

I pulled my shirt up and looked at my own torso. It was covered in raw and bloody wounds and bruises. Looking at my wrists, they looked the same. I could see the broken skin where the clasps would have cut in to my wrists if I had been the one wearing them.

Stamping its hooves, the deer tried to nudge me forward and I nodded. The creature was showing me what I needed to see. It was showing me what was happening to Satara and I knew I had to get there before it was too late.

***

The well dressed man and the hooded man stood outside the tattoo parlour and both lit cigarettes. They knew the piper inside had the situation well in hand but something felt wrong. Something felt off with the whole thing. They had been sure that Satara knew where the blade was. He was known as the man that knew everything. You needed information, you went to him. It was as simple as that yet now, they were sure he didn't know. It was such a shame to have to hurt him but sometimes, violence is the only thing you have to get you the answers you seek. That's how life worked in their part of the world. Hell, it's how life worked in a lot of the human world too, it's just that theirs liked to hide it's vicious nature under the guise it furthering the humans various causes. It was pathetic. Why they couldn't just accept their nature was beyond them. At least they were true to themselves and did whatever they had to do to make sure they survived. Never matter, all of this would soon be changed for the better if Mother and The Family get their way. That was certainly something for them to look forward to at least.

The well dressed man jolted backward and held his chest before breathing heavily. With a twitch of his hood, the other man looked at him quizzically.

"He's on his way. Naz is coming."

The hooded man nodded slowly, opening his jacket to ensure his hand was as near to his gun as possible but the man in the suit shook his head.

"No. This needs to happen. Mother has seen it all so let it run its course."

They both looked at each other before putting out their cigarettes under the heels of their expensive shoes and walked away, with the well dressed man whistling under his breath.

***

Mother sat in her gown at the head of the table. She made sure to have a tantalising array of food arranged on the table in various shapes and sizes, which the other Family members were happily devouring before her very eyes. This was a time for celebration. This was a time for praise. This was a time for decadence and over indulgence.

Webber was sat quietly at the opposite end of the table, quietly picking at her food. She wasn't hungry at all, the guilt had seen to that, but she hadn't wanted to seem ungrateful to Mother.

"My sweet Webber, is the food not to your liking?"

She looked up at Mother with a hesitant look on her face. The entire table had stopped eating, some in mid bite with remnants of food hanging from their spit and grease covered faces, and all were staring at her expectantly.

"Yes Mother, thank you."

Mother tilted her head and looked at her.

"Is your heart not full of joy?"

Webber nodded slowly, trying to hide the sinking feeling in the pit of her stomach.

"Then why are you not rejoicing with us at the knowledge we will soon be rulers and not hiding in the shadows like common street trash?"

She hadn't realised and had seen no movement but Trent was now stood behind her with his hands on her shoulders.

"Yes daughter of mine, why are you not rejoicing?"

Webber looked over her shoulder and looked at Trent before turning back and looking at Mother, her fingers absent mindedly picking at the food on her plate. Her eyes flicked to each person on the table as if waiting for their reactions to help her choose her response. No help came.

"Did we have to kill Martel? Was he truly a danger to us?"

Trent tightened his grip slightly on her shoulders, making her stiffen in her seat.

"What he knew could have been dangerous to us all and I wasn't prepared to risk the lives of any member of The Family. When the storm does rain down on us all, I know not all of us will be there at the end. I'm not naive nor am I stupid. We will face losses and we will celebrate them with honour and gratitude but I wasn't prepared to risk anyone before we embark on that journey."

Webber nodded. She couldn't fault the reasons but she was still struggling with him having been taken. He was a good man and a good friend but at the end of the day, she knew that his would not be the first death and nor would it be the last before this was said and done.

"Thank you Mother."

Trent patted her shoulders and took his place next to Mother but before he sat, he raised his hands out to everyone.

"Now, let us continue to feast before the door to battle opens for us all. Do it for blood. Do it for Family."

The whole table roared in celebration and every hand grabbed as much food as they could, shoving as much as possible in their mouths.

Chapter Thirty One

Sopor looked up as Rhea approached the table and he put down his quill before shutting the book he was writing in. The leather bound cover with simple lettering on the front seemed at odds with the ornate look of the quill.

Rhea ran her hand over the book and looked almost lovingly at it. Sopor placed his hand on top of hers.

"Can I help you Rhea?"

Slowly, she looked up at Sopor and raised an eyebrow.

"Why do you write in this thing, even after all these years?"

Sopor seemed taken aback by the abrupt nature of her question but stroked her hand in an attempt to reassure her.

"You know why Rhea. This book, and many others like it, tell the story of our kind. Each and every one of us. Fairies, pixies, elves, deities, all of us have our stories and our histories in these books and each time they are passed down, I have to write our stories in them with each incarnation of ourselves."

"So tradition is why you do it?"

"I suppose you could say that yes but that would over simplify it."

"Tradition is merely the absence of free will amongst the simple minded Sopor."

He looked towards the door towards where his guard would normally be stood watching over him. Sighing, he remembered that he had sent him to guard Michael's room.

"Rhea, what are you talking about?"

Removing his hand, he tried to reach for his horn without Rhea noticing but she snatched his hand with hers, gripping his wrist with a strength that surprised even himself.

"I'm doing this for two reasons and two reasons only Sopor. It's not personal."

He struggled to get his hand free from her grip but tried to looked defiantly at her while she looked at him emotionless, her eyes burning with an intensity that he had not seen from her before.

"No Rhea, not with them. Please think before you do something you'll regret."

Rhea raised an eyebrow slightly before a flash of silver took Sopor by surprise and she let go of his wrist. His hands raised to his throat as blood gushed out, splashing the book and Rhea while she watched him fall.

"Naz is the one who did something to regret. He played our hand Sopor. He has made us do this and he alone."

The panicked look in Sopor's eyes begged Rhea for mercy. She shook her head as the blood ran from his wound and coloured his robes in a violent parody of an abstract painting as she crouched with one knee on his chest.

"Don't worry Sopor, I know you can be reborn. We all know that of your kind. Mother and Trent can do the same. You're not special. Not even remotely. I also know one other thing. You can't be reborn if your head is removed from the body and is desecrated with the marks of the black arts."

Sopor's eyes widened in terror. He tried to grab at her, tried to push her off of him but his strength was flowing from him with each drop of blood that he lost on the cold, stone floor.

"Goodbye Sopor."

Slowly she started to carve away at his neck with a clinical precision that surprised her and closed her eyes in ecstasy as the head came away from the body. Holding it up in the candlelight, she smiled and readied her knife to start carving the symbols she'd need in to the flesh. Time to get to work.

***

Jim rushed towards the door of the bedroom but before he could get his hand on the door handle, Michael rushed out of the wardrobe and tackled him to the floor. Fists rained down on Jim's face with a furious abandon giving him no time to protect himself.

Michael laughed as he grabbed Jim's face in his hands.

"You are weak. You all are. There was a chance to kill me but instead, you try to save me. You try to save all of us. That's where you went wrong."

Jim gripped Michael's arms tightly and forced himself to speak.

"No, it's all of you that have succumbed to hatred that are weak. That is where you all went wrong, not me."

The door burst open and Sopor's guard burst in but before he could say anything, a blade appeared from the front of his throat in a shower of blood and he fell to the floor, revealing Rhea behind him.

"Leave him Michael. I want him left to send a message to Naz that all of this is and always will be his fault."

She aimed a kick to his face and laughed as Jim closed his eyes and slipped in to unconsciousness before raising Sopor's symbol covered head to show Michael and threw it on to the bed.

"Now to have some fun."

Michael smiled as he pulled the blade from the dead guard and Rhea pulled his sword from his scabbard.

"Do it for blood"

"Do it for Family."

Chapter Thirty Two

Mother paced up and down the room a couple of times happily humming to herself before stopping in front of the mirror to admire herself and running her fingers over her face. The blood baths were working wonders for her complexion. In fact, if she hadn't have lived through it herself then she would never have known she'd come back from the dead.

Trent and Jacob both marched in to the room and knelt in front of her with their palms up in the usual show of respect. She hadn't seen Jacob since the meeting in the church and he looked just as nervous in her presence as always, if not a little more so.

Jacob smiled shyly and dabbed at the sweat flowing down his forehead with his handkerchief before trying to discreetly slide it back in to his suit jacket.

"Mother, thank you for the pleasure of your time."

Mother raised an eyebrow at him in mock annoyance and gestured at him to be quicker at getting to his point as he stumbled over getting the next set of words out.

"We've heard from Rhea. The plan went ahead without a hitch and Sopor has been dealt with accordingly."

"Fantastic, thank you Jacob. You may go join the others now."

Dabbing at his sweat covered face again, he couldn't hide the sheer delight on his face as she praised him and had to stop himself from skipping out of the room in delight. Trent shook his head and shrugged.

"Why do we keep that waste of space about?"

"Well my darling Trent, you never know when you will need a lawyer around, especially when you use your talents a little too freely on your jaunts to town."

Trent couldn't help but smirk. It was indeed true, he'd been careless with his last couple of feeding's but that was half the fun of it all. The chase wasn't more fun than the catch, far from it. The whole thing was fun as was seeing the fear turn on to resigned acceptance of their impending death in their eyes.

Mother clicked her fingers to get his attention and he grinned at her, hoping that would disarm her a little.

"Go anywhere nice there Trent or was I merely boring you in to a coma?"

"No, no, pray continue beautiful."

"With Sopor out of the way, we are clear to call forth the door for our ancestors to ascend to our realm."

"And then the humans will truly see us for who we are."

"For blood, for Family."

***

The two men sat in the restaurant staring out of the window at the tattoo parlour and waited for their order to turn up. Yes they were doing a job but there wasn't a rule against making it enjoyable.

"Are you sure we should be doing this?"

It was the man in the hood that spoke first. Normally he was a man of few words but clearly not tonight.

"Of course. Mother said do whatever it takes to distract Naz and hopefully find that blade in the process."

"And sacrificing the piper like this?"

"Fuck him, the guy's an arrogant idiot."

The hooded man nodded as the waiter brought over their order. The waiter scurried away after they both gave a cursory thank you then went back to looking out the window as a strange shimmery shape walked past.

"It's starting so why not get comfortable?"

The man in the suit stabbed a bit of lasagne with his fork and raised it to his mouth and watched.

***

The deer had gotten to the tattoo parlour before Naz, deliberately walking past the restaurant window to make sure the two idiots inside had seen him. They couldn't have been more obvious if they tried.

He sighed to himself. No matter what he tried, no matter how many times he reached out to Naz, he just wasn't getting through. Something was blocking his messages and that left Naz helpless. He didn't like that. Naz was the key to all of this and they couldn't afford to lose him.

Tilting his head, he saw Naz walking towards the parlour with an unsure look on his face. The deer knew this was some kind of trap, it had to be with those two useless wastes of skin and bone watching on in the restaurant. Why else would they be there? He knew he couldn't warn him though, it was hard enough getting Naz to see him and it left him exhausted each time. This one, Naz was just going to have to do on his own.

***

I looked at the door handle in front of me. I don't know how but I just knew that I was in the right place. In fact, it felt like I had been led here by that deer but he disappeared to fuck knows where leaving me with no idea what I was going to do, especially if Satara was hurt in there. I can barely look after myself let alone someone who is possibly badly injured.

Second guessing yourself as always Naz?

That voice. The time spent with Rhea, Jim and the others had been calm all things considering and had been a nice diversion without that voice drilling in to my head at every opportunity.

Don't be ungrateful, I'm giving you the pleasure of my company and don't you remember that saying? Mother knows best?

"Fuck you, you're dead so stay that way."

It's funny how little you actually know Naz.

I opened the door and slowly walked in, taking the time to duck behind the till. Closing my eyes, I tried to listen for any clues as for where Satara was but all I could hear was some strange flute music. He really didn't seem the sort to blare that sort of music out. Was I in the wrong place?

The music came to a crescendo and then abruptly stopped and I saw a small man walk out and stand just in front of me while he held a phone to his ear.

"I said I'd call you when it was done. Have I called? No."

I knew better than to let him see me so I tried to crouch lower as the man turned his back to me.

"You can tell Mother he knows nothing about the blade. I'll call when he's dead."

He slammed the small phone down on to the surface just about my head making me jolt slightly but then the room went completely silent. I counted to ten and slowly started to get to my feet when a kick hit me in my ribs with enough force to send me careening in to the chairs in the waiting area with a painful thud, driving the air out of my lungs.

I rolled on to my hands and knees gasping for breath and tried to crawl but the man followed me slowly with his hands behind his back and a mocking look on his face.

"So, you're the infamous Naz that I have heard about. You don't look like much."

Another kick to my ribs sent me back down to the floor, where I curled up in to the foetal position and tried to cover my head and face.

"I really don't see why everybody is so scared of you. There's no way a pathetic little ant like you could possibly stop The Family. We were all born to rule Naz, not to hide away from prying human eyes."

Spitting on the floor, I noticed some blood mixing with my saliva and raised my hand to my mouth. I'd split my lip on the way down. Looking up, I saw the man looking at me. I was under no illusion, he was going to kill me but he was taking his time and was going to enjoy it.

While looking at him, I pushed myself back as he lunged at me narrowly missing me on the way down. I prodded him with my foot and realised he wasn't getting up. That's when I saw the blood starting to form around his body and I started to panic, scrambling to get away from the body until my back hit one of the chairs.

"You're welcome."

Chapter Thirty Three

Snow stood over the body of the piper with her pistol in her hand and unscrewed the silencer. She wasn't one for being subtle with her weapons but this wasn't the time or place for a loud gunshot to be heard.

Behind her, Aithling held up Satara. He was leaning heavily on her with his eyes half closed but a strange, almost contented smile on his bleeding face.

"I know you'd come for me my dear boy but I wasn't expecting the cavalry to turn up for little ol' me too."

Snow cleared her throat.

"We're not with him and we're not with you. We just don't want to be around when Mother brings the weight of Hell down on all of us and to stop that, Naz and you have to not be dead."

Aithling looked at Naz and then at Satara.

"I wouldn't stay here if I were you. Naz, take Satara and we'll clean this shit up."

Naz rose to his feet with his eyes darting between Snow and Aithling. Indecision ran through him when a reflection in the window caught his eye. The deer shook his head and sniffed, clouds of condensation covering a small part of the window display making it look misty.

Snow, Aithling. I wish I could say I was surprised that you're here but I always knew you weren't strong enough to follow us. I should have known you were too weak to lead. You will pay for this dearly. Cherish the days you have left on this world because there won't be many of them left.

Naz jolted backwards and realised that Mother's voice had come from his own mouth. Aithling and Snow were looking at him with uncertain looks on their faces while Satara was trying to stand with as little support as possible.

"Mother is linked to him but he's getting stronger at blocking her."

Snow and Aithling looked at each other and nodded.

"Then in that case, we're out of here."

Satara sat down in one of the chairs and nodded a grateful smile at them as they stopped halfway through the door. Both Aithling and Snow looked at him and then looked at Naz.

"They can't know where we're going or where the knife is going either. We may not agree on a lot of things with your lot but we can agree that Mother needs to be stopped. There are ways and means to get what we want but this is certainly not one of them and not what I want to be involved in."

Naz was sat slumped over with his head in his hands as flashes of light flashed through his mind and various words repeated and echoed in his mind.

"Very well. God speed and good luck ladies."

"There are none of either where we're going."

The bell jingled as the door shut behind them and Satara looked at Naz with a concerned expression on his face.

"Hey, you're meant to be fussing over me not the other way around my dear. I'm the one who got tortured by a man with extremely boring music taste."

Naz looked up and gently ran his fingers over the wounds on Satara's face.

"I've got a very bad feeling about all of this. We need to get back to the coffee house and we need to do it now. I can't help but think all of this is rather too convenient."

Satara sighed and rested his hand on top of Naz's before lifting it, kissing its palm gently and resting it back on Naz's lap.

"My dear Naz, I fear you might be right so let us not rest on our laurels."

***

The two men left the restaurant as Snow and Aithling walked past. This was going to be far easier than they thought.

Following them at a few steps back, it was easy to keep up with them both. In fact, Snow and Aithling seemed unsure where they were going. The hooded man pointed discreetly at the slight bulge in the side of her jacket.

"She has it. She has the blade."

The well dressed man nodded as the two women walked in to an alleyway and gestured that they should follow them, turning into the alleyway themselves. It was empty.

Before they could even say anything to one another, the hooded man fell and his head rolled away from the body, hitting the metal bin with an echoing clang before turning in to dust. The well dressed man fell to his knees with the blade in his chest.

"Do it for blood. Do it for Family."

Those struggled words were the last he would ever speak as he slowly crumbled in to a dark pile of dust like his partner and Aithling quickly wiped the blade on the inside of her jacket.

"Two down, no doubt many more to go."

Snow nodded towards the opening of the alleyway and started to walk quickly out of there. Aithling afforded herself one last look at the piles of dust before turning quickly on her heel and catching up with Snow.

She looked Aithling up and down, playfully shaking her head and pointing at her dust smeared cheek.

"You missed a bit."

Chapter Thirty Four

Mother pushed past her hand maiden with such force that sent her sprawling to the floor, dropping the contents of her tray over the floor with a loud thud. She looked at the maiden with a reproachful look.

"Oh do get up and tidy up after yourself, you silly girl."

The maiden scrambled to pick everything off the floor as Mother paced around angrily muttering to herself. She knew Aithling had somehow taken the blade. She'd placed members of The Family all over this city so there was no way Aithling would have been able to get away with taking it without being noticed. What had surprised and angered her was the simple fact that Aithling had used the blade against some of her own kind. That had been an unwelcome revelation to say the least. Mother had expected her to take the blade and try to keep it for herself as a bargaining tool. Snow turning up was another unexpected intrusion that she hadn't foreseen either. No matter, it wouldn't stop the plan.

She turned and glared at the maid still crawling about trying to pick up the remnants of the tray contents. Moving quickly, she grabbed her letter opener and roughly slid it across the maid's throat, watching the arc of blood spraying forth in satisfaction.

Watching her fall to the floor gurgling, Mother leant over her watching the blood flow from the jagged cut before running her tongue slowly over the wound itself and sighing deeply as the blood flowed in to her mouth. After a couple of near euphoric gulps, she stood up and walked to the mirror, looking at her reflection as she brushed the hair away from her eyes. The blood had created an almost abstract pattern on her lower lip and chin so she lightly touched it with her finger. Trent was most certainly right, the young ones do taste electric.

The mirror shimmered and she reached her palms out to it as an image of the coffee shop came in to focus. Oh yes, this was going to be worth watching.

***

Webber walked down the long corridor quickly, cursing the reverberating sound of her footsteps every inch of the way. This was not a place that you could creep around in, that much was sure. Her eyes darted around the darkness. The torches on the walls didn't give out much light but it was enough to create shadows out of everything.

She gave the corridor one last look before opening the door to her room slowly and took a deep breath. This had been her room since she was young. In fact, it had been so much more than that. It had been her room, her school and even where she had learnt of the history of her people since Mother had brought her here.

The sparseness of the room hadn't bothered her until she had been sent out to make a life for herself and started to fit in to the every day comings and goings of the humans. They lead such full lives that they seemingly had everything they needed yet it all seemed so very wasteful. The minute anything didn't work the way they wanted, they threw it out without a second thought. They did the same with people. If someone looked, sounded or acted different then they were regarded as little more than trash to be thrown on the ever growing pile. At the heart of it all however, she couldn't help but feel almost a pang of envy.

Throwing her backpack on to the simple wooden bed, she started throwing her clothes in to the back as quickly as possible. The sooner she filled this bag, the sooner she could be out of here.

The sound of a throat clearing made her look up from her bag, revealing Trent standing in the entrance of the room closing the door behind him.

"Going somewhere Webber?"

Her grip tightened on the bag as she stared at him. His face didn't give away any emotion at all and her face mirrored that. She had never trusted Trent and wasn't going to start doing so now.

"Well, we don't want to arouse suspicion with Martel being dead do we?"

Still Trent stared at her without showing anything other than nodding slightly.

"Quite right Webber. Go on as normal."

She could feel the relief running through her but tried her best to conceal it. Now was not the time to give anything away. All she had to do was get out of here and then she'd be safe.

Trent grabbed her wrist tightly and stared at her with a sense of mistrust running over his face slightly.

"Mother may trust you but I don't. Remember that."

He squeezed her wrist a little tighter with each word before letting go and walking out the room. Turning back, he allowed himself to smirk slightly.

"I'm also not as blind to your machinations as you appear to think I am. It would serve you well to remember that as well Webber."

The door shut and Webber stared at it for what felt like an eternity before breathing out. She hadn't even realised that she had been holding her breath. A tightness had grabbed hold of her chest, feeling like something was pressing down on her.

Turning back to her bag, she fastened her it closed and slid it on to her back. The familiar and reassuring weight helping her to calm her breathing as she put her hand on to the door handle and turned it.

A sense of finality ran through her as run the decision through her thoughts. When all of this started, she was prepared to follow Mother and The Family blindly. She was a full believer of everything she had been told. It had even driven both her and Aithling apart despite being both believers. Then they hurt Michael and she still didn't know where he was or even if he was alive at all. Hearing Aithling have doubts started to pour fire on to her flames of doubt. Them killing Martel was the last straw. He hadn't deserved that for merely doing his job. Yes he had clues as to what was really going on but he had no way of proving it so why kill him? It was all too much and all too far. All she had wanted was for the humans to see them as they truly are, not as people hiding away from them and now The Family were going to make them pay.

Shutting the door behind her, she rushed down the corridor without looking back. Her heart started to beat faster and her breathing was nearing panicked levels but there was nobody to stop her. She didn't even see Trent as she left the church building behind her, determined to never go back there.

Chapter Thirty Five

Satara was a few paces ahead of me as we walked to the coffee shop. I was amazed at how quickly he was moving despite the amount of pain he was clearly in but I also couldn't shake the bad feeling that we were about to be led in to another trap. As if sensing my trepidation, he turned to look at me and smiled.

"My dear Naz, you cannot fear the unknown as nothing is certain."

I couldn't help but think, rather ungratefully, that he sounded like some self help guru on a local access television channel. The deer was walking next to him but something weird was happening within him. Where he was once translucent, he was starting to become more substantial. He was starting to look like he was really there and not some strange, fractured part of my imagination. Colours were swirling around in his body and making him seem both there and far away.

Naz.

That bloody voice again. She was back.

It's not too late to stop what will happen to you. I can protect you from all of this.

The buzz saw like vibration in my head was making my mind feel like it was going to explode. Her words ran through me, feeling like little pins were being forced in to my eyes. I don't know how but when I next opened my eyes, Satara was holding me in his arms and looking in to my eyes with a worried expression on his face.

"Welcome back handsome."

I looked around confused. How long had I been out for? It had only felt like seconds between hearing her voice and waking up like this.

Looking at Satara's arms around me, a sense of safety made my heartbeat quicken as I looked up at him. I don't know why but I had the urge to kiss him so I pulled myself up and gently kissed his lips. He smiled back down at me.

"While I appreciate the sentiment Naz, now isn't really the best time to be getting all loved up my dear but when we get through this, and we will, you can buy me a drink and maybe spend a little time getting that loved up feeling."

My cheeks flushed bright red and I found myself laughing despite all of the horrific stuff that had happened to us all since we met. Seeing me laughing, he laughed too. Several people walked past us looking confused but for now, it felt like just the two of us existed and it felt nice.

"It was Mother, she was telling me she could save me from what was about to happen."

"And do you believe her?"

"I don't know what I believe any more, especially when I don't know what's real and what's not."

Satara stroked my face gently as I leant my face in to the palm of his hand.

"Everything is real and everything is imagined. That is the wonderful secret of life but also one of the most painful things to have to deal with."

Hearing the sound of hooves on the concrete, I looked at the deer. His entire body had turned solid and he turned to look at me. Snorting air from his nostrils, he nudged me with his head. The look of sorrow in his eyes unnerved me.

"See what I mean Naz?"

Satara gestured towards the deer.

"And remember, every person and every thing has a story. Even him."

The deer nodded slowly and started to walk in front of us in the direction of the coffee shop. Satara followed closely behind him but I couldn't help myself. I stayed a few paces more than necessary behind them in a futile attempt to starve off the feeling that something was badly wrong. It felt like something was missing but I couldn't place my finger on just what that something was.

Suddenly, a bright flash of light burst in front of my eyes. It dulled to reveal a scene of pure and utter bedlam. There were sounds of fighting, echoes of screams running through everything I was seeing. Splashes of blood both appeared and disappeared in quick succession. Then it all went black.

"Something's wrong. Satara, something is very badly wrong. We have to get there now."

Without saying a word, the deer and Satara started to run as quickly as they could towards the darkened form of the coffee shop. The lights were all off, leaving it to look like little more than an empty shell. The door was thrown open violently as Jim rushed through it with blood covering his face as he fell to the floor. By the time I reached him, all I could hear was his voice weakly muttering three words that chilled the blood in my veins.

"They're all dead."

***

Mother sighed contently as she watched the bedlam unfold in the scene projected from the mirror. Everything was going exactly as she had foreseen and soon, it would be time to call forth the ones who came before her.

The loss of the blade didn't matter. She knew that Aithling wouldn't have the courage to use it against her. Deep down, she was a coward and was running away with her little friend. They'd find her, there was no doubt about that and when they did, not only would they take back the blade but they would make her pay for her insolence too.

Mother ran her hands over the mirror's frame. She'd owned this thing for more years than she could possibly remember yet it always brought a flicker of happiness in to her heart whenever she looked at it. It was said to be cursed by the most bitter of witches and that made it possible for only those with the darkest of hearts to be able to see in to it at will. Curses, hocus pocus, simple parlour tricks to amuse and confuse the masses. That's all religion was when you boiled it down to the bare bones of it all yet it still yielded great power to those who had the ability to use it.

She'd spent years honing her powers. Years building The Family in to who they would soon become. Years of rebirth after rebirth. All those years were building to now, to the result they all wanted more than anything.

It had nearly ended after her first rebirth. She had been young and stupid back then. Her head had been turned by a pretty face and she'd let herself be distracted by what she had mistakenly thought was love. He'd been a simple farmhand but she'd found she couldn't take her eyes from her and before long, they were sneaking off for little rendevous but she should have known better. In fact, she knew that they would get caught sooner or later and someone would have to pay the price and pay the price he did.

All of that was of little consequence now. It had sent her down this road and she was fated to be here. Each time Naz died, she had grown colder to the human kind. She had witnessed the ferocity of their anger towards one another first hand. She had seen him driven to suicide, had seen him murdered by a lynch mob. The world was such an ugly place. That hate had grown and festered inside her. Now, this was her chance to clean it all away. She could rule over them and they would soon learn that hatred would just grow more hatred in return. They would learn to accept her kind as the magical beings that they were. If they didn't, if they chose to continue down the path of self destruction that they were intend on travelling down then so be it. That would prove to her that they don't deserve to be in this world. She would wipe each and every one of them out without a second thought.

Raising her eyes again to the mirror, she took a deep breath. This was the beginning of the end but for whom? Only time would tell and that time was now.

Chapter Thirty Six

Webber stood at the bus station and tearfully looked at the time table in front of her. In thirty minutes time, she would be out of this city. In thirty minutes time, it felt like such a momentous amount of time yet in reality, it was next to nothing really. She just wanted to leave all of this behind. The strange thing was, she still believed that Mother knew best. She still believed that all of this would hopefully make the world a much better place for all of them. It's all she had ever wanted yet she couldn't shake the feeling that she was to blame for all the pain she was feeling. Martel was dead because of her. Michael was gone because of her. Aithling had disappeared with the blade and she knew that Mother wouldn't stop until she found her. She wanted no part of that. She didn't want to see her sister suffer the way that Michael had.

A hand gripped her shoulder tightly and Webber closed her closes before sighing. She knew it had been too simple and just prayed that that Trent would make it a quick death for her.

Turning around, the expression on her face changed almost immediately.

"Going somewhere sis?"

Webber threw her arms around Aithling, holding her tightly and she felt the tears come hard and fast. To her surprise, Aithling stayed holding her only moving to rest her head near her ear to whisper to her.

"It's all gone to shit, I see that now. If Mother succeeds then all we have is each other. You, me, Snow. If we stick together, we might just be all right."

"And even if we're not, we'll be together."

Webber couldn't help but find herself chuckling between sobs. Snow had never been one for optimism.

"As long as we have the blade then Naz still has a chance to stop her."

Webber looked up at her sister with a surprised look on her tear streaked face.

"How?"

Aithling ran her hands over her little sister's face, wiping the tears away tenderly.

"The curse. He's fated to be in a never ending cycle of death as long as Mother is still there. She brought the curse down on him by laying with a mortal so surely he can be the one to undo it all. As far as I can understand it, he can break the curse by surviving her but if she brings her previous blood line down in to this world then that will be the end."

"But how will he break the cycle?"

"I don't know but he will. He has to. He just has to."

Aithling checked her watch. It was nearly time for the bus to arrive so she turned to look at Snow.

"You ready?"

Snow nodded and grabbed her bag as the bus pulled in.

"Let's get out of here before the shit hits the fan. It's their problem now, not ours."

***

It was only Sartara's hand across his mouth that was preventing him from sobbing in front of Naz and the deer. He looked at Naz comforting Jim then looked back at the wall. Sopor's body was nailed to the wall, surrounded by the bodies of the fairies that were drained of their colour and sparkle. It looked like a grotesque butterfly collection surrounding a headless body in a Jesus Christ pose.

Sopor's head wasn't too far away as Satara's eyes took in all the carnage. It had been left on one of the tables with two candles jammed in to the eye sockets in an abstract attempt at an altar.

In front of the head was a phone with the words 'play me' written in blood next to it. Looking back over his shoulder, he could see Naz trying to calm Jim while the deer sniffed around the room.

Picking up the phone, he found a video already on the screen and pressed the play button. The screen was focused on a figure nailed the fairies to the wall around the Sopor's body, his laughter mixing with their screams as their blood and magic spilled down the wall in front of him. Then a familiar voice started talking.

"I'm sorry it had to happen like this. I truly am. When I was with all of you, I must admit, I nearly lost sight of what was important. I nearly lost sight of what I was really here to do and that was to stop you from preventing the inevitable."

Rhea stepped in front of the camera, her face covered in blood, ash and tiny specks of sparkling colours from the fairies bodies. A sickly smile was plastered over her face in an effort to mock those watching.

"Naz, you're cursed. You know that. Death follows wherever you walk. It was on so easy to show you that. Part of me even felt sorry for you while I struggled to keep you alive long enough for all of this puzzle to fall in to place."

Naz looked up at the mention of his name and the realisation that the voice was Rhea hit him hard, leaving him breathless.

"Satara nearly worked it out. Now Jim was easy, we just had to play on his pathetic need to help the helpless. Yes, Michael had to make the ultimate sacrifice but it played right in to Jim's worthless attempts to heal everyone and everything but Satara, you were smarter than I gave you credit for. I had to get you out of the way first and for that, I needed some help. I'm hoping the piper didn't do too much lasting damage, I mean after all, you are one of our kind."

Satara looked at the phone with a look of pure and unadulterated fury in his eyes. Naz looked at him in disbelief that Rhea had done all of this. Jim looked around the room and continued to sob while blaming himself.

"Now I know all three of you very well I feel so Mother had me plan this very carefully."

Michael turned around and walked across the room so he was now in clear focus next to Rhea herself.

"We have carved the ritual markings in to the walls around you although, let's be honest, you probably haven't even noticed them. You're probably too distracted by our attempts at improving the decor of this shitty little coffee shop. Personally I feel our attempts help cheer up the place don't you Michael?"

"For once Rhea, you and I agree."

"While this has been fun, you'll find that Michael and I are long gone but the markings are going to allow for you all to have a couple of visitors that you will be very familiar with now that the protection Sopor provided this place with has been dealt with. So to that end, I bid you all farewell."

The video stopped and Satara threw the phone to the floor, leaving it to bounce and slide across the wood. He turned to Jim and Naz and knelt in front of them.

"I will rip that bitches throat out, I swear it on my life and that of my ancestors. She will pay for this."

Before anyone could answer, a blue light started to swirl in the room and the furniture started to shake, knocking everyone to the floor. Satara grabbed for his knives, only realising then that they were still at the tattoo parlour. Cursing himself, he stood in front of Naz and Jim protectively as laughter started to come from the blue light.

Chapter Thirty Seven

Tendrils of crackling blue light extended from the mirror towards Mother, wrapping themselves around her arms and legs. A feeling of electricity ran through her entire body, making her feel more powerful than she had ever felt.

The blue light dragged her towards the mirror as the light became stronger and brighter than before. In each tendril, she could see the faces of her ancestors and the faces of her previous selves. They were becoming more and more powerful as they pulled her towards the pulsating mirror.

In amongst the moving blue shapes, she could see Naz, Jim and Satara cowering and shielding their eyes as the bolts of colour flicked towards them. She could also make out Sopor's body on the wall and surrounded by the bodies of his fairy brethren. A tad overkill on Michael and Rhea's part but they had done well in fulfilling their part of the plan, wiping out those who only wanted to be equal and not be their true selves.

The tendrils around her arms and legs jerked and stretched out so they covered the entire limbs. They felt like they were pulling her apart as they dragged her towards the scene in the mirror. The faces in the the dark blue screamed silently as if calling out to her.

With a final jerk, she was pulled through the mirror violently and the room fell silent as the face reverted back to normal glass.

***

Trent stood in the doorway. He'd seen the entire transformation of Mother before she went through the portal. It had seemed like the blue light had enveloped her but she was laughing.

Slowly he walked over to the mirror itself and placed a hand on it. It felt cold to the touch but made his skin feel like it was burning. Pulling his hand away, he looked at the red blister on the palm of his hand. It was shaped like a screaming face, making him step away from it while staring at the now weeping wound on his hand. The pus wept from the blister, running down his hand and wrist creating a pattern down his arm. Slowly the pus started to twist and move in to letters adorning his skin like an oily yellow tattoo.

Veni ad me.

Come to me.

A blue light flashed in front of him and once again the tendrils made their way from the mirror's surface, this time ripping at his clothing and at his skin leaving bloody marks on him. Trent started to struggle but the more he moved, the tighter they held him, cutting in to his limbs and body.

He tried to scream out and call for help but one of the tendrils pushed itself down his throat, silencing him and pulling him roughly forwards.

A smell of burning flesh started to permeate the room as his skin started to burn and fall away in smouldering, bloody strips on to the floor as a voice started to rumble through his mind.

"Iasion, son of the Gods. You have chosen to defile our bloodline by becoming an incubus in the pursuit of knowledge and power. That very knowledge and power have corrupted you to the point of no return so go. Go join your queen and rule over your dominion be beware of the pure of blood for that will strike you down like a thunderbolt from thine own hand."

His body jerked violently and forced its way through the mirrors surface, his bones twisting and snapping with each movement of the powerful blue tendrils before his mind went completely black.

***

The bus ride was not smooth in the slightest. Rain was lashing down against the windows, creating an almost calming beat as the raindrops hit the glass. At the front of the bus, the driver leaned forward to try in vain to try to see the markings on the road before cursing and pulling over just as a series of blue lightning bolts carved shapes in the sky above them.

"Sorry folks, it's safer for us to wait this storm out."

The passengers all groaned at the news. They were all as eager as each other to leave this city but the driver was right. This was one of the worst storms they had seen in decades. The rain was lashing across the road so hard that it was near impossible to see where the road ended and the land either side of them began. For all they knew, they could either be in the middle of the city or out in the countryside. There was no way to be sure as nobody could see a damn thing out the windows.

Even when the lightning struck, the brief flash of light didn't give anything but a momentary glimpse to the terrible conditions outside.

Aithling looked at Snow with a worried expression on her face.

"We're too late. They've already started to pull themselves through."

Snow looked out the window and grimaced as the lightning once again flashed and carved the sky in two.

"We're in this whether we want to be or not Aithling. I should have known better than to think we could outrun this."

Webber yawned and rubbed her eyes. She always had the gift of being able to sleep anywhere, no matter what was going on around her. One trait that Aithling was definitely jealous of.

Snow looked at her tired face and tried to look sympathetically at her. She was only young but she had played a big part in this going so far. There was blood on her hands, Snow was sure of that and knew that debt would have to paid before long. They may be different to the humans in a lot of ways but when it came to revenge, they were more similar than they would want to admit.

"Webber, where is Mother going to pull through the others? Do you know?"

She nodded and looked worried.

"Below Sopor's coffee shop. With him out of the way, she'd be near all the books of the history of our people. The words within those books with give her the power to call down her previous selves as well as our ancestors."

"Out of the way?"

Webber sat forward with her head in her hands.

"He's dead. Rhea and Michael killed him and carved the dark symbols in to his severed head to reverse the spell of protection he'd put over the coffee shop. They were all wiped out. Him, the fairies, the guarding race. They were all wiped out."

Snow nudged Aithling and nodded towards the driver. While the storm was raging outside, the driver was sat completely still. She looked around the bus. The rest of the passengers were all sat as if paused in the middle of whatever they were doing. Looking out of the windows, Aithling saw that the people outside were still too despite the weather soaking them to the skin. The scene looked almost comical with some of the people outside stopped in mid stride trying to run to somewhere dry.

"Snow, we're involved in this whether we want to be or not. We should get to them and help Naz. We do have the blade after all."

Despite the bravery of her words, the fear of what she was saying was written all over Aithling's face. So much for a quick get away.

Webber looked at them both sadly.

"They killed Martel too. He was no threat to anybody."

Snow rested her hand sympathetically on her shoulder. She could tell that she was blaming herself and if she was brutally honest, how naive she was had played a part in his death but now wasn't the time for blame. Now was the time to try to stop Mother.

A groaning at the front of the bus caught their attention as the driver started to jerk and convulse before falling to the floor, his body moving at horrific angles. The cracking of bones, the snapping of tendons shouted like gunshots in between the thunder cracks and flashes of lightning.

Snow and Aithling stood up and started to slowly move up the aisle, keeping their eyes on the body every step of the way. The rest of the passengers stayed still, staring off in to the distance. As the body arched on the floor, a tearing sound make them both take a step back as skin started to tear away from itself and opened up like a cocoon. A bug like creature stepped out of the corpse and hissed angrily, pointing at Webber.

"This concerns you not. I am merely here for her."

Aithling stole a glance at her. The look of terror and recognition on her face told her all she needed to know. Smirking at the now familiar weight of the blade in her jacket, she stepped forward.

"That's who killed Martel" Webber said with a sad tone in her voice. She was glued to the spot as the fear she felt held her in place.

The creature whipped it's long green limbs at Aithling but she deftly dodged the attempt, hearing the metallic clang of the impact as it hit the metal bar. She'd heard of these creatures before. They could burrow in to your mind and steal your thoughts and memories, making them one of the best creatures to use if you were tracking someone down. She was surprised that they were working for Mother however. They were normally solitary in their nature but she knew, just like everyone else, they had a price.

Rolling gracefully forward, she aimed a well placed kick to the creature's knee as she reached for the blade but the creature was quicker than she thought. Another of it's limbs wrapped painfully around her other wrist.

Before Snow could take a step forward, a blue light surrounded the creature, spikes of it driving their points through its body. As it opened its mouth to scream out in pain, one of the spikes drove its way through its tongue, pinning it to the bus floor with a metallic clang. Within seconds, the blue light was shining through the creatures body and it started to melt before their very eyes, leaving a wet bubbling mess on the floor.

Accepting Snow's offer of her hand, Aithling stood slowly and stared at what remained of the creature. The bubbling of the viscous remains started to get quicker so they both took a step back. It moved and flowed in the shapes of curved letters.

Quia sanguinem, pro domo

Sic incipit

They both looked at each other and nodded.

For blood, for family.

It begins.

Chapter Thirty Eight

The ground shook after our feet as every single thing around us vibrated and reverberated. Blue light flashed all around us, illuminating the room and giving it an eerie atmosphere.

I struggled to my feet, helping Jim up as I held on to the nearest table and looked at Satara in the hope that maybe he had some idea of what to do. He just stared back at me with concern before walking through the door towards the stairs. With hesitation, we both followed. The three of us had no weapons, no plan and no clue as to what was happening.

You know where I am. I'm not hard to find.

Was this the start of it all? Was she really trying to become the keeper of souls that Satara mentioned when we first met in that strange place between our world and the next?

I am the mother of darkness and the haunter of dreams.

I had no idea what we were walking in to, only a whole load of hearsay and stories that were little more than myths and legends.

Even after all you have seen, you still don't believe?

As I followed behind Satara, I could see the anger coursing through his body. Rhea had been his friend. More than his friend in fact. He had helped to raise her after she'd been abandoned by her family and she has done all of this. Between her and Michael, they had butchered everyone, leaving the three of us to make sense of it all and for Mother to have the opening she needed.

Rhea is one of my greatest creations. She was the daughter that I'd always wanted but never managed to birth myself. It didn't take much convincing for her to see the beauty in the future I was promising her. Michael will be richly rewarded for his sacrifice he has made for our cause. He will be written of in the new history books and seen as a saviour of our kind.

The whole corridor had changed since I was last here. After the brutality of what we had seen upstairs, it was as if the whole life had been sucked out of here. The colour had drained too leaving it drab and devoid of hope.

The only hope that will survive is for those who follow us Naz.

Blue light lit up the end of the corridor as it flicked out of the doorway to the room where I had met Sopor. The talons of light reached out to us as if inviting us in but there was no love in the invitation. Quite the opposite.

Something was telling me that not all of us were going to leave this room alive. It was a horrible feeling of inevitability, leaving us feeling like nothing we were about to do was about to make even the tiniest bit of different to the result.

Come on in Naz. Come to mummy.

***

Trent felt like it he was falling through a never ending sense of nothingness. It didn't feel like gravity was pulling him down, it just felt like nothing existed under his body as he spun and turned no matter how much he flicked his feet out. His hands tried to grab on to something, anything, but just found his fingers moving feebly instead.

The blue light that had dragged him in to the mirror, tearing at his skin and searing its mark on to him for eternity had disappeared leaving blackness in its stead. He'd long since stopped screaming, it had seemed pointless to scream when there was nothing but a void to shout in to.

Silence had stabbed its way through him, shocking him at first but now, he had started to welcome it. Trent knew that all of this would end soon but for now, he was content.

***

Blue flames and light flicked through the veil between this world and the next, leaving its mark wherever it touched. Screams of the ancestors could be heard through every crack of the lightning, through every clap of thunder.

The voices were calling out. Someone in pain, some in ecstasy although the two were so close together that no sane person could tell the different any more.

Faces pressed themselves out of the shadows and through the light, leaving a translucent mask of their features. Soon their kin would see them for the first time in centuries when they came through in to their world. Despite their minds having been long lost to time, they couldn't help but wonder what had changed in the world since their last visit.

Yes it was true that they had been watching proceedings from afar. They'd seen horrific crimes committed by humans against their own kind. They'd seen cities both rise and fall. Governments come and go. Gods and deities being long since forgotten by the masses. That's not what had called to them however. A long voice through the darkness had asked for their return, begged in fact. She had beguiled them with stories and promises that their majesty was to be returned to them. She had sworn that the humans would be easily scared and forcing in to adopting the old ways, leaving the door open for their kind to rule over them like cattle. That's why they were here.

Her voice had a bitter quality to it and that they liked, it had welcomed them and beckoned them in to her world. Even as deities they were bitter at their treatment from the humans. In the days long past, they had flocked to them for help, for mercy. When the crops failed, they were on their knees in the myriad of temples built in their image.

When the storms came and threatened their safety, they were once again on their knees. It was endless and empowering, keeping them well fed and satisfied on their pedestals that the humans had placed them on but now, everything was different. Nobody but tourists visited their temples and even then, that was just to laugh at their legends and their powers.

The power ran through the blue bolts and charged the entire room with an electric crackle as the floor cracked and began to open up. Slowly, Mother clawed her way through and stood looking around the room. Michael and Rhea had served her well, leaving her a way to enter where the sacred place Sopor kept the books of their time lines. He drew his power from them, maybe she could do the same.

Books flew off of the shelves, landing open on the table in front of her with the pages flapping and turning before she suddenly slammed her hand on and they all stopped moving. The words seemed to dance across the page.

The Legend of Kybele

The story where the Gods showed themselves to be vengeful, spiteful creatures and little else. The story where she learned the greatest lesson of all. It was her story and hers alone.

***

The name of the man had long been lost to history but it didn't make his story any less important.

Kybele had noticed him day after day toiling in the field and felt a mixture of pity for how hard he was having to work and an denable feeling of attraction as the sweat ran down his bare back.

It was unadulterated animal attraction for her and nothing more or so she told herself. Each day she walked past his field in the hopes she'd catch a glance at him, not knowing that he was trying to do the same himself.

Eventually, neither one of them could deny themselves any longer and it turned from innocent chats to a lot more. She knew that they would eventually get caught by the Gods but for now, while they were distracted by the sheer amount of worship in the temples, she would take full advantage of it.

They lay together under the oak tree, watching the branches sway in the breeze, their clothes in a tangled heap on the floor.

Before they could say anything, a kick hit the man in the ribs and drove the breath out of his lungs in an awkward gasp as Iasion stood over him.

"You have lay with my woman. She is linked to me and me alone."

Struggling to pull her dress back on, Kybele laughed.

"He has indeed Iasion."

He pulled his hand back and slapped her hard across her cheek, making her laugh more as he forcibly placed his hand on her stomach.

"You are now with child woman, a bastard of a half breed."

Iasion turned and looked at the man disgusted as he watched him struggle to his feet. This human man was no warrior, that was for sure. He was little more than a lonely farm worker and yet he seduced his Kybele. He had lain with her, leaving her belly full with his seed and child.

Pulling out the blade, he grinned and muttered a curse under his breath before pushing it slowly in to the man and opening his belly up, his guts spilling out in front of him.

"You will forever live in the middle world racked with the pain you feel now. That will be your punishment."

Kybele placed her hand on his and pushed the blade in further while kissing Iasion on the cheek.

"And now we feast."

The man was lucky that for now, his soul was dead as they ripped his flesh with their hands and teeth but soon, he would be reborn, cursed to walk through the world alone and in pain.

***

Satara tried to open the door to Sopor's room but it was blocked as if something was pushing it shut from the other side. Tongues of flickering blue light moved around their feet as they all tried to push the door open but to no avail.

Grunting with effort, Satara slumped to the floor and thumped it with his fist out of anger and frustration.

As he sat on the floor, more light flowed from under the door and circled around them all before starting to flow up Naz's body and wrapping itself around him tightly. Jim and Satara grabbed him quickly as the light jerked, pulling them through the door as if it had never existed.

Hello boys, glad you could join me.

Chapter Thirty Nine

I couldn't believe my eyes. Mother was being held in mid air by the blue light that had followed us since we got back to the coffee shop. Books where everywhere. On the table, on the floor and even on Sopor's throne.

My legs tried to walk but I was held in place by the weirdly magnetic feeling blue light that was wrapped around me.

Satara and Jim both stood frozen to the spot as faces started to push themselves through the crack in the concrete floor, each face a different deity from the books.

I am Alpha, I am Omega, I am all things. Mother of death, keeper of souls and I command you to come to me ancestors. I command it.

Each word felt like a stab in to my mind, my eyes and my brain.

Naz, my child, it's not too late to follow me, to serve at my right hand.

Squeezing my eyes shut, I willed myself to ignore her voice. I willed myself to be strong enough to withstand anything she would try to do to me.

Mother was reaching her hand out to me. I couldn't see her but I could feel the movement of her fingers near my face as my entire body pulsed and moved towards her involuntarily. As much as I tried, I could feel myself drawn towards her.

Her hand stroked my face before trying to force my eyes open.

Naz, look at me. All of this is for you and me. We could rule over everything together. The humans could pay for all they have done to themselves and to us.

The door smashed open as the deer ran in to the room, a look of anger on it's dirty face as it ran towards her, its mouth opening and closing as if trying to scream something as loud as it could but any sound was drowning out by the constant hum of the energy around us.

My eyes were wide in terror as Mother picked the deer up and with one flick her of hand slammed him hard against the wall, laughing as his body crumpled on to the cold floor and twitched besides us.

Did you really think that would work farm boy?

She turned her attention to me and pulled me closer until I could see the spit hanging from her lips as she smiled.

Ignore that dirty old thing. He's no longer of any importance.

She looked at Jim and Satara, both of whom were struggling to get to her but looked like they were moving in slow motion.

Oh how tedious.

A blue bolt sizzled from one of her fingertips before she flicked it towards Jim. It hit him hard, sizzling as soon as it made contact with his skin before impaling his hand and thudding in to the wall behind him, leaving him hanging like a broken marionette.

Satara, you're like a cockroach, always there and always unimportant so do what you will. It will have absolutely no bearing on what happens next.

His face was absolutely seething with anger as Mother flicked her hand towards him but instead of bolts of energy, she just held him in mid air in a crucifixion pose and laughed.

All of this has just been far too easy. You were all just so trusting of whoever walked in to your little world and now look. You are all falling like a cheap and tacky set of dominoes while I am here ready to rule over my new dominion.

I couldn't help but try to ball my hand up in a fist and throw a punch towards her but my arm wouldn't move no matter how hard I tried.

Oh Naz, you and your anger management problems. Watch that temper of yours my dear boy or you'll get yourself in to the kind of trouble that you won't be able to get yourself out of.

My mind was starting to feel like it was burning inside my head with each moment of her speaking. With each moment of her lecturing us.

The deer slowly stirred slightly on the floor. Jim struggled to pull the bolt out of his hand as he hung, impaled on the wall. Satara floated in mid air, the blue light making him look like some kind of neon version of Jesus Christ while I just stood there looking like an angry, confused statue.

The faces that had been coming out of cracks in the floor were beginning to form themselves in to bodies as another body, but this one was bloody and bruised, pulled itself through the gap.

Oh Iasion, how pleased I am to see you my love or would you rather I still called you Trent?

He dusted himself off as he panted in pain. The flaps of skin that those weird blue tendrils had pulled from him were oozing down his body as he looked at Mother.

I am forever yours my lady.

Trent knelt in front of her and held his palms out in a mark of respect.

Good boy, you know that's exactly where I like you.

Before Trent could answer, Aithling ran in to the room brandishing the ceremonial blade, slamming it in to Mother's chest with a scream of anger.

A look of shock passed across Mother's face as she pulled the blade from her body and the wound closed, leaving nothing but a slight speck on her pale skin. Aithling fell backwards looking confused, her mouth opening and closing and only managing to repeat the word what over and and over.

Did you really think that blade would stop me?

"But the curse…"

Do you believe everything you read Aithling?

Mother threw the blade to the floor, letting it land with an echoing thud.

It may work on some of you but I'm so much more than that. Besides, it's me that put the curse on it when I helped slit that dirty human's stomach open and watched as his guts spilled to the floor. It was rather enjoyable I must say but enough reminising for now.

Mother kicked out at Aithling, sending her tumbling backwards in to Snow and Webber. Snow pulled her pistol from her pocket but before she could fire it, Mother had melted it in front of her very eyes.

The blue bodies of her ancestors, of the gods and goddesses who came before her, were now fully formed and stood pawing at her body. She looked at them with a smirk.

You all think I've called you here to restore you to your former glory don't you?

They were nearly climbing over themselves to get closer to her in the sheer desperation to be as close to her as possible.

Oh sweet, misguided fools. You're here to power me. To worship me as I take rule over all that you see before you.

This was my chance. I could feel her distracted mind detach from mine and for a split second I was free. Knowing it was now or never, I threw my body towards the blade on the floor. It may have not worked for Aithling but maybe it would work for me.

It was the moment Mother's eyes met mine that I knew I'd made a terrible mistake as she drove the blade in my chest. I didn't have time to say anything as my world went black for the final time.

Chapter Forty

The scream that came from Satara's throat roared through the air, taking everyone by surprise. He freed himself from the the clutches of the light and ran to Naz's side. He knelt down and stroked his cheek gently as warm tears streamed down his cheek, dripping on to the floor.

Ok, enough is enough. Bow before me and watch as I make this world in my image.

Blue bodies surrounded her, still trying in vain to paw at her like helpless puppies trying to get their master's attention. Nobody else moved except for the deer that struggled to its feet while Mother watched in interest.

You're stronger than you look. That ends now.

She flicked her hand up, opening a wound in the deer's throat. He gargled quietly as the blood poured from him like waterfall before falling to the floor for one last time.

Anyone else or can I continue?

Snow was stood staring, unable to move. Webber was checking on Aithling. Satara was weeping over the body of Naz. There truly was nobody left.

Good. About time you all showed me some respect at last.

Mother raised her hands, palm up, towards the ceiling as it started to crack. More blue figures started to come through the cracks, screeching and moaning loudly with the effect of pulling themselves through.

You will all serve me.

The deers blood flowed across the floor and around one of the books on the floor. The edges of the pages started to turn red as they soaked up his blood and words started to stand on the page.

Satara looked through his tear soaked eyes at the seemingly floating letters that spelled out one word.

Abomination.

With the letters pointing up towards Mother, Satara saw the blade still in Naz's chest then looked back at the book. It felt like it was calling to him.

Call forth the hungry, the forgotten, the powerless and absorb in to me. I am the keeper of souls and you will sustain me with your will.

Mother was distracted with the ceremony. This could be the chance they needed but he would have to be careful. Subtly, he gestured at Aithling, Snow and Webber that he was moving towards the book before closing his eyes and pulling the blade slowly from Naz's body.

Snow nodded before taking a step forward and kneeling in front of Mother. Webber did the same while Aithling lay moaning and holding her ribs.

So we have two willing sacrifices do we? What a pleasant surprise.

Sliding over next to the book, Satara chanced a glance with them. Snow and Webber both looked at Mother with defiance in their eyes. He blinked at them, almost in thanks, as he raised the blade above the book, the words formed in front of him.

Destroy her history, destroy her.

Snow looked at him and smiled. Mother turned to look at him but it was too late. Satara plunged the blade deep in to the pages of the book as it screamed out in pain. Trent backed away slowly, holding himself against the wall as the room started to shake. He'd been brought through to serve with her but he wanted no part of this. He was no angel, of that he was sure, but he knew deep down that Mother needed to be stopped. There would be a way to rule but this was not it.

He took the noise and distraction of the book as his chance to run from the room and not look back. If had have looked, he'd have seen Mother jerk and slam to the floor in pain. Her scream drowned out by that of the book. She gasped and held her chest, pulsating blood seeping through her fingers.

Help me. I brought you here, help me. Help your keeper of souls.

The blue figures all stood around her and watched as she started to melt and fade before them. They too started to fade as they all converged on Mother, pulling her disappearing flesh from her bones before dragging her back through the ground, leaving only the four survivors behind in a now silent room.

Epilogue

A Year Later

The world would never know how close it had come to ending. Nobody could ever know. That much was sure. The weird thing is, even if the humans did know, would they have believed?

When the ancestors had started to come through, the world had momentarily stopped so what felt like hours had actually been a split second of time but what had been a blink of the eye for some, had been the most horrific moment of their lives for others.

Satara stood at the graveside and ran his hand over the stone. He had spared no expense for Naz's gravestone. The humans may not have known it but he was a hero and a hero deserved the best send off that money could buy. There had only been four of them at his service but wherever he was, Satara knew that Naz would be smiling down at them. He had become part of their family after all.

"I miss you Naz. I don't know when or how but I know we'll get that drink together one day. I promise and I don't break my promises. I'll see you again soon."

A small movement caught Satara's eye and he looked up. A small bird looked at him. It tilted it's head at him and chirped and he smiled.

"We've rebuilt the coffee shop. Myself, Aithling and the others. The coffee hasn't improved though."
The bird had one blue eye and one green that seemed to sparkle in the sun light. Behind it was a deer who stood gracefully in the background, watching Satara with interest on its face.

He stood up to go with a slight grimace. It may have been a year but old wounds certainly didn't heal fast.

The bird shimmered and disappeared. The deer shimmered and disappeared as Satara watched their essence form together. Naz and the farm worker stood next to each each other smiling, the farm worker with his hand proudly on Naz's shoulder before disappearing altogether.

***

Trent sat in the park enjoying the silence of it all. He'd pulled his collar up to hide the scars on his face from those infernal blue lights. The burns had been deep but he'd survived. Mother wasn't so lucky.

He'd always enjoyed watching people go by, watching strangers go about their personal business without a care in the world yet the park was strangely empty. He had wanted to stand up, feed and regain himself once more but that would have to wait. It wasn't something he'd be able to do alone no matter how much the ignorance of the humans angered him. He would just have to be patient.

The cold feel of a blade against his throat made him stiffen as he let out a sigh. He had always known this was coming, he just thought there would have been a little more time.

"I have a promise to keep Trent and I don't break a promise."

The blade cut through his skin easily and he fell to his back as the blood soaked the grass as she knelt down beside him. She had waited a long time for this and had made sure that this part of the park would be empty and if not, well, Snow and Webber were watching out for her so she smirked and patted his cheek playfully.

"I know you'll rebirth and come after me. I accept that but this, this is purely for my own, purely selfish enjoyment so be a good boy and wait there a moment please."

One by one, she placed pen after pen in to the bleeding, gaping wound before taking a step back to give herself the chance to not only admire her handiwork but to also smile at the shocked look on his face.

"I told you I'd put my pens there."

She turned and walked back to Webber and Snow.

"Coffee?"

***

Michael and Rhea sat in the rental car in the motel car park. They had driven from place to place but still, something had drawn them back to this place.

An elderly man carrying a mop and bucket walked past them cheerily whistling to himself as Michael stared at him from the dirty car window.

"Are you sure this is the right place?"

Rhea nodded and got out the car. Michael followed her, his long jacket floating in the wind as they walked over to one of the motel doors. Rhea tapped her knuckle against the wooden door before opening it while he looked around to make sure the weird looking old man had gone.

A woman was sat on the bed hunched over and breathing heavily. You could see the scars that criss crossed her back through her blouse. The old fashioned television set was playing the final moments of a news piece about Aithling's book being a literary surprise that still sat at the top of the best seller list as Michael's lip curled in annoyance at her name being mentioned.

"You called for us?"

The woman nodded and turned to face them before smiling. Rhea and Michael looked respectfully back at her before kneeling with their palms face up.

She walked slowly and painfully over to them both and placed a hand on each of their heads. Gently, she started to stroke them before whispering.

"For blood, for family."

They both looked up at her in reverence.

"Yes Mother."

Printed in Great Britain
by Amazon